IMPROPER DELIGHTS

"Oh, Philip," Tender amusement lit Sarah's eyes as she reached up to touch his cheek. "My white knight, always having to rescue me."

Philip turned his head and pressed a kiss into her palm. Sarah gasped and would have pulled her hand away, had he not held onto it. "Madam, it has been my pleasure."

"H-has it?"

"Come here." His arm slipped about her waist, pulling her close against him, and his gaze caught hers. "You are a beautiful woman, Sarah Pembroke."

"Philip." Sarah pushed at his shoulders, to no avail. "Someone will see."

His head bent; his lips slid along her jaw, to her cheeks, her eyes. "No one will care."

Sarah's knees were growing decidedly weak. "But—"

He kissed her quickly, once, twice, leaving her aching for more. Then his lips came down on hers and he was at last kissing her as he had the day her horse had run away with her. There was no anger in this kiss, though, only passion, desire, and something more . . .

DISCOVER THE MAGIC OF REGENCY ROMANCES

ROMANTIC MASQUERADE   (3221, $3.95)
by Lois Stewart

Sabrina Latimer had come to London incognito on a fortune hunt. Disguised as a Hungarian countess, the young widow had to secure the ten thousand pounds her brother needed to pay a gambling debt. His debtor was the notorious ladies' man, Lord Jareth Tremayne. Her scheme would work if she did not fall prey to the charms of the devilish aristocrat. For Jareth was an expert at gambling and always played to win everything—and *everyone*—he could.

RETURN TO CHEYNE SPA   (3247, $2.95)
by Daisy Vivian

Very poor but ever-virtuous Elinor Hardy had to become a dealer in a London gambling house to be able to pay her rent. Her future looked dismal until Lady Augusta invited her to be her guest at the exclusive resort, Cheyne Spa. The one condition: Elinor must woo the unsuitable rogue who was in pursuit of the Duchess's pampered niece.

The unsuitable young man was enraptured with Elinor, but *she* had been struck by the devilishly handsome Tyger Dobyn. Elinor knew that Tyger was hardly the respectable, marrying kind, but unfortunately her heart did not agree!

A CRUEL DECEPTION   (3246, $3.95)
by Cathryn Huntington Chadwick

Lady Margaret Willoughby had resisted marriage for years, knowing that no man could replace her departed childhood love. But the time had come to produce an heir to the vast Willoughby holdings. First she would get her business affairs in order with the help of the new steward, the disturbingly attractive and infuriatingly capable Mr. Frank Watson; *then* she would begin the search for a man she could tolerate. If only she could find a mate with a *fraction* of the scandalously handsome Mr. Watson's appeal. . . .

A Maddening Minx
Mary Kingsley

ZEBRA BOOKS
KENSINGTON PUBLISHING CORP.

To Sarah Willett Matlock —
First fan, fast friend.
Thank you for all your encouragement.

ZEBRA BOOKS

are published by

Kensington Publishing Corp.
475 Park Avenue South
New York, NY 10016

First printing: March, 1992

Printed in the United States of America

Chapter One

"Why are we stopping?" Sarah Chadwick called out the carriage window.

"There's a tree blocking the road, miss." The coachman, big and burly, jumped lightly down to the road as the carriage came to a stop and walked back to her, tugging at the brim of his cap. "Must have been a storm hereabouts to bring it down. But don't you worry, miss—Us'll have it up in a trice."

"I'm sure you will." Sarah gave the man what she thought was a polite smile but which made him blink, and leaned back against the cracked leather squabs, leaving the window curtain open. Old and poorly sprung though it was, the carriage had at least the advantage of being private. Sarah had managed to adjust to many deprivations over the past four years, but sharing a cramped stagecoach with various and sundry strangers, many in dire need of bathing, was not one of them. When she had been turned out of her position as governess at Rockhill Grange in Norfolk—and most unfairly, too, though she no longer felt quite the same indignation at the injustice as she had—she had determined to leave in style. Thus, she had hired a carriage for the long ride to Gloucestershire and the house of her former guardian. It was the last extravagance she would be able to afford for a long, long time.

Sarah's lips quirked in a wry smile. Extravagance, indeed. Once she had dressed in satins and silks and muslins and traveled in carriages upholstered in fine-cut velvet or buttery soft leather. That had been before Papa's death, though, when she'd had all the world before her and enough money to enjoy it. Now she had neither, and yet, she felt oddly content. Almost happy.

It was taking an unconscionably long time for the men to shift the tree, she thought, and leaned out the carriage window to check on their progress. Ahead on the road the coachman and his helper, holding stout branches to use as levers, stood by the tree, apparently discussing the best way to move it. A strange spot for a tree to fall, she thought, craning her head to see. Here the road ran between two steep banks so that there was no chance of driving on the verge to avoid an obstruction. Overhead the trees, still blooming with summer foliage, nearly met, making the road dim and cool. To the side on one of the banks, the vegetation rustled. Some animal, most likely, Sarah thought, sitting back and resigning herself to a long wait. There was no real rush. For the first time in ages she was at no one's beck and call, and the freedom was wonderful.

Sarah stretched luxuriously, sticking out her legs in a most unladylike manner and regarding the toes of her scuffed, serviceable half-boots. No more obnoxious children to attempt to teach some semblance of manners and knowledge. No more mistress to look down her nose; no more master to leer and make improper suggestions — and occasionally to act on them. Why, Sarah couldn't for the life of her tell. Certainly she was no beauty, no pink and gold pocket Venus or raven-haired Incomparable. No, her hair was simply brown. There was no other word for it. And straight, too, rarely holding a curl. Her eyes were also brown, looking out from a face that was well-enough proportioned, she supposed, but not in any way remarkable. Neither was her figure, which was too full, too rounded, ever to attain the sylphlike proportions dictated by fashion. Some men, she decided, as she had in the past, would make advances to anyone. Usually she had managed to fend them off, with no one the wiser, but not this time. This time, Mrs. Ramsay, outraged at finding Mr. Ramsay and Sarah in what appeared to be an improper embrace, had had no compunction about turning Sarah out of the house without a character. As if she'd been a willing participant in what could have been her own rape, she thought indignantly, though she was confident she could have fought Mr. Ramsay off. Men, she thought contemptuously. It would be best to have as little dealings with them as possible.

Outside the coachman gave a shout, and Sarah leaned back. Must have been the tree going. They'd be on their way soon, then. And what would happen then, she wasn't certain. She hoped Sir Edwin Staples, her former guardian, wouldn't mind taking her in and helping her find a position. Otherwise she didn't know what she'd do. She had little money and fewer prospects, and her future was uncertain at best. By all rights she should be blue-deviled. Instead, she felt a tremendous elation. It did no good to sulk and complain about things that couldn't be helped, as she'd oft told her obstreperous charges. She always tried to keep cheerful, but this feeling was different. It was exhilarating, and it had grown since leaving Norfolk, as if she were heading towards something tremendously wonderful and exciting, something special, just for her. She couldn't, at that moment, wait to discover what it was.

More shouts from outside. Sarah, lost in dreams of the future, ignored them. Thus, she had no hint that anything untoward was about until the carriage door was wrenched open. Startled, she found herself staring at a roughly dressed and rather dirty man with a kerchief wrapped around his lower face and an evil-looking gun in his hand.

For a moment Sarah simply stared, unable to believe this apparition, and then her teacher's instincts, honed by the years spent in a schoolroom, took over. "What do you think you are doing with that?" she snapped, holding out an imperious hand. "Hand it over this instant."

The man's hand involuntarily moved forward, then jerked back. "Wot?" He gawked at her and then turned, calling to someone out of her sight. "Cor blimey, it's a woman!"

"Shoot anyway!" a voice yelled back, and for the first time, Sarah felt a cold thrill of fear. What had happened to the coachman and his assistant? Though she'd heard no shots, they must have been overpowered in some way, else they would have come to her assistance. She was alone, and she was in danger.

"I'll have no truck with killing a woman!" the ruffian shouted, and at that moment, Sarah acted.

"No!" Without warning, she threw herself at him, grabbing for the gun. He fell back several paces, startled by this unexpected attack, and a huge, meaty arm went about her waist, clamping her close against a powerful chest garbed in clothes that were none too clean. Frantically Sarah kicked out, but to no avail.

"Cor blimey, mate, she's a wildcat!" the ruffian shouted.

"Shoot, damn ye!" the second voice yelled back, just as a strange, unearthly howl split the forest's silence.

"No!" Sarah cried again and with her free arm clawed for the gun. Several shots rang out, and she was falling, falling. Her last conscious thought, before the darkness descended upon her, was that now she'd never know the wonderful fate that had been in store for her.

The passengers of the curricle's first indication that something was wrong ahead was the shouting. Philip Thornton, Marquess of Pembroke, expertly checked his team of perfectly matched bays and peered through the forest's gloom. "Sounds like a bit of bother ahead," he said mildly.

"Highwaymen, think ye?" said his companion, a red-headed giant of a man.

"In this area? Hardly. More likely an accident. Shall we see?" The marquess's tone continued mild, but his face was set as he reached into the pockets of the curricle for his pistols, kept primed and loaded for just such an eventuality.

"I'll not say no," the big man said frankly. "Aye, I'd welcome a fight, after what happened at—"

The marquess turned and fixed him with a look that had been known to make lesser men quail and then relented with a laugh. "Aye, Geordie," he said, mimicking the other man's broad Scots burr, "I'd not say no, either." And with a flick of the wrist, he set his team into motion quickly, but under expert control.

A fine thing, Geordie thought, holding his own pistols at the ready, that his lordship could still drive to an inch, considering what had happened to him. Yes, and his shooting hadn't been affected either, for all his lordship only had the one good eye now. A good man to have beside you in a fight, he thought, and leaned forward, eager to leap into the fray.

The curricle swept around the curve into the section of road the marquess liked least, where the steeply sloped and overgrown banks hung over the road. A perfect spot for an ambush, he'd always thought, and now he was being proved right. "Highwaymen, by God!" he exclaimed. "But why—"

"Look ye!" Geordie said, his accent broadening as one of the ruffians, the one who stood near the carriage, suddenly dragged out the passenger. "A woman!"

"War, Geordie!" Philip's face was grim, but there was a light in his eye. "You take that one."

"Aye, my lord!" Geordie jumped down from the curricle with surprising ease for a man of his size and began running, howling the Scottish war cry that had put fear into England's enemies on the battlefield. Running towards them from the downed tree and the felled coachman was another ruffian, shouting something to his companion, but the sound of that war yell stopped him. His eyes grew wide and then, without a second thought, he turned, scrambling up the bank and disappearing into the underbrush. At that moment there were several shots, and the man near the carriage fell, the woman crumpling to the ground beside him.

"Fine shooting, my lord!" Geordie shouted.

Philip shrugged, shoving both pistols back into his pockets as he went down on one knee. He hadn't lost it, then, the ability to use both hands in a situation such as this, even with just one eye. The instinct, the skill, were still there. "See to the ruffian," he said tersely, and reached out to turn the woman with long-fingered hands that were both capable and gentle. And then, he simply stared.

So much had happened in the few moments of the encounter that Philip hadn't realized how much he had taken in. By the woman's gray stuff gown, buttoned high to her neck, and her untrimmed bonnet, he had assumed her to be an older gentlewoman, fallen upon hard times, perhaps. The face that stared up at him, though, was absurdly young, the features perfectly composed and serene, in spite of the blood streaming from the wound in her temple. Oh, God. Was she? No. A hand placed over her heart found not only a strong, steady beat but a delightful soft roundness, as well. Philip snatched his hand away, though the impression of that softness lingered. She was a beauty, and he hadn't the slightest idea who she was.

"Ye did for this one, my lord," Geordie said, rising from where he had been kneeling by the ruffian and coming to stand by Philip. "How is she?"

Philip probed lightly at her temple and then drew back. "A flesh wound, I believe. She'll do."

"Thank God for that, sir. D'ye ken who she is?"

"No, I've no idea." *Not that I know so many people around here,* he added silently. The girl could be anyone, a farmer's daughter, though he rather doubted that, or even, judging by her dress, somebody's governess. The only thing he was certain of, after looking at her fingers bare of rings, was that she was unmarried. That gave him a curious feeling of satisfaction, though he didn't know why. "We can't leave her here. Nothing in her bag to say who she is?"

"No, sir." Geordie backed out of the carriage, a portmanteau in his hand. "Nothing." Uneasily, he glanced around. "I mislike this, my lord. It's getting dark—"

"I know. And we cannot leave this girl lying here, no matter who she is." Philip bent and hoisted the unconscious girl over his shoulder and rose easily, though he wasn't nearly so large or strong as Geordie. "We'll have to go the back way to Havenwood. I'll take her and send help back."

"Aye, sir. I'll see to the others."

"Good man." Carefully Philip deposited the girl on the seat of the curricle and then climbed in himself. It was a good thing that his horses were tired after a long day on the road, else they might have bolted by now. So much for his quiet return to his home, he thought wryly, setting off, an arm around the girl to support her. She was very still, and that worried him. The handkerchief he'd used to bind the wound was already soaked through with blood. He thought she wasn't badly hurt, having seen enough injuries in his time, and yet, suppose he were wrong? He had to get her to shelter, and help, soon. Whoever she was, and that question was intriguing him more by the minute, she certainly was disrupting his life and the quiet retreat to his home he'd planned. And that, oddly enough, didn't bother him at all.

She was floating, drifting, at peace, relaxed. Why had she complained about the coach? Quite clearly it was a superior one, well-made and well-sprung. It gave an amazingly smooth ride, almost as though she were lying on a bed.

She *was* lying in bed, Sarah realized, and a soft one, too. For a moment her confused mind reeled. She was in her own bed, and her maid would awaken her in a moment with chocolate and muffins, and Papa was downstairs, already starting the day's work. But, no, Papa was dead, she thought, with a wrench of loss stronger than any she'd felt in a long time. Where was she, then? This was much too soft a bed to be her governess's pallet. Unless Mr. Ramsay had succeeded in getting her into bed, after all, and —

That made her open her eyes, and what she saw confused her even more. The room in which she'd awakened was unknown to her. Not any bedroom at Rockhill Grange, that was for certain; Mrs. Ramsay's taste was nothing like this. The room was decorated with a cheerful simplicity that pleased her. Bright chintz drapes hung at the casement windows, open against the late-summer warmth of the day. The bed in which she lay was a simple fourposter with a net canopy, and over there, in the corner to her right, was an equally simple washstand. And, at the foot of her bed, in a comfortable-looking wing chair, sat a man dressed all in black, in profile to her.

The sight of a man in her bedchamber should have startled her at the least, but instead it was oddly comforting. She *knew* this man, somehow, knew the way his dark, straight hair fell

11

across his forehead, knew the way his skin would darken in the summer sun, knew that the fingers that held his book would be long and elegant, and yet strong. Something settled in her, then, a feeling of peace. The sense she'd had before, that she was heading toward something wonderful, returned. Stronger now, though, because she'd found it.

And then, though she had made no sound, the man turned toward her, and she saw his eye patch.

Chapter Two

Sarah gave a little shriek, startling herself in the hush of the room. The man paused in the act of rising but then continued with unhurried, almost graceful movements, carefully marking his place in the book before laying it down. She was right, she thought dazedly as he came toward her. He did have long, strong fingers.

"Good morning, madam." He was unsmiling, and yet, in spite of that, in spite of the eye patch that gave him almost a sinister look, Sarah felt no threat from him. His good eye, startlingly bright and blue, was calm and steady. This was a man one could lean on. "I trust you are feeling more the thing."

"I — yes." Face flaming, Sarah reached behind herself to plump up the pillows, trying in some way to meet this man on more equal footing. The movement sent such a sharp stab of pain through her head that she gasped. She fell back, eyes closed, and set herself to endure.

A moment later, she felt a cool cloth being laid across her brow. "Is that better?"

Sarah opened one eye, cautiously. This was all very odd. "Yes, thank you," she said, as meek as the schoolgirl she once had been. "What happened to me?"

"I was rather hoping you could tell me that." The man drew a chair forward. "May I sit?"

"Yes, of course — whatever are you doing in my room?"

Something that might have been a smile briefly appeared at

the corners of his mouth. "I was wondering when you would ask me that."

"Well?" she demanded, in her best schoolteacher voice.

The smile flickered again. "Rather, madam, you should ask yourself what you are doing in my house." He paused, his face growing wary. "I am Pembroke."

She frowned. "Oh. Have we met?" Perhaps the blow to her head, whatever had caused it, had addled her wits, but she had no memory of this man. She was certain she would, no matter what had occurred to her.

"I believe not. You are—?"

"Sarah Chadwick—oh!" She shot up in bed, and the pain stabbed at her again. "Ouch." She subsided against the pillows, her face very white. "This hurts like the devil."

"It should. You were shot."

"Shot!" Suddenly, it all came back, the carriage, the fallen tree, the ruffian reaching for her. "My uncle, he'll be worried—"

"You've relatives in the neighborhood, then." Pembroke leaned back, and Sarah didn't know if she heard relief or disappointment in his voice.

"Yes. Sir Edwin Staples. Well, he isn't really my uncle, but he was my guardian. Before I came of age, of course."

"Of course." There was nothing in Pembroke's voice out of the ordinary, and yet she had the strangest feeling that he was laughing at her. "I shall see he's notified. Though I fear this will do your reputation little good."

"Really?" Sarah tilted her head, regarding him for a long moment.

"You don't ask why," he said, finally, apparently uncomfortable under her scrutiny.

"No."

"You aren't curious, then?"

"Oh, curiosity's one of my besetting sins," she said cheerfully. "But I've other things on my mind just now. My uncle—"

"Yes, that is a problem."

"It needn't be. He doesn't know I'm coming."

"Oh?" Something that might have been curiosity sparked in

14

his eye. "I see. In that case, it might be best to say nothing. I was serious when I spoke of your reputation."

"Really?" She looked at him again, and her eyes, which had been dull with pain, began to sparkle. She dearly loved a mystery, and here she was, right in the middle of one. "Very well, if you think it's wise. And if you don't intend to ravish me."

Pembroke stared at her a moment and then grinned. She should have been insulted, Sarah thought, at the implication that she was not desirable, but the old pain was blotted out by the sheer pleasure of seeing his taut, tight face relax. He looked younger, freer, and remarkably handsome. Again that sense of something wonderful about to happen caught at her and then faded.

"Trust me, Miss Chadwick. I am not the monster some people believe me."

"No, do they?" Sarah tilted her head. "Because of the eye patch?"

"That, and other things." His face was tight and wary again. "No, Miss Chadwick, I assure you. You are safe with me. No matter what others might say."

"I'm sure they're wrong," she said warmly, "whoever they are. And I do hope my uncle isn't one of them."

Pembroke shrugged. "It is of no moment. He won't hear of this unless you wish him to. My servants won't talk."

"Then they are unlike any servants I've ever known."

Pembroke's face relaxed briefly. "Nevertheless, they'll keep quiet. And when you do return to your uncle's house, I'll explain how you came to be here, of course."

"It doesn't matter." She yawned, startling both him and herself. "My reputation's not so very important." Another yawn.

"I'm tiring you." Pembroke rose. "I would like to know what happened to your carriage, but it can wait."

"Yes." Sarah snuggled deeper into the pillows, savoring the luxury of sleeping in such a soft bed again. "This is a haven."

Pembroke shot her a look, but she didn't see. "Rest easy, ma'am. No one will disturb you here."

"Mmm. Thank you," Sarah muttered, and closed her eyes. A moment later she was breathing deeply, sound asleep.

Philip stood by the bed a moment, staring down at her. By all rights he should leave her to the care of his housekeeper, but not yet. Not yet. A most unusual woman, Miss Chadwick. Apart from that first shriek, she'd shown little interest in his injury, as if it didn't even exist. Remarkable. And really quite remarkably attractive. Younger than she would have him think, too, in spite of her evident command of herself. "Well, Miss Chadwick," he murmured, reaching out to tuck the comforter more closely about her with a tenderness at odds with his fierce appearance, "it seems you and I will be speaking again."

Pleasure so filled him at the thought that he gazed at her a moment longer, unable to move, and then turned sharply away. Not for him, he reminded himself as he left the room, quietly closing the door behind him. She was not for him.

"Good morning, miss." The woman advanced into the room with measured tread, a tray held out before her and her skirts, the same iron gray as her hair, rustling sharply about her. "I hope you are feeling better this morning."

"Yes, thank you." Sarah leaned back against the pillows, folding her hands meekly in her lap. The woman reminded her irresistibly of the headmistress of her last school, the one who had always been so quick to catch out a younger, and freer, Sarah at some mischief.

"His lordship said as I'm to give you breakfast." She set the tray across Sarah's lap with a thump that would have made another invalid wince. Fortunately Sarah was made of sterner stuff. "If you'll be wanting anything else—"

"I am Sarah Chadwick." Sarah held out her hand. After all, she was no longer that silly schoolgirl to be intimidated by the same stern face she herself had used on her pupils. "And you are . . . ?"

"Mrs. Stevenson, miss," the woman said unwillingly, and dropped a token curtsy. "His lordship's housekeeper."

"Really? Then I must congratulate you on your work, from what I've seen of this house. It really is one of the

16

most comfortable I've seen in a very long time."

"No thanks to me." Mrs. Stevenson set herself to drawing back the drapes, allowing golden sunlight to stream into the room. "Some people just don't know when to stop poking their noses in where they don't belong."

Sarah picked up a piece of toast, rather surprised to discover that she was ravenous. "His lordship, you mean? But why would he be concerned about the ordering of the house?"

"You may well ask. Not natural, it isn't, him being so involved. And those things he makes! How he ever thinks of them, I don't know. If he'd only let a body do her work—"

"He sounds a most extraordinary employer," Sarah murmured, dipping her head to hide her smile.

"Too much so, if you ask me!" Mrs. Stevenson exclaimed, and then looked abashed. "But, there, you didn't ask, and I'd much appreciate it, miss, if you don't tell his lordship what I said—"

"Does he not treat you well, then?"

"Oh, as to that, he's fair enough, I suppose." Her voice was grudging. "Pays a good wage and always comments on work well-done. But lord help you, miss, if something's out of order, or if I touch one of those precious machines of his."

"Machines?"

"Aye, machines. Instruments of the devil, if you ask me. Why, there's a machine to write two letters at once, not that he needs that, him being able to write with both hands and all, and that contraption he calls a dumbwaiter and—but you won't be interested in that," she said, suddenly reverting to the same stiff demeanor she had worn upon entering.

"It sounds most unusual, Mrs. Stevenson. I wonder you bother to stay?"

"Oh, comes to that, he's fair enough. Not many would pay what he does. But then, not many would work for him, neither."

"What does he pay you?"

"Thirty pounds, miss, not that it's any of your concern! Now, if you'll excuse me, I've a deal of work to do."

"Of course," Sarah murmured, watching as Mrs. Stevenson

trod out the door, her interest piqued by the picture she was getting of her reluctant host. Thirty pounds per annum was indeed a handsome salary for a housekeeper, which could mean either that Lord Pembroke was extraordinarily generous or that he had difficulty keeping servants. Both, perhaps? And those machines Mrs. Stevenson had mentioned with such disapproval—whatever could they be?

Thoughtfully, Sarah finished her breakfast, only half-noticing the quality of the bacon, larded with little fat, or the fine texture of the bread or the fragrance of the tea that proclaimed it the best, and properly brewed, too. She had landed herself in an odd situation this time, and no mistaking. To have been shot—shot!—and then to have ended up in this house was adventure such as she had never supposed would happen to her. And, she decided, pushing the tray away, while she was here she might as well make the most of it. Soon enough it would be back to meager governess fare for her, and a life ordered by someone else. While she could, she would take advantage of her freedom.

Her head throbbed a bit as she rose, but she ignored it, opening the wardrobe and finding her clothes there, neatly cleaned and pressed. Whatever else Mrs. Stevenson might be—did she ever smile? Sarah wondered—she kept a well-run house. Still, Sarah couldn't keep from making a face as she pulled her gray stuff gown over her head. Dismal thing. She wondered if she would ever wear bright colors again.

Feeling a bit like an interloper, Sarah opened her door and stepped into a wide corridor that stretched vast distances in either direction. She hesitated for a moment and then, on impulse, turned to her right. Lord Pembroke certainly didn't stint on comfort; the carpet was thick under her feet and sconces set in the wall, gas-lighted ones, she noted with surprise, insured that this hallway would never be dark. She wondered what anyone would say should she be found wandering about the house, but she wasn't really doing anything wrong. Was she?

The corridor abruptly opened onto a landing, and again she hesitated. Then, marshaling her courage, she started down the curving staircase, finding herself in a square entrance hall, floored with flagstones. Across from her another set of stairs rose, leading probably to another wing. Just how big was this house? she wondered, and turned to the inner door.

At that moment, the clock over the doorway struck the hour, and she looked up. Not only was the time displayed, but the day of the week, as well. "Goodness," she murmured, and her gaze rose higher, to the ceiling. To her complete surprise, a compass was mounted there, for what reason she could not guess. "Well, Sarah, you've landed yourself in it proper this time, I'd say," she murmured, and pushed open the door.

Immediately she found herself in a vast, circular space tiled in marble. Again she looked up and was delighted to see that this room had no ceiling, only a dome high above with a gallery running around it about halfway up. Stained glass set in the dome sent shafts of color into the immense space, gilding the marble busts set in niches in the wall and changing her gown from drab to bright as she revolved, laughing with pleasure: crimson, gold, vermilion. Then the color faded as the sun went behind a cloud, and she returned to earth. This was likely the center of the house, with wings extending to either side. A most remarkable house owned, she was beginning to suspect, by a most remarkable man.

Doors set into the circular walls beckoned, and she gave into her curiosity. One opened into a handsome dining room, furnished conventionally, if attractively, with a mahogany Hepplewhite table. Not so conventional were the botanical prints on the wall, rather than the customary hunting scenes. Sarah closed the door and opened another at random, finding herself in a room filled with sunlight. The far wall was entirely glass, and everywhere there were plants, many of which she couldn't identify. Since the room faced south, it would be a delightful place in which to sit in winter, but just now it was stifling. She closed the door with relief and went into another room, the drawing room. There she stopped, very still. Facing her across the length of the room was a portrait of the most beautiful woman she had ever seen.

19

She paused for a moment on the threshold and then quietly closed the door behind her. It had somehow become imperative that no one know she was there. Save for a leather upholstered chair with a desk attached to it, the drawing room, too, was furnished conventionally, painted in pale colors with straw-colored draperies at the windows. The focal point of the room was obviously intended to be the portrait over the mantel.

Unable to stop herself, Sarah walked toward it. The woman in the portrait was young and radiated an impish kind of self-confidence that made Sarah feel inferior. Golden curls clustered about her head, her mischievous smile displayed deep dimples, and her eyes—her eyes were those of a woman in love, Sarah knew instantly, though she herself had never really been in that happy state. Who was she? Standing on tiptoes, Sarah searched the gilt frame for a nameplate, but there was none. It was important to her, somehow, to learn the woman's identity, even more important to learn who had painted it with such obvious love. This house had presented her with a great deal of puzzles to be solved, but none mattered more to her than this.

Sarah gazed at the portrait a moment longer, aware as she had rarely been of her own plain brown hair and eyes and her less-than-perfect figure and then abruptly turned away. So far she had met no one in her tour of the house, but now the skin at the back of her neck was prickling. For some reason she couldn't fathom, she'd rather no one see her studying the lady of the portrait.

In the hall again, safe from prying eyes, she headed on impulse toward the other stairs. Her headache was returning and she was beginning to tire, but something more than mere curiosity drove her on. There was a secret at the heart of this house, and it was somehow very important for her to learn what it was.

This wing was unlike the other; no carpets lined the wideboard floor, and the sconces were plain. Sarah's sense of intrusion began to grow, yet from down the corridor came a sound that piqued her curiosity further. It was a steady, rhythmic sound, thump, thump, thump, and it drew her inexorably along the hall to a room whose door stood ajar.

Sarah's curiosity failed her. She wanted nothing so much as to run back to her room and safety. But she had always told her pupils to have courage, and it would be hypocritical for her to run away from one little room. With a thumping sound, of course. It was that, more than anything, that made her push at the door. "Hello?" she called.

There was no answer. Growing braver, Sarah opened the door more fully and stepped into what was surely one of the most amazing rooms she had ever seen.

Like the hall downstairs, it was circular, and she guessed that it was in a tower. Heavens, what was this house, a castle? She found the source of the thumping sound almost immediately. Set against one wall was a printing press, apparently running by itself. To her left, a skylight set in the wall let in northern light, touching on an easel covered by a drop cloth. Sarah's fingers itched to lift the cloth and see what was beneath, but even she wasn't that brave. Besides, there was so much more to see in this room! On one long table were all kinds of apparatus, the uses of which she couldn't even begin to imagine, and piles and piles of papers, each covered with a distinctive, spiky scrawl. A small table nearby held a quantity of wax, several keys, and scraps of metal of indeterminate origin. More plants lined the windowsills. Shelves held large glass jars such as she had seen in apothecary's shops. And there were books. Oh, and so many books, set in cases far enough from the windows to prevent any damage from the sun, books bound in morocco leather or cloth or even paper, all looking well-used. Sarah's head whirled as she slowly began to move down the shelves, staring at such treasure. Books on electricity, the Americas, botany. Books in Latin and Greek, as well as French, Spanish, and Italian. Books in English, too, all meticulously grouped together and all irresistible. Sarah was just reaching out for one on the education of children when the door suddenly slammed open. She whirled, her hand to her heart, the book falling to the floor, and faced a formidable-looking Lord Pembroke.

Sarah's heart began to pound. Before she hadn't been afraid of him, but now she was, a little. It wasn't so much the eye patch, though that added to the fierceness of his appearance, but the sense she had that he was very, very angry. He was garbed all in black again, black pantaloons, black waistcoat, with only the brilliant white of his shirt relieving his somber appearance; that, and the brilliance of his eye. And he was, she realized again, a very handsome man, eye patch or no.

"What are you doing in here?" Pembroke demanded, and Sarah's fear drained away. He sounded like a petulant little boy, and heavens knew she had faced enough of them in her day.

"I told you," she said cheerfully, stooping to pick up the fallen book and ignoring the way her head throbbed. "Curiosity is my besetting sin."

She may have imagined it, but she thought she saw a smile twitch at the corners of his mouth. "I see. Did no one ever tell you that curiosity killed the cat?"

"Now, my lord, with all you've done in this house, can't you come up with something more original than that?"

This time, there was no mistaking it. He did smile, if only for a moment. The tension between them eased perceptibly as he stepped towards her. "You're not afraid of me," he said, sounding bemused.

"No. Should I be?"

"No. But then, you're new to the neighborhood."

"Ah. A mystery."

"One that the local tabbies will happily solve for you," he said bitterly, and went on before she could speak. "Very well, madam, I grant you your curiosity, since it's a trait I happen to share. You may go anywhere you like in this house. Except this room."

His voice was so firm that Sarah knew there was no disobeying it. She had gone beyond what was allowed. "Very well. What are you printing?"

Philip's eye flicked toward the printing press. "It is of no moment. Now, madam, may I escort you to your room? You are looking a trifle peaked."

"I feel peaked," she said frankly. "But, no, thank you, sir, I can find my own way." Giving him a quick smile, she dropped a curtsy and then edged by him. "You have a most unusual house, my lord."

"Thank you. Oh, and Miss Chadwick. . . ."

Sarah paused by the door. "Yes?"

"I would be honored if you would dine with me tonight."

"Why, I would be pleased to, sir," she said, smiling. "And perhaps then you'll tell me what you're printing."

"What?" he exclaimed, but she was gone, whisking about the door in a swirl of gray skirts. The smile that had threatened before grew wide, until it was almost a grin. "Minx," he muttered, and turned away.

The smile faded. She would leave soon, and with her would go something he hadn't even known was missing from his life. But he would endure, as he had before. He had rebuilt his world very carefully, and only now did he realize how fragile it was. No one would be allowed to destroy it or his precarious peace of mind. Not even Miss Sarah Chadwick.

"Good evening, miss." The maid bobbed in the doorway. "Mrs. Stevenson says as how I'm to help you get ready for dinner."

"Goodness!" Sarah couldn't help from smiling. How long was it since she had needed a maid? Too long. For so many years now she had been fending for herself and could very well do so tonight. Except—except for him with whom she was dining. "Very well. What is your name?"

"Millie, miss." The maid bobbed another curtsy and came to fasten the long row of hooks on Sarah's best gown, another gray, though of silk. "A lovely gown, miss, and lovely hair. Shall I dress it for you?"

"You can try." Sarah sat at the dressing table and smiled at the maid, whose eyes were as curious as her own. "Though I warn you now, it won't take a curl."

"We'll see. Proper lucky, I am," Millie went on. "All of us wanted to serve you, and Mrs. S. chose me."

23

"Really?" Sarah bit back a smile. "Am I so interesting, then?"

"Lord love you, miss, nothing so exciting has happened around here in a long time! Imagine being set upon by highwaymen!"

"Yes, well—"

"Be different if his lordship entertained." Millie picked up a pair of curling tongs, which Sarah eyed with trepidation. "Keeps to himself when he's here."

"Does he?" Sarah said cautiously. She was well aware of the impropriety of discussing her host with one of his servants, but, again, curiosity had gotten the better of her.

"That he does, miss. Never has visitors, never goes out. And he never talks to anyone, does he? But he knows everything that's going on. It's not natural, I'd say."

"But he's a good employer?"

"Oh, yes, miss, long as you stay out of his way. Has a proper temper, he does. I heard you made him smile."

"Yes, so?"

"He doesn't do that too often. There, miss." Millie stepped back. "What do you think about that?"

"Why, Millie, it looks quite nice," Sarah said in genuine surprise. Her plain brown hair had been caught in a fashionable cluster of curls atop her head, held there by a cherry ribbon that somehow brightened the rest of her ensemble. "I almost feel fashionable."

"You look fine as fivepence, miss, if I do say so myself. Good enough to dine with the Regent himself."

Sarah laughed as she rose. "Hardly likely, Millie. But then, a few days ago, I'd not have expected this, either."

"Lord love you, miss, who can blame you? I wouldn't want to dine with his lordship, and that's for certain." She shuddered. "Fair frightens me, he does."

"I find him most pleasant," Sarah said sharply, fixing Millie with her governess's eye. This exchange of improprieties had gone on long enough. Never mind that she herself had felt just the slightest bit scared of the marquess this afternoon. He was just a man.

Pembroke was waiting for her in the great circular hall when she came down. The westering sun turned the stained glass colors more mellow, and Sarah looked up, smiling. "I do adore your dome. All those lovely colors."

A smile touched Philip's lips. "A fancy of mine, I fear."

"I like it. Though this must be cold in winter."

"We heat with steam. Come. Shall we go in to dinner?"

"Yes, thank you." Sarah laid her fingers lightly on his arm and was surprised to find it hard-muscled. A deceptive man, lean, but not weak. She must remember that.

Philip seated her to his left at the dining table, rather than at the other end. Conversation while dinner was served was light and general: the recent developments in the ongoing war on the Peninsula; the latest doings of the Prince Regent; and, of course, the weather, which had generally been good. It was this last subject, to Sarah's surprise, that seemed to bring him to life. It had been a perfect summer for planting, and he expected a good harvest come fall. He sounded, in fact, just like a farmer, and that image was so incongruous with his appearance, elegant in black evening clothes, that she smiled.

"I'd not have thought you a farmer," she said.

"But I am, among other things. Everything you see was grown on this estate."

"It looks delicious," she said, as the entrée, lamb with minted jelly, was set on the table. Steam rose from silver serving dishes containing various vegetables—fresh peas, new potatoes cooked just until done and sprinkled with parsley, and slices of a green vegetable Sarah couldn't identify. "However does your cook manage to keep everything so warm?"

To her surprise, he grinned. "By something Mrs. Stevenson absolutely detests. Do you see that door, there?" he asked, turning, and she followed his gaze to see a small door set into the wall, about midway between floor and ceiling. The footman who was waiting on them was taking food from it. "It's called a dumbwaiter. Cook puts the food in it—the kitchen is in the basement—and then by means of ropes and pulleys it comes up here."

"Really?"

"Really." Philip smiled at her surprise. There was nothing hidden about this woman. Everything she thought, felt, showed on her face, and she approached life with an enthusiasm that had long ago left him. He didn't know whether to envy her or to feel superior.

Sarah shook her head in wonder. "How ingenious." She had assumed that, as in most houses of this size, that the food had to be carried upstairs and down long corridors before it reached the dining room at best only warm. Heavens knew in the days of her come-out, she had eaten enough such meals. The marquess's contraption made dinner infinitely more enjoyable. "Did you design it?"

Philip took a sip of his wine. "Yes."

"Oh." Sarah, too, sipped at her wine, a fine burgundy that she was quite enjoying after her years of more meager fare. "It's a very well-run house."

"I hire only the best."

"And pay them well, I'll wager."

Philip set down his wine glass. "Tell me, Miss Chadwick. Is outspokenness one of your sins, too?"

"Oh, yes. It's got me into trouble any number of times."

This time, he did smile. "I can imagine."

Sarah found it hard to look away, so real was the feeling of closeness between them. An intriguing man. A clever one, obviously. A man who loved color, and yet a man who seemed to wear only black. "Do you always wear black?"

"Yes. Do you always wear gray?"

"Only since I became a governess."

"A governess. Ah. I should have known." He sat back, and again Sarah suspected that he was laughing at her. "No, we'll have coffee in the drawing room," he said to the footman, who was placing the sweet, a trifle, on the table. "Are you on holiday, then?"

"No." She made a face. Philip noticed again how mobile her features were and how expressive her fine, dark eyes. "And, as I lost my last position—I'd rather not say how—I decided to come back to Sir Edwin's until I find another. Though I don't particularly want to."

26

"Why not?"

She made that face again. "No real reason," she said, not meeting his gaze. "And then my carriage was set upon by highwaymen, and—"

"We'll speak of that in the drawing room, I think. If you are ready?"

"Of course." She rose, intrigued again. Now why wouldn't he wish to discuss the attack here? Surely it must be common knowledge in the neighborhood by now.

In the drawing room, Philip stood beside the leather chair she'd noted earlier as he waited for their coffee to be served. Sarah, ignoring both footman and marquess, drifted over to the painting that hung over the mantel, unable to stay away. Who was she trying to fool? Even in her best gown with her hair fashionably curled, she was no match for this beauty.

The door closed behind the footman, and they were alone. "Won't you have a seat, Miss Chadwick?" Philip said.

"Of course." Sarah gave the portrait one last look and then turned away. "Who is she?"

Philip paused for just a moment, and his voice when he spoke was rough. "She was my wife."

Chapter Three

It hit Sarah like a blow. His wife. Of course. A man such as he, handsome, wealthy, titled, would naturally have married a beauty, in spite of his various eccentricities or his eye patch, married her and kept her happy, by the look in the woman's eyes. Sarah suddenly felt very jealous of that.

"She looks happy," she said, babbling before she could stop herself. "Like a woman in love."

"She was," Philip said, in such an odd tone that she turned to look at him. "But, come. I want to hear more about your accident. It's not usual to have highwaymen in these parts."

So his late wife wasn't to be a topic of conversation. He must have loved her very much, Sarah thought, and felt that swift upsurge of jealousy again. Not that she had any right to be jealous, she reminded herself, sinking gracefully onto the sofa of straw-colored satin, the silk of her gown glistening just a bit as it settled around her. "I don't believe they were ordinary highwaymen, sir. I don't know what highwaymen would want with me, anyway. I certainly have little of value."

"Did they try to rob you?"

"No." Sarah frowned, trying to remember. After her day exploring and the wine she had had at dinner, her headache had returned, and it was difficult to think. "I don't remember it very well."

"I don't wonder. Do you have any enemies?"

"Who would a governess have for enemies, sir? I assure you, even my former charges didn't dislike me so much."

He didn't smile. "Regardless, you were attacked. If robbery weren't the motive, then what did they want?"

"I don't know. Not me, certainly. They wanted a man."

"Is that what they said?" Philip said sharply.

"Ye-es. No. Now I remember, a little. One of them, the one who grabbed me, said he thought it was supposed to be a gent they wanted."

"A gent." Philip sat back in his leather chair, and then, putting his foot against the floor, spun the seat partly around and back. "A gent. You're certain that's what he said."

Sarah was staring. "That's a most unusual chair, sir."

"Yes. A gent."

Something about the tone of his voice made her look at him. "You know something about it, sir?"

"No." Philip rose. "You must be tired. You do realize that for your reputation you'll have to stay here until your wound heals?"

"Yes," Sarah said, though she knew quite well the scar could be covered by her hair. She didn't want to leave this house. Not just yet.

"Then I'll bid you good night."

"Thank you." She curtsied; he bowed, watching her go as she left the room. Then he turned, facing the windows.

"Did you hear that?"

"Aye, sir." Geordie stepped out from behind the drapes. "And next time, sir, don't be askin' me to go skulkin' behind curtains like some thief. It's not something I'd do for just anybody."

"I know that, Geordie." Philip smiled. "I thought it was best this time."

"Aye, sir. She is a bonny thing, isn't she?"

"I hadn't noticed. What do you think of what she said?"

Geordie's face instantly sobered. "Got me worried, sir. Not many people use that road beside you."

"You think it was meant for me, then."

"I don't know, sir. All I'm thinkin' is, we got trouble."

"So it would seem," Philip said, but it was not of the highwaymen he thought. Instead he saw expressive dark eyes lit with curiosity, a sweet smile, and, underneath the governess gown, a figure that could drive a man to distraction. Now *that* was trouble, yet somehow he didn't mind letting her stay until she had completely recovered. Not at all.

"Sir?" Geordie said, and Philip realized he had been talking. "What should I do about it?"

"What can we do? We haven't found the other ruffian, and unless we know who hired them, it's pointless."

"Then you'd best be on your guard, sir."

"I intend to be." Philip drained his coffee. On his guard against those expressive eyes, that lush figure. Not for him. Such as she would never again be for him.

Sarah healed quickly. She would not have stayed abed even if she hadn't; the only effect she had from her adventure was a headache, and what was that? A mere trifle. Ladies like Mrs. Ramsay might allow themselves to be prostrated by such a thing, but Sarah didn't have, or desire, that luxury. There was always too much to do, too much to see.

Except that there really wasn't much to do in this huge, unusual house. Whatever else she was, Mrs. Stevenson was an efficient housekeeper, and the staff was industrious. And quiet, so much so they were almost invisible. Sarah had no doubt that below stairs they were buzzing speculatively about her, but when she chanced to meet any staff, she would be met with a bowed head and a brief curtsy or bow. It was, Sarah acknowledged, a well-run house, beautiful in its own way— and empty. Empty of life, empty of laughter. She actually found herself missing her former charges; at least they would disrupt the almost tomblike hush that pervaded the mansion.

Sarah shuddered at the thought and reached almost at random for a book from the library shelf. The book room was not at all like the marquess's bizarre workroom with its technical and foreign books. Here one could find, more conventionally, the classics and, somewhat to Sarah's surprise, the most recent novels. Odd how the marquess seemed to know everything that was going on, though he so rarely left the house. He rode early in the morning, alone, she was told, never went out in company, and certainly never received guests. Likely he was the major focus of gossip and interest in the neighborhood because he did so little. Likely she, too, was a topic of conversation, she thought ruefully, but that was nothing new.

She had at last found to her delight a novel by the author of *Sense and Sensibility,* called *Pride and Prejudice,* when the bookroom door opened and Philip came in. Without seeming to see her on the library steps, he crossed the room and stood in front of one of the cases, frowning a bit. Sarah wasn't certain whether to make her presence known or not. She saw so little of him. They met only at dinner, and conversation then was always general. Sometimes they even lapsed into silence, which, because of her gregarious nature, was hard to endure. She had been there nearly a week, and she knew little more about her host than she had when she first met him.

What she did know was there was something about him that compelled her, drew her to him. It wasn't just that he was handsome; heavens knew she was far past the age when mere good looks would sway her. No, there was something more about him, a leashed energy that she saw manifested in the odd and various contrivances he had set up in the house, and the sense that underneath his brooding, forbidding exterior was an actual flesh and blood man. After all, she had seen him smile once or twice; though he never seemed to laugh. What, she wondered, had caused him to lock himself up in this mausoleum of a house, never to leave again?

"Ahem." She scrambled down the stairs, and Philip, who had just reached for a book, turned, startled. "I'm sorry, sir, I didn't mean to surprise you," she said, her eyes widening as she saw the title of the book he had chosen. *"The Secret Marriage?"* Sarah's eyes sparkled. "Oh, surely not! Don't tell me that you actually read such gothicky stuff."

She could swear that faint color had spread across his cheekbones. "It was out of place," he muttered, turning to replace the volume, and she quickly reached out to lay her hand on his arm. He looked down at her hand and then at her, and for a moment the world stopped. "I'll just put it back."

31

Sarah began breathing again, though she felt oddly light-headed. The continuing effects of her concussion, she supposed. "Please don't. I was only funning you. I fear my tastes aren't the highest, either."

Philip glanced down at her book. "You'll enjoy that. Tell me, Miss Chadwick. Do you quite enjoy funning people?"

"Oh, quite," she said cheerfully. "Most people take themselves much too seriously, haven't you noticed? I've always found that laughing makes things easier."

Philip gazed at her for a moment and then smiled. "Very well, Miss Chadwick, I admit it. I do read gothics."

"There, now, what was so very difficult about that? Even geniuses need to relax."

"I'm hardly that, ma'am," he said, crossing to a chair.

"Nonsense, of course you are! But I'm glad to see you do something for pleasure. Life is so dull else, don't you think?"

"Are you implying my life is dull?"

"Well—"

"I do a great deal for pleasure, madam."

"Such as?"

He smiled, sitting back with his legs crossed and his fingers steepled. "You are a most vexing woman. Very well, if you must know, I ride in the morning."

"Looking at your estate. That's work."

"I also enjoy tinkering in my workroom."

"Also work."

"Not if you enjoy it." He stared at her and shrugged. "Very well. What would you consider pleasure?"

"Oh, I don't know. Socializing, of course, taking a walk for the fun of it, playing games."

"Such as chess?"

Sarah made a face. "Much too slow. No, I was thinking of a good hand of piquet."

"Piquet! You hardly look the type to enjoy gambling."

Sarah smiled. "Another of my vices. I'm quite good at it, you know."

"You are a most unusual governess, Miss Chadwick." He looked at her measuringly, and Sarah knew he was trying to puzzle her out. "Very well. Piquet it will be."

"Now?" Sarah said, as he rose and went to the library table.

"Why not?" He withdrew a pack of cards from a drawer. "No time like the present, is there? Or are you scared you'll lose?"

"Nothing of the sort! Very well. I'll take your challenge, sir. Except—"

"Ah. Need a concession, do you?"

"You needn't sound so odious," she said, sitting on the chair he held out for her. "If you must know, I haven't much money, so we'll have to play for chicken stakes."

"I believe I could manage a penny a game." He sat across from her, his face calm, his hands expertly shuffling the cards. Something about the sight of his long, elegant fingers sent a shiver through her. What would they feel like, touching her?

"Miss Chadwick?"

"Hm?" Sarah looked up, aware that he'd been speaking while she'd been staring at his hands and thinking the most improper things. To her chagrin, she could feel herself blushing.

Philip watched the color rise in her face with interest. "I said, do you want to cut for the deal?"

"Oh. Oh, yes, of course." Sarah reached for the pack to cut it, won the cut, and elected to receive, giving her the advantage. "Carte blanche," she said, looking at her cards after he had dealt them.

"Really?" he said, in a slow drawl that made her blush again.

"You know quite well what I mean," she said severely. "I haven't a king, queen, or jack. That's ten points for me. And I'm not asking to be anyone's mistress."

"No, Miss Governess, ma'am." He marked her points down on the scrap of paper he was using to score, ignoring the look she shot him, and the play continued. The first game was a cautious one, each feeling out the other's skills and neither gaining the one hundred points needed to win. After that, though, the competition sharpened. Philip, who accorded himself a decent player because of his mathematical sense,

33

was put on his mettle by Sarah's fierce, concentrated play. He should have guessed, he thought, watching her gnaw on her lower lip as she decided which card to discard, that she would be as intense at this as she was in everything else. Nothing halfhearted about his Sarah. His Sarah, indeed. She was a person who belonged strictly to herself in a way he hadn't thought any woman could. Having her here this week had been a blessing unlooked for.

"Pique," she said, breaking into his reverie.

"What? I don't believe it. Let me see."

Sarah showed him her cards. "You sound piqued, sir."

"Ha. Definitely a pique, damn it."

"Why, Lord Pembroke, you swore."

"I am not accustomed to losing at cards."

"Then it is high time you learned. Repique."

"Damn!"

"Really, sir, I can't countenance such language."

Philip looked up sharply at the repressive, governess's tone of her voice to see her eyes sparkling with mirth. Something happened within him, an unfamiliar pressure building in his chest. It was a feeling almost of bubbles rising, and it was so strong that he had to give into it. Putting his head back, he laughed. "You are definitely a minx," he said. "Do you realize I haven't any points yet, and you need only ten more to win?"

"Yes, and that would double the value of the game."

"Baggage. You shouldn't be a governess, you know. You should set up your own gambling establishment."

She gave him a quick look. "I don't think so."

"Point," he said, showing her his cards. "You've not won yet."

Sarah drew a card from the stock. "And you've still to reach fifty. Capote."

"What?" He stared at her cards and then put his head in his hands. "All right. I concede."

"Good." She pulled in the cards and began to shuffle them. "I believe that's tuppence you owe me, sir."

"Where in the world did you learn to play?"

"From my father. He was a very smart man."

"Was?"

"He's been gone these two years past."

"I'm sorry."

"I do so miss him sometimes." She set out the deck for Philip to cut. "Do you know, perhaps I *should* open a gambling establishment."

Philip looked up quickly at that. "I was only jesting."

"Yes, but if I can continue winning tuppence—"

"You'd end up in a workhouse in no time."

"Not unless players like you came to play."

"Ha. And where would this be?"

"Oh, in London, of course," she said, arranging her cards by order of suit. When there was no answer, she looked up to see his face gone very still. "Well, there's no profit in doing it in Bibury, is there? London is where the money is. If I'm to do it, I should do it right."

"Strange to think of you in London," he said, to himself.

"But you'd come and visit, of course. Wouldn't you?"

He dropped his cards on the table and walked to a window. "No."

"Just like that, 'no'? Do you plan ever to leave Havenwood?"

"Not really, no."

Sarah folded her cards together. "What a waste."

He turned, his face savage. "What do you know about it?"

"Enough to know you're wasting your talents staying hidden away," she said, refusing to be intimidated by his fierce glare. "What are you so afraid of?"

"I fear nothing, madam."

"No? Then why do you never go out in company?"

"Madam, I am warning you—"

"Why do you hide away, and why have you never remarried?"

He stared at her for a long moment. "I believe you are quite recovered from your injury?"

Sarah looked startled at the change of topic. "Well, yes, but—"

"Then I believe it is time you journeyed on to your uncle's home."

35

"Oh, dear, I've offended you. I am sorry, I didn't mean to meddle—"

"Your maid will help you pack, and I'll see the carriage is brought round," he went on inexorably. "Now, Miss Chadwick, I suggest that you see to your packing."

A look at that stony face told her that further protestation would be useless. "Yes, sir. Thank you for letting me stay."

"You're welcome," he said, and turned back to the bookcase, quite effectively dismissing her.

Sarah stood for a few moments and then turned, laying her book down on the library table and blindly making her way to the door. She didn't think she had ever been so summarily dismissed, and it hurt almost as bad—no, worse than—than her come-out in Cheltenham. But, no, she wouldn't think of that. Nor would she give up. Since she would still be in the neighborhood, perhaps she would see him again.

She turned at the door. No, likely she wouldn't see him again, and it was her own fault. "I'm sorry," she said to his unresponsive back and went out, knowing she had blundered badly. Her interlude at Havenwood was over.

She was gone.

From the gallery that ran around the dome, high above the marble floor, Philip watched out the window as Sarah drove away. Or, rather, was driven, as he had driven her away. That was just as well. He had no room in his life for a cheerful, curious, and altogether too-attractive woman.

The carriage was long out of sight and even its dust had settled before Philip turned away. He could go back to the book room and retrieve the book he had chosen, but he had lost his taste for reading; he could go to his workroom and tinker with his latest project, a latch that would hold doors open automatically, but he knew he wouldn't be able to concentrate on it. He felt odd, restless, guilty. What he'd done was the right thing, of course. Of course. How quiet the house was, though, how empty, though in the brief week of her stay Sarah had made little noise, little trouble. And yet, her going left a void.

He finally decided to return to his room. It was nearing the dinner hour and he should change, though why he bothered, he didn't know. For a moment, a voice came back to him. *Do you always wear black?* He pushed the memory away. Black quite, quite suited his mood.

In his room, he pulled off his coat and walked over to his shaving mirror. Yes, he did need another shave, damn it, he had such a heavy beard. He was about to ring for his valet when he stopped, caught by his reflection. For a moment he studied himself and then, with great deliberation, reached up to untie the cord of his eye patch.

He forced himself to look at his scar quite unflinchingly. It was a fact of his life now, there was no denying that and no use railing against the fate that had taken so much from him. Dispassionately he studied the scar, turning his head so that he could see it from every angle, the puckered flesh, the closed lid. It was ugly. *He* was ugly, maimed for life, a pariah, and he didn't deserve happiness. Especially if it came in the form of a brown-haired, brown-eyed girl who had made him laugh for the first time in a very long time. She deserved better than him. That was why he had sent her away.

Enough of self-pity, he scolded himself, and tugged on the bellpull to summon his valet. He was what he was, and he would simply have to accept it. Sarah Chadwick was not for him. She could never be.

"Sarah!" Sir Edwin Staples waddled down the shallow steps of his manor house, the local Cotswold stone gleaming golden in the late afternoon sun. He looked every inch the country squire rather than the hardheaded businessman Sarah knew he was, in his top boots and buff tailcoat, the buttons of his waistcoat straining. "My dear, why didn't you let me know you were coming? I'd've sent my carriage for you," he said, frowning as the carriage that had brought her drove away. "Is that a hired rig?"

"Yes," Sarah lied, without a second thought. So her presence at Havenwood wasn't known. Pembroke's servants must be well-trained, indeed, not to spread such news through the neighborhood. She couldn't help but be relieved, and yet, a little disappointed, as well. This past week had somehow been one of the most significant of her life.

"I didn't know myself I was coming," she went on, turning her face so his kiss landed on her cheek. "I'm afraid I've come to ask for your charity, Uncle. I've lost my position."

"And a good thing, too." He patted her hand with his moist, pudgy one. "There's no need for you to be working at all, Sarah. You know you always have a home here."

"We've been over this, Uncle. You know why I choose to work. Papa's debts are not yet paid."

"If you would but let me help you, child—"

"No. Papa's debts are mine to pay." She stopped in the hall, glancing up, wishing wistfully for stained glass. "I won't argue with you, Uncle. If you wish to wrangle on this, then I'll have to leave."

"You always were a stubborn puss, eh?" Sir Edwin pinched her cheek as if she were still a child, and she stiffened. "I can't think what Benjamin was about, leaving you in such straits."

"What Papa did is past," she said firmly. The fact that Benjamin Chadwick, successful merchant, had died, not only insolvent, but in debt, was something she had ceased to wonder at. It had only added to the shock of losing her beloved father so suddenly from a brain fever to find that she, who had never lacked for anything, was suddenly penniless. Thus her dependency on Sir Edwin, her guardian, which had fueled her determination to work. Papa's debts were her problem.

"Oh, very well, very well. But you know you are welcome here as long as you wish. No need to go out looking for work just yet."

"So long as Papa's creditors hold off. But it would be nice to have a holiday," she said, more to herself than to him.

"Then you shall. Now let Mackie show you to your room. You must be tired after your long journey."

Sarah's smile was strained. "Yes, I am a trifle fatigued." In fact, her head was pounding terribly, proof that she hadn't yet fully recovered from her injury. Worse, though, was the shock

38

of leaving Havenwood so quickly, which had not yet abated. "Thank you, Uncle, for letting me stay."

"Anytime, my dear," he said, smiling.

The smile faded, however, as Sarah disappeared up the carved oak stairs. Great heavens, this was a contingency which he'd not planned to deal with just yet. The pangs of conscience, which he usually managed to suppress, would not be stilled this time. What was he to do about Benjamin's daughter?

"Everything looks lovely, Mrs. Watson," Sarah said, surveying Sir Edwin's dining room with a practiced eye. A cloth of pristine whiteness was spread upon the mahogany table. Upon this Mrs. Watson, Sir Edwin's housekeeper, had placed chrysanthemums in silver bowls, as well as the best beeswax candles. Covers had been laid for eight, including Sarah and Sir Edwin himself. On the evening after her arrival at her guardian's home, Sarah was about to be introduced to the neighborhood.

Mrs. Watson bobbed a curtsy as Sarah turned to Sir Edwin, standing with his legs braced apart and his hands tucked into his waistcoat pockets. "But you needn't have done this just for me," she went on. "I don't plan to be social while I am here."

"Nonsense, nonsense, you're my godchild, after all. Have to do the right thing by you, what?"

There was a rather odd note in his voice, making Sarah turn to look at him, but his face held its habitual expression of unimpaired geniality. Impossible to know what was going on behind those shrewd, sharp black eyes, so at odds with his beaming smile. "Oh, very well, since it seems I'll be here for a while. Until I find another position."

Sir Edwin frowned. "Now, child, as to that—"

"Uncle, I'll not argue this with you," Sarah said, as if speaking to one of her former charges. "Now. Tell me about our guests tonight."

Sometime later, sitting at the foot of the table, Sarah assessed the guests for herself. There were the Reverend and Mrs. Crabbe, who were, unfortunately, aptly named. Sarah could imagine Reverend Crabbe preaching fire-and-brimstone sermons while his wife indulged in gossip. There were also Squire Abbott with his wife Lady Amanda and their two children, Basil, of an age with Sarah, making calf's eyes at her throughout the evening, and Winifred, who would be making her come-out in Cirencester next spring. Lady Amanda's eyes were cool and watchful, but humor sparked in them whenever she glanced towards Mrs. Crabbe. Sarah thought that she might be able to have a friendship with her.

They weren't the only people Sir Edwin could have invited, of course. The Earl of Bathurst lived nearby, but he would never have attended such a simple affair even if he were at Cirencester Park, his estate, instead of in Brighton. There were other good families, solid English stock with decent estates and pedigrees stretching back centuries, and there was, of course, the Marquess of Pembroke. However, though he was by title, if nothing else, of the highest rank in the neighborhood, there was little known of him.

"How was it you came to leave your position, Miss Chadwick?" Mrs. Crabbe asked when they had been sitting for a time, her voice sweetly malicious.

Sarah smiled. "I found it didn't suit me. But, tell me," she said, diverting attention away from herself, "I noticed a most unusual house on the way here. I couldn't see much of it, but it looked something like a castle. Who lives there?"

For a moment, as the sweet, a syllabub, was served, there was silence. Glances were exchanged around the table and then Mrs. Crabbe spoke up. "That terrible monstrosity? That is Havenwood, my dear. You must avoid it at all costs."

"Now, Mrs. Crabbe, we should be kindly towards the marquess," the vicar said. "He is, after all, a fellow human being in Christ—"

"Yes, and didn't he tell you he didn't believe in such nonsense when you went to pay him a call? Imagine! He's not Church of England!"

"Imagine," Sarah murmured, bringing her napkin to her

mouth to hide her smile.

"A perfectly dreadful man," Mrs. Crabbe went on with relish. "Oh, of course, you don't know of whom we are speaking, my dear. The Marquess of Pembroke. And why he chose to settle here, I can't think!"

"I rather like him," Lady Amanda said, in her cool voice.

"Well, he quite terrifies me," Winifred put in, ignoring the minatory look her mother gave her. "That terrible eye patch he wears, it quite frightens me! And when you think of all he's done—"

"Winifred, dear, I don't believe Miss Chadwick is interested in local gossip." Lady Amanda's voice was icy.

"Pardon me, Lady Amanda, but I think she should be forewarned," Mrs. Crabbe interrupted. "After all, who knows what might happen should she meet with him?"

"Which will not happen," Sir Edwin said, beaming down the table towards Sarah.

"Heavens, he sounds most ferocious," Sarah said lightly. "Is he really so evil, then?"

"Really, Miss Chadwick, you wouldn't like him," Basil said, his voice earnest.

"I see. But what is it he is supposed to have done?"

There was again a little silence, and again it was Mrs. Crabbe who broke it. "Well, dear, one doesn't precisely know. And one must be charitable, of course; it is the only Christian thing to be, but one must wonder when one hears the rumors and the stories."

"And what rumors are those?"

"Why, that he killed his wife, of course."

Chapter Four

"Oh, surely not!" Sarah exclaimed, such horrified surprise in her voice that the others turned to look at her. "He wouldn't do a thing like that."

"Why, do you know him, dear?" Mrs. Crabbe said, with malicious sweetness.

"I — no, of course not." Sarah took refuge behind her napkin again. "It just seems unlikely since he's a marquess."

"I say, wouldn't be the first time someone noble did something wrong. And got away with it," Basil put in.

"I think we're being uncharitable to our neighbor," the Reverend Mr. Crabbe said, and Sir Edwin nodded.

"Indeed, indeed," he said. "No one knows the right of things. Must admit, though, the circumstances were dashed suspicious."

"What happened?" Sarah asked, some of her composure returning. What they were saying couldn't be true. The man she had known so briefly surely couldn't be capable of such a thing, sinister appearance or no. Could he?

"No one is quite certain," Mrs. Crabbe said, her eyes sparkling, "but it was a horrible thing. A fire, you know. They say the bed curtains went up and she didn't have a chance."

"Oh, no!"

"To be fair, he tried to save her," Squire Abbott pointed out. "It cost him his eye."

"But however did such a thing happen?" That beautiful woman, dying in such a horrible way, and her husband, injuring himself trying to save her. Sarah felt she understood the marquess a great deal more than she had just yesterday. Poor man. Poor, poor man.

"I'm sure I don't know," Mrs. Crabbe said. "Possibly he knocked over a candle. Or perhaps worse."

"Worse?"

"You wouldn't know, my dear." Mrs. Crabbe's voice darkened. "That house of his, filled with contrivances of the devil. Who knows what he did?"

"It doesn't do to meddle with the natural order of things," the vicar intoned. "I shall speak about that in my sermon this Sunday."

"But surely there was an inquest," Sarah said, looking from the vicar to his wife, filled with a sudden distaste for them. Listening so avidly to tales about a man she knew was suffering and condemning him.

"Of course there was an inquest," Sir Edwin said. "It was ruled an accident, and that's all we need to say."

"Except for the rumors," Mrs. Crabbe said, and her eyes were bright again.

"Oh, come now, Lavinia, you know that is the merest gossip," Lady Amanda said.

"No smoke without fire, I always say. Particularly in this case." She tittered at her own joke, though no one joined in. "And when a man's honor has been insulted in such a way — well, it's no wonder he did what he did."

Lady Amanda glanced at her daughter, listening closely, and then at Sarah. "Perhaps we should leave the gentlemen to their port now."

"What? Oh. Oh, yes, of course." Sarah rose, wondering what the rumors were, wondering why Lady Amanda hadn't wanted to speak of them. Good heavens, this was all such a tangled mess, she thought dazedly, leading the ladies to the drawing room. Surely it wasn't true.

She hadn't a chance to learn more, however, for Lady Amanda set Winifred to playing on the pianoforte and then determinedly turned the conversation to other matters. Though Mrs. Crabbe looked disappointed, Sarah was relieved to chatter of the happenings in Bibury, the nearby village, and to learn more about her other neighbors. She had just received a great shock, and she needed time to assimilate it. What could Pembroke's wife have done to make his performing such a heinous deed seem likely?

After their port, the men joined the ladies in the drawing room, and conversation became general. Basil Abbott made calf's eyes at Sarah again—she couldn't, for the life of her, imagine why—and Winifred prattled about her forthcoming come-out. Mrs. Crabbe gossiped some more, the vicar pontificated, Lady Amanda smiled coolly, and the squire and Sir Edwin talked of farming. It was not, Sarah thought, the most edifying evening, especially not after her stay at Havenwood. She must find a new position soon.

Sir Edwin was locking the massive oak front door with an equally massive key when Sarah wandered into the hall. "Uncle? Could I ask you something?"

Sir Edwin turned. "Thought you'd be for bed, girl. A good evening, wasn't it?" he went on, taking her arm and walking back with her into the drawing room. "I think young Abbott rather fancies you. You could do worse, you know."

"Ye-es." Sarah sank down onto the tapestried stool in front of the empty fireplace, her chin resting on her hand. "Uncle, is it true what they said? About the marquess?"

"Perhaps, perhaps. Mind if I smoke?" Sarah shook her head, and he took out a cheroot, rolling it between his fingers. "Why do you ask?"

"Oh, I don't know. I would just think that if the man's done such a thing it's surprising he's allowed to stay in the neighborhood."

Sir Edwin nodded. "My thoughts exactly. Shows proper spirit in you, girl. Trouble is, we don't really know he did anything. Can't bother a man just because of some rumors or because he's unpleasant."

Of course not! Sarah thought, but for once she held her tongue. Best to appear to agree with Sir Edwin for now. Best not to let on that she knew more than anyone suspected about the mysterious marquess, though she felt rather a coward for not having come to his defense. "What were the rumors?"

"Harrumph." Sir Edwin made rather a job of lighting his cigar, puffing on it until it was drawing to his satisfaction. "Not fit for a young lady's ears, Sarah. Just accept my word that he had cause."

"To kill his wife?"

"No, no, of course not, of course not. But cause to be angry, anyway." He looked down at her, and let out a sigh. "You always were a curious little puss," he said, reaching down to pinch her cheek, which she endured. "All right. The rumors were his wife had a lover."

Oh, the poor man! Sarah's heart instantly went out to the marquess. He was a good man, and such a thing must have wounded him deeply. "But would he really have killed her?"

"No one knows. Coroner's jury acquitted him, as I said. But he had cause." He hesitated. "Aye, he had cause."

"This didn't happen here, did it? Surely you would have told me in one of your letters."

"No, no, happened in Kent, thereabouts. The Pembrokes have had their seat there for years. But after what happened, he had to leave. Came here, property he'd inherited from his wife, tore down the house already there, and started building that Gothic place. A very strange man." He pulled on his cigar. "Keeps to himself, never speaks to anyone, never even goes to church."

"Well, if he expects people are going to run him off, as they must have done in Kent, then you can hardly blame him, can you?"

Sir Edwin laid down his cigar and surveyed her shrewdly. "What's got you so exercised about this, girl? You don't even know the man."

"No, I don't. But I do know how scandal and innuendo can ruin one's life, and it's not fair."

"Aye. Fair. Well, life isn't fair, girl, as you yourself know. And sometimes a man is driven to do things he wouldn't ordinarily do," he added softly.

"You don't really believe he killed his wife?"

"Who? Oh, Pembroke. Who knows?" He shrugged his massive shoulders and turned to her. "Are you happy, Sarah?"

"Happy?" Sarah looked up in surprise. "I don't know. I think content is a better word."

Sir Edwin frowned. "But all you lost, girl, all you had to give up."

"Oh, as for that, I never was much success socially, was I? Great big girl that I was." Sarah smiled, as if the past held no pain for her. "I only regret that Papa's name was so tarnished. I still can't believe that he actually stole money to cover gambling debts!"

Sir Edwin shifted uneasily in his chair. "Quite, quite. A shock to us all."

"And yet you never held it against him, Uncle, though he was your partner in the mill."

"We must think he was misguided, child. Or ill."

"Yes, I know."

"I want to make it up to you, Sarah, you do know that? Stay here until you're settled. Perhaps we can find you a husband."

Sarah laughed and rose. "But, Uncle, don't you know I'm quite on the shelf by now? No, I'm best suited to being a governess. In fact, I posted letters to several employment agencies in London today."

"I see. Well, no hurry, no hurry." Pushing at the arms of his chair, he rose. "I'm for bed. Now don't you worry about Pembroke, girl, he won't bother you. I'll see to that."

Oh, would he, indeed? "Thank you, Uncle," she murmured, and suffered his brief kiss on her cheek before making her way to her own room.

Very early the next morning, Sarah rode a piebald mare down a leafy lane, heading, she hoped, in the direction of Havenwood. After only a few days in the neighborhood, she still wasn't sure of her surroundings, but one thing she did know. After last evening, she had to see the marquess again. Even if it meant riding a horse.

"Easy, girl. No, don't do that! Oh, why won't you listen to me?" Sarah said, sawing at the reins and jouncing in the saddle, certain that at any moment she would fall off. It looked a very long way to the ground, and the last thing she wanted was to appear before the marquess looking bedraggled and undignified. Though heavens knew he had seen her in such a state before and, in any event, why should it matter so? He was just a man, a neighbor whom she feared had been cruelly wronged. That was what had impelled her to rise early this morning, put on her outmoded, but barely used, riding habit, and actually go down to the stables. That was all. Wasn't it?

Sarah had never learned to ride. She had lived all her life in town, having been born in Cirencester. Her only contact with horses had come during her brief visits to Sir Edwin's home. She distinctly remembered the long-suffering groom who had been assigned to teach her to ride and the torture the lessons had been for both of them. One of the few advantages of her being a governess, she'd often thought, was that no one expected her to ride. Thank heavens. Great, nasty beasts, horses were, even though the groom had assured her that Nancy, the mare she was riding, was old and placid. "If that is so, someone forgot to tell Nancy," she muttered, sawing at the reins again as the horse showed an unaccountable tendency to prance sideways. Perhaps she should have let the groom accompany her after all; perhaps she shouldn't have intimidated him with her best schoolmistress look into allowing her to go alone. It wasn't as if this were an assignation, after all. Heavens, no, of course not, she thought, but her insides were quaking with a mixture of nerves, anticipation, and excitement at the thought of seeing *him* again.

It was exciting to be free, to have all the time in the world at her disposal, and not to be at the beck and call of grubby little children and their demanding mamas. Soon enough it would be back to that for her, but not yet, not yet. For now she could enjoy this moment, the sun streaming through the leaves, the rush of the nearby river Coln, the little cottages with their flaked-stone roofs and rose gardens, the occasional sight of the Cotswold hills, green and leafy with few hints of the gold they would soon become. Summer was almost over, and she was determined to enjoy all she could of it.

So engrossed was she in her surroundings and so intent simply upon staying mounted, that she was startled when a twist in the lane brought her to a break in the trees, making her catch her breath. From her vantage point on the small hillock a marvelous vista opened to her, a chessboard of fields crossed with dry walls of Cotswold stone, fields planted with corn and rye and other vegetation. Sheep grazed in a far-off pasture, fat and woolly, and the scudding clouds sent dappled shadows down upon them. And there, off to her right, were the arches and towers of Havenwood.

Seen from here, it was quite a remarkable sight, dark granite so rare in an area known for its golden stone. It really did look like a castle, with its turrets and towers, and though it should have looked alien, out of place, somehow it belonged exactly where it was. At the same time it presaged change and a future quite unimaginable. Mentally she saluted Pembroke's genius. The excitement that she had contained within herself all morning suddenly welled up, filling her again with that marvelous sense of something wonderful coming to meet her. It made her bounce in the saddle, which proved to be her undoing.

In most circumstances Nancy was the most placid of horses, but, like all horses, she could sense an inexperienced hand at the reins. She knew she was the one in control. Or, perhaps, some of Sarah's excitement communicated itself to her, for she suddenly set off at a gallop, down the hillock, splashing through the ford and heading straight toward one of the low stone walls, veering off only at the last moment. Sarah shrieked and grabbed at the reins. "Stop! Oh, stop, I say! Nancy—"

The horse went on heedless, galloping down another narrow lane, little more than a foot path. Sarah held on tightly, knowing she was powerless over the animal and hoping she would not fall off. She would, she thought somewhat prosaically, have some discomfort in sitting down for the next few days.

At first the sound of hooves pounding behind her blended with those of her own mount, but then they came closer, developing their own cadence. A man was there, dressed in black, mounted upon a white horse, and his hand, strong and capable, reached out to grab the reins from Sarah's nerveless fingers. Nancy tossed her head, but there was no arguing with the firm grip on her reins. She slowed, and then, still tossing her head as if to say she were doing a great favor, came to a stop. Sarah's breath came in great gasps of relief, and her legs felt like India rubber. She wanted nothing more than to slide to the ground and dissolve into tears, quite like the silly young miss she was not. Instead, she turned and forced herself to smile into the sardonic face of the Marquess of Pembroke. A knight on a white charger, she thought, dazedly.

"Good morrow, sir," she said, quite cheerfully. "It seems you are always having to rescue me."

"Good morning." Philip relaxed his grip on the reins. Instantly Nancy bolted forward, and both he and Sarah grabbed again for control. "However did you let this old slug run away with you?"

"Did you think that was what she was doing?" Sarah laughed, and even to her own ears it sounded artificial. It was somehow very important for her to appear at her best before this man. "Heavens, no! I simply wanted a gallop."

"Oh." He sounded unconvinced but didn't press the matter. "And what are you doing out so early in the morning?" he said, taking up the reins of his own horse and setting it to a walk so that Sarah had no choice but to follow.

"Oh, I thought I'd learn my way 'round. I'm not very familiar with this area."

"Really? I thought you were born here."

"No. I lived in Cirencester until my father died. Sometimes we would come out to visit Uncle Edwin, but I never really did see much of the neighborhood. Whose fields are these?"

"Mine."

"Heavens! What a great estate you must have!"

"Quite. You've been on my land for some time."

"You saw me?"

"There isn't much that happens here I don't know about."

For some reason that made her want to shiver. She remem-

49

bered the talk of the evening before and his own servants' attitude toward him. He was only a man, for heaven's sake. "It's always that way in the country," she said cheerfully. "At least, it was in Norfolk. I suppose because so little else happens that everyone talks about everyone else. Human nature, I suppose."

"Quite."

The eye with the patch was closest to her, but she was certain, from his tone of voice, that the look on his face was wary. "We had guests to dinner last evening," she chattered on, unnerved by his silence, "and I got quite caught up on the local gossip."

Beside her, Philip came to a sudden stop. "I see," he said, and set his horse to the gallop.

"Pembroke!" Sarah called, and slapped the reins. Nancy took one step forward and then refused to budge. "Oh, you nasty thing, why won't you pay attention to me? Pembroke! Please! Wait for me."

Something in her voice must have reached him, for Philip at last stopped, turning his horse crossways and looking back at her with that same sardonic gaze. He really did look quite sinister, and yet Sarah wasn't the least afraid of him. "Why?" he asked.

"Couldn't we get off these nasty beasts and just talk?"

"Why should we?"

"Because I can't ride, damn it!"

Philip stared at her a moment and then, to her chagrin, put back his head and laughed. "I was wondering when you would admit that," he said, riding back to her.

"Well." Sarah reached up to smooth her hair and her ruffled dignity. "I did grow up in a town, you know. You needn't laugh."

"You make me laugh. Sarah."

"What?" Sarah's eyes rose and held his gaze. Something in his expression took her breath away. "What is it?"

"Nothing. Very well, let's get off these nasty beasts, as you put it, and talk."

"Pray don't laugh at me," she said, but her voice was breathless rather than disgruntled as he came around to her side and held his hand up to her. His grasp was firm, strong, warm, a hold on which one could rely. A man on whom one could rely? Ridiculous thought. Sarah smiled her thanks at him and busied herself with brushing down her habit before walking on slightly shaky legs to the stone wall where he was already perched.

For a few moments they sat in a silence that was somehow companionable, warmed by the sun at their backs, entertained by the chorus of birdsong. "Know everything, do you?" Philip said, breaking the silence.

"Yes. Yes, I'm afraid I do—or as much as the neighbors know. I know how things can get garbled and confused—"

"Oh, it's all true." He cut across her words, effectively silencing her. "About how my wife died, about how I lost my eye. But I didn't kill her." He turned and gazed at her, unblinking, and the force of his one good eye, blazing blue at her, was almost impossible to face. "I swear that to you. Whatever else happened, I could never have hurt Anne."

"I didn't believe it for a moment," Sarah said, conviction ringing in her voice.

"Thank you for that. Most people aren't quite so charitable."

"A bit of scandal, you know. Tends to liven things up." She leaned forward, her hands clasped upon her knees. "How did it happen?"

"I'm not certain, even now. All we know for sure is that a candle fell against the bed curtains and Anne's nightrail caught fire."

"Oh, no!"

"I tried to save her, but she was so badly burned—"

"That beautiful girl."

"I tried to save her," he said again, his fingers going to his eye patch and then dropping. "There was nothing I could do. She died the next day."

"I am so sorry." She paused. "When did this happen?"

"Three years ago. I was on leave from the Army at the time. After this happened," he indicated his eye, "I wasn't much good to them." He paused. "I don't know when, really, the rumors started. At first everyone was very sympathetic and kind. But then one Sunday after I'd started going out again, I went to church and my nearest neighbor cut me dead. Most astonishing thing that ever happened in my life. Even the vicar was cool when I shook his hand, and he owed his living to me."

"Surely there was an inquest," she said, as she had the night before.

"Of course there was, and the verdict was death by misadventure. But still . . ." He looked off into the distance. "Neighbors, old friends, were never at home if I chanced to visit or were cool. Nor did anyone stop by to see me, after paying their condolence calls, of course. All quite perplexing. It was Geordie, finally, who told me what was going on."

"Geordie?"

"Geordie MacLeod. I don't expect you remember him, but he helped rescue you from those ruffians. He was with me in the Peninsula, and he stayed on after Anne's death. He was the one who heard what was being said."

"That you'd caused the fire."

"Yes. And that I'd killed Anne," he said, speaking the words that Sarah had left unsaid. "All nonsense, of course, but how do you fight rumors? Especially with something like this." He pointed savagely towards his eye patch.

"But you were hurt, you couldn't help that."

"Nonetheless, you must admit it gives me a piratical air."

"I've always rather thought pirates were much maligned," she said, and he laughed again.

"Perhaps. But it isn't so funny, you know, when one of your maids crosses herself each time she sees you, or makes the sign against the evil eye."

"As bad as that?"

"Worse. You see, Anne was a considerable heiress."

"Oh, dear."

"I was a second son, you know. I never expected to inherit the title, or Thornhill. Then my brother was killed at Vimiero, and that about did my father in." He glanced away.

"They're right, I think. In a way, I am responsible for Anne's death."

"Oh, nonsense! Whyever would you feel that way?"

"Because the candle that started the fire was on my side of the bed."

Sarah couldn't help it. She let out a snort of laughter, earning a furious glance from him. "Oh, I am sorry, but it's such a little thing to be so guilty about—"

"It should have been me." He pounded his fist on his knees and rose, walking a little away from her. "Damn it, it should have been me."

"But it wasn't, and you can't undo the past," Sarah said calmly, making him turn and look at her. "Are you going to spend the rest of your life feeling guilty because you survived, and she didn't?"

"I don't know." He dropped down beside her again, rubbing his hands wearily over his face. "I just don't know."

Pity welled up inside Sarah. "What you've had to go through," she said.

"Don't waste your pity on me." His voice was dry. "When things got too bad, I left Thornhill in the hands of my agent and came here."

"Havenwood."

"Precisely. Havenwood." Silence fell between them again. "I expect you think me a bit of a coward, hiding away as I do."

"We all handle things in our own way." Sarah wrapped her arms about her knees. "When my father died, it was a great shock. He wasn't old. It was a brain fever of some sort that carried him off. That was bad enough, being left alone, but he left a lot of debts behind."

"And you didn't know."

"No. In a way, though, I was glad. It gave me something to do, something to hold onto. Uncle Edwin offered to help, of course, but they were Papa's debts, not his."

"Ah. Now I understand."

"What?"

"Why you went out as a governess."

53

"Well, I've always been a managing type of female, as I'm sure you realize."

"Oh, quite."

"Pray don't laugh at me. It gave me a way to handle things, do you see what I mean? Working was the way I handled Papa's death."

"While I retreated within—"

"And created contrivances of the devil."

Philip laughed. "Is that what they call them?"

"Mrs. Crabbe does. Oh, if only others could see you like this, they'd surely know you couldn't be capable of such dreadful things."

"A man may smile and be a villain."

"Yes, well, don't start quoting Shakespeare to me. If you gave other people a chance—"

"On the contrary." His voice was cool. "It is they who won't give me the chance. Except for you." His gaze was quizzical. "I wonder why?"

"Because I met you before I heard the rumors, of course. And you don't fool me, you know," she went on, as he was about to speak. "When you have nasty, grubby schoolboys playing tricks on you, you soon learn what is bravado and what is real malice."

Philip laughed again. "A rare set-down, madam. That puts me in my place."

"Oh, dear. I didn't mean—"

"Never mind." He rose. "I must be getting back."

"I suppose I should, too. Breakfast will be soon."

"Will you be all right? Getting back, I mean?"

"Oh, I don't intend to ride. I'll lead Nancy, if she'll let me."

"Good." An awkward little silence fell. "Well, then, Miss Chadwick—"

"Will I see you again? That is, may I walk here again?"

"It's a public footpath, even if it is on my property," he said, but Sarah saw behind the cool, impersonal words, heard a note in his voice that hadn't been there before. A note of hope, of interest? Her spirits lifted immeasurably.

"Oh, good. I do enjoy an early morning walk."

"Do you?" He mounted his horse and raised his hand to her. "Good day to you, Miss Chadwick."

"Good day, sir. Happy contriving."

His laugh floated back to her as she rode away. Really, quite a remarkable man, so personable and kind under that stern exterior he had created for himself. No wonder, poor man, after all he'd been through, she thought, taking her horse's reins and turning back toward Sir Edwin's house. It really was quite unfair, and she could understand why he had retreated from the world. But . . . three years. It had all happened three years ago. Surely it was time, even for him, to come out of seclusion.

Sarah nodded her head determinedly as if discussing the matter with someone. Of course it was time. And while she waited to hear word of a new position, perhaps she could do something about this situation. *Oh, what fun!* She could hardly wait.

Chapter Five

"I'm not to be disturbed, Mackie," Sir Edwin said as he closed the door of his study behind him and locked it. "Not even by Miss Chadwick." Especially not by Miss Chadwick. She was the source of his current worry.

Taking out his handkerchief, he mopped at his forehead, though the room was cool. He hadn't meant things to go so far, really, he hadn't, and now he was faced with the consequences of his actions. It had been easier while Sarah was away, but her return had reawakened the old guilt that had lain dormant these past years. It was because of him, and him alone, that she was penniless.

He wiped his brow again as he unlocked a drawer in his desk and pulled out several leather-bound books, records of what had really happened to the mill he and Benjamin Chadwick had owned together. There had only been that one time, that one little time, when he had been in low water and had needed money badly. And it could have happened to anyone. Perhaps he should have known better than to go into that gambling hell in London—certainly he should have known better—but for a sober, church-going man it had held out a dangerous allure. Besides, he'd accounted himself skilled at games of chance. Before the end of the evening, however, he'd been so deeply in debt that he'd had no idea how he would repay it. And a gentleman, of course, always repaid his debts, even if he were in trade.

It was then that he'd thought of taking money from the mill.

Well, after all, it was his money too, wasn't it? Hadn't he worked just as hard as Benjamin to set up the mill and keep it running? He would borrow it for just a little while. To be on the safe side, however, he had labeled the expenditures he used to cover his act as having been authorized by his partner.

And that was where the trouble started. Who would ever have expected that Benjamin would be carried off so quickly at a relatively young age? And before he, Sir Edwin, had had a chance to pay back even a tenth of the money he had borrowed. The mill had nearly gone into bankruptcy, then, but he had managed to secure a loan that had rescued it. Since then, Sir Edwin had kept his dealings strictly honest, fervently thanking God at church every week that he had not been caught and even more fervently forswearing gambling. He had been very lucky.

All would have been well were it not for Sarah. The business would have gone along quite fine and no one would have known of any irregularities in its financing. Sarah, however, her father's only heir, had not only been left penniless, Benjamin's money being nearly all tied up in the mill, but she had been stunned to learn that her father was not the honorable man she'd always thought him. Sir Edwin had nearly spoken up, confessing to what he had done, but he had managed, just in time, to hold his tongue. It was all water over the dam. He liked Sarah, had never meant to harm her. He would make it up to her. Sarah, however, had proven stubborn and independent, insisting that it was her duty to discharge her father's debts, and had gone to work as a governess. Sir Edwin had been left alone with his conscience.

Gradually, though, the guilt had eased. He had quietly repaid the money he had taken—and really, why bother? it was all his now, anyhow—and he had been able to soothe himself with Sarah's infrequent, cheerful letters into believing she was happy. Maybe she'd been meant to be a governess; her one season had been a disaster, and since she'd broken her engagement to the Pollock boy there'd been no other suitors. No, Sarah was all right, he'd told himself, until she'd unexpectedly shown up at his door.

And that brought him back to his problem. Sir Edwin put his head in his hands and groaned over the account books. What in the world was he going to do about Sarah?

"Not a thing a body can put his hands on, sir," Geordie said, reaching again for his tankard.

Philip briefly smiled. "Still spoiling for a fight, Geordie?" he said. The two men were sitting in the drawing room, more like the old companions they were than master and servant, their faces carefully averted from the portrait over the mantel. The fortunes of war were strange, Philip had often thought. In the disastrous retreat from Corunna, back in 1808, over frozen mountain passes, their friendship had been forged. "Here in peaceful Gloucestershire?"

"Aye, that I am," Geordie admitted frankly. "You must admit, sir, powerful strange it was that a carriage was attacked on that lane just when we were supposed to be there. And ye heard Miss Chadwick. They expected a man."

"True." Unexpectedly, Philip smiled. Miss Chadwick. Sarah. A most astonishing young woman. In spite of the rumors, truths, and half-truths that swirled about him, in spite of the possible danger to her reputation, Sarah contrived to take early morning rambles every day during which they invariably met. He suspected that Miss Chadwick had something of the crusader spirit in her and that he was her current project. He didn't mind, though. She made him laugh. It had been a long time since anyone had done that. Besides, she was so damnably pretty . . .

"Sir," Geordie said, breaking into his thoughts.

"Hm? Excuse me, Geordie. I'm afraid I wasn't attending." He sipped at his burgundy, the only ration of spirits he allowed himself, to cover his emotions. "You were saying?"

"I'm saying it's damned suspicious, sir. As I —"

"As you've said before. I know. I agree, the ruffians were waiting for someone, but we don't know for whom."

"I think we do, sir."

"Who would wish me harm, Geordie?" He set his glass

down, and his lips tightened. "God knows I bring enough of that on myself."

"No, sir, there I don't agree. Ye've had some bad luck—"

"Luck!" Philip's laugh was bitter. "You might well call it that. Why do you stay, Geordie?"

Geordie leaned back. "Well, sir, my mam always said it would have to be a powerful fate that got me, big as I am. Figure if I could survive Corunna, I could survive anything."

"Even an employer who makes contrivances of the devil?"

"Sir?"

"Nothing," Philip said, but his face had relaxed. "I would like to know who is behind this. If we'd been able to talk to the highwaymen, find out who hired them—"

"Aye, sir, but with one dead and the other gone, wasn't any chance of that. But, sir—"

"What?"

"I've heard that Charles Grantham was seen in Bibury."

Philip's glass stopped halfway to his mouth. "Anne's brother? Good God, you don't think—"

"And could be he was at Thornhill."

"We don't know that for certain. And he has friends in the neighborhood. Though he resents it that I inherited this property."

"He resents everything about ye, sir. Remember—"

"Yes, yes, he swore revenge after Anne's death. But I never believed that, Geordie. Charles has a temper, but—"

"And he's never forgiven ye, either."

Philip's fingers reached up absently to rub at his eye patch. "It's hard to believe, Geordie. After all, it's been three years."

"Aye. But some things die hard. We should watch him, sir."

"Perhaps. But we once were friends." He drained his glass. "Did the primers get off to London all right?"

"Yes, sir, saw them into the mail coach myself. Sir, if the people hereabouts knew what you were doing, writing and printing books to educate their children—"

"They would still spurn me. Nothing so powerful as rumor, you know." He rose. "If you'll excuse me, Geordie, I had some thoughts on that new door latch I was telling you about. I shall be in my workroom, if anyone wants me."

"Aye, sir." Geordie lifted his tankard in salute as Philip left the room and then turned, looking fully and deliberately at the portrait of Lady Anne, his lordship's late wife. There, if you asked him, was where a lot of the trouble had started. Oh, beautiful she'd certainly been, charming and sweet, but there'd been something about her Geordie'd not quite trusted. Not that you could tell his lordship that, oh no, besotted as he still was with Lady Anne. Geordie had hoped for a time that Miss Chadwick—but she had her own life, and it apparently did not include the marquess.

Geordie drained off his tankard and then rose, picking up Philip's empty wineglass and heading toward the kitchen. Wasn't much he could do for his lordship; the marquess had to find his own way back into life. In the meantime, however, Geordie would make sure that he could live that life in safety. He took his self-appointed mission seriously. No one would hurt his lordship, or his name wasn't Geordie MacLeod.

It had come at last, the news Sarah had both desired and feared. It seemed a certain family, far off in Yorkshire, was in desperate need of a governess, and she apparently was perfect for the position. If she decided to take it—and why shouldn't she? the wage offered was quite good—she would have to leave for London soon and then for her new home. Heavens knew when she would return to the Cotswolds, if ever.

It was early morning. With the letter from the employment agency tucked into her pocket, she slipped quietly out of the house and headed off over the dew-soaked grass, pulling her sturdy cloak tighter around her. September had come to the Cotswolds, and with it had come cool nights that changed the leaves of the beeches on the wold to a gold that rivaled and complemented the golden stone houses. Soon it would be winter, and she would be gone. Winter in the Yorkshire Dales. The thought made her shiver.

She was sitting on a rock by the river Coln, not far from the footpath, when she heard hoofbeats. Turning her head, she saw Philip on his white horse. *My white knight,* she thought fondly, though lately he hadn't had to rescue her from anything. Lately, in fact, he had proven to be a good companion and the only person to whom she could really talk. She would miss him when she left.

"Good morning, Miss Chadwick." Philip dismounted gracefully and tethered his horse to a tree. "You're out early today," he said, as he did every morning.

"Summer's over," she said, rising and going to walk by his side down the leafy path. "Harvest here must be beautiful."

"It is. The Harvest Home celebration is enjoyable. Or so I've been told."

"I wish I could be here to see it."

Philip stopped. "You've had news?"

"Yes." Wordlessly she handed him the letter from the employment agency; wordlessly he unfolded it and read it slowly, carefully. With equal care, he returned it to its envelope. Sarah, leaving. He had known the day would come, but he had let her laughter and the golden days of late summer seduce him into believing that this idyll would last forever. Now, it seemed, she was right. Summer was over.

"It sounds a good position," he commented, strolling beside her again, his hands tucked into his pockets.

"Oh, it is. The wage is more than fair. Which makes me wonder just how difficult my job will be."

"Ah. There is that. But they must have faith in you, to teach the social graces to a merchant's daughter."

"Lord help me. I can only hope she isn't heavy with spots on her face and a decided liking for all the wrong colors." She stopped, shaking her head. "No, I am being unfair. As if I were such a great success myself."

Philip looked back at her. "Weren't you?"

Sarah laughed, the sound free and easy. She could laugh about it now, much though it had hurt at the time. "Heavens, no! Would I be a governess, else?"

"There is that." He cast her a sidelong look, something she'd gotten used to. There were times she even forgot he didn't have two good eyes. "Didn't you ever wish to marry?"

"Oh, of course I did. When I was young and foolish and believed I was beautiful. That was Papa. He always told me I was, when the truth —" She shrugged. "In truth, it was his fortune that made me attractive."

"Are the young men around here blind?" he demanded.

She laughed again. "I'm no beauty, sir. I came to terms with that a long time ago. My aunt tried — she sponsored me at my come-out — but, God bless her, she has no taste. My clothes were terrible, and that only made matters worse."

"But wasn't there anybody? I can't believe all the young men were so foolish."

Sarah shook her head, remembering almost with fondness how she had appeared, the year of her disastrous debut. She had been plain, dressed in ruffles and furbelows that had only served to accentuate her overblown figure. And her hair, no matter what anyone tried, would not hold a curl. "There was one, but —"

"But?"

"It didn't work out," she said lightly. "And then when Papa died quite penniless you can imagine what happened."

"Yes, I'm afraid I can. But, Sarah." She stopped, turning to face him. "Surely this isn't what you want to do with your life, taking care of other people's children."

She didn't meet his gaze. "What else is there for me?" She turned away, and he had no choice but to follow. "Oh, Uncle Edwin would let me stay, of course, but let us be honest, sir. I have no money, no family background. Nothing, in short, to make me the least bit eligible. My chances of marrying are about as remote as — as your flying to the moon!"

Philip's lips twitched. "I do wonder, if the balloon design I've been working on —"

"Oh, now you are funning me! My heavens, look at that, you're actually smiling!"

Philip's smile widened under her teasing and then faded. "Surely, though, there must be something else for you."

"If so, I don't know what it is. At least in this way I have a chance to control my life."

"Always at someone else's beck and call."

"Nothing in life is perfect."

This is. The words were so powerful that for a moment he thought he'd spoken them aloud. These last few weeks, finding someone who cared not a jot about his appearance or his past, had been a respite from the world he had inhabited far too long. He had grown fond of Sarah in that time. He might almost say he — no, he didn't love her. Love was something that had died with Anne and that he would never feel again. He would, however, miss Sarah a great deal when she left.

"When do you go?" he asked.

"I don't know. I haven't decided whether I'll take the post. I suppose I probably will. But within a fortnight, I would think."

A fortnight. "Sarah," he began, and she turned to him, something sparking in her eyes.

"Yes?"

"Ah, nothing." He turned. "I must be getting back. I've things to do."

"Oh, yes. The balloon to the moon, perhaps?"

He smiled slightly. "Perhaps."

And wouldn't he just love that, to be able to fly away and not have to face the problems of living on this earth anymore? Sarah thought and then instantly felt contrite. In the few weeks of their acquaintance, she had grown to respect, though not to understand, his reticence. She had teased him about it at first and then chided him and then, belatedly acquiring wisdom, left him alone. He had to find his own path in life as did she. If her path led her to Yorkshire, so be it. She knew, though, that she would be leaving something very precious behind when she left.

They parted amicably, and Sarah tromped through the lanes and over the fields until she reached Sir Edwin's house. In the breakfast parlor, Sir Edwin had just sat down to a substantial meal of sausage and eggs. "Good morning, Uncle," she said cheerfully, sitting down across from him.

"Good morning." Sir Edwin eyed her covertly behind his tankard of ale as she requested breakfast from the footman. She was looking uncommonly pretty this morning, even dressed in gray; her cheeks were pink and her eyes sparkled. Not for the first time he wondered where she went on her morning walks and whom she met. "And what are your plans for the day? A visit with Lady Amanda and Miss Abbott again?"

"I'm not sure." The light faded from her eyes, and she reached for a piece of toast from the rack, crumbling it onto her plate. "I've some letters to write. I had one from London yesterday, you know."

"Yes, I know." Wasn't much went on in his own house he didn't know about, especially when it concerned Sarah.

"I've been offered a position, Uncle," she said abruptly. "A good one with good money and what sounds like few responsibilities."

"Oh, aye, have you?" He strove to make his voice casual. "And where would this be?"

"Yorkshire."

"Yorkshire." He set his tankard down with a bang. "Girl, have you lost your mind? Yorkshire, and in the winter?"

"It's a good position," she repeated.

"Which you know full well you don't have to take."

"What would I do instead?" She flung her arms wide. "I suppose I could stay here and act as your housekeeper, but Mrs. Watson seems to have things pretty well in hand. I don't think either of us would like it."

"Basil Abbott seems to fancy you."

"Oh, please." The look she gave him was withering with scorn. "Besides the fact that he has nothing in his head besides horses and hunting—and don't deny it, you've had to listen to his hunting stories, too—I doubt very much the Abbotts would allow him to marry me. Oh, don't mistake me, I like Lady Amanda very much, but what sort of prospect am I? A father who was in trade and died with scandal hanging over him, and not a penny to my name? Not to mention my lack of beauty. Oh, don't protest, you and Papa always doted on me too much! I know myself, Uncle, and, unfortunately, I know the world. My chances of marrying are nonexistent."

"I wonder." Sir Edwin looked at her oddly as he set down his tankard. "Yes. That would solve all our problems. Don't know why I didn't think of it before."

"What?"

"Sarah, I know whom you can marry."

"Whom?"

"Me."

Chapter Six

"You!" Sarah gaped at him, and the footman who had been about to set her plate before her let it drop with a clatter. "Uncle Edwin, surely you can't be serious."

"Think about it, Sarah." Sir Edwin leaned over and grasped her hand in a grip too hard for her to break. " 'Twould solve all our problems, yours, mine, and, forgive me, m'dear, but you'll not do much better with a father in trade. I'd have a wife and mayhaps a family, and you'd have a home. You'd never have to worry about taking care of someone else's brats, Sarah, never have to worry about money, I'd see to that. And it's fitting, since —"

"But you're my uncle!" Sarah twisted her arm free and wrapped it around herself, nursing the place where he had grabbed it with her other hand.

"Not really. There's no relation, Sarah. Think how suitable it is —"

"I can't. I can't."

"Ah." Sir Edwin leaned back. "I understand. Maidenly modesty and all that. Of course you wouldn't agree right away, it wouldn't be right in a lady of quality. But just you think about it." He rose, laying a heavy hand on her shoulder. "You'll see it's right, m'dear. Now I'll leave you to think about it." And with that he swooped down and planted a moist kiss on her cheek and left the room, his heavy tread somehow jaunty.

Sarah sat very still, stunned, managing only by a great effort of will not to scrub at her cheek. Marriage! No question that she would like to marry someday, in spite of what she had said to both the marquess and Sir Edwin that morning. To have her own home, her own children—but the man of her dreams, though he had always been shadowy, certainly looked nothing like Sir Edwin. Good heavens!

"Will that be all, miss? Or would you like more tea?" the footman said, and Sarah looked up. Too much to hope that he would keep the news of this to himself. His eyes were avid and eager, and she could tell he was bursting to be the first to tell this news to the household and thus to the neighborhood. By this evening, she would be engaged to Sir Edwin in everything but fact, and the very idea filled her with such repugnance that she stood up abruptly, her chair scraping back. She couldn't do it, she wouldn't marry him, but who was there to help her, who could she talk to who would understand—?

Philip. The name came to her from nowhere, though she had never before called the marquess that, not even in her mind. Philip, though he hid from the world, was no fool. Philip, the first real friend she had made in many a year, would understand her dilemma and might even be able to counsel her about it. Yes. She would go to Philip, and she would do it now.

"Miss?" the footman said, as she strode toward the door, her eyes unseeing. "Is something wrong?"

"What? Oh. No. Go tell everyone, I know you're dying to," she said, and walked out.

Havenwood's door was opened by Mrs. Stevenson, who stared incredulously as Sarah pushed by her. "Is the marquess in, Mrs. Stevenson?"

"Miss Chadwick! What in the world? No, his lordship's not in. That is, he's not at home to visitors—"

"Then he's in his workroom. No, don't bother to show me, I know the way."

"But, miss!" Mrs. Stevenson called, as Sarah ran up the stairs of the south wing. "You can't go up there! Miss! Well!"

Sarah ignored her, though she knew Mrs. Stevenson would soon be adding her morsel to the local gossip. She had to find Philip, and no one was going to stop her. "My lord," she said, knocking hastily on the door of Philip's workroom and pushing it open. "I know I shouldn't be here, but—oh!"

From across the room Philip looked up. He was standing behind a long table, his hands braced on it, and he was studying a book open before him. Beside him stood a giant of a man with red hair whom she didn't know. It was his presence, and the fact that he'd taken a step toward her which somehow seemed menacing that had made her stop.

"Miss Chadwick?" Philip straightened, only mild surprise in his tone. "Why are you here?"

"You're busy. I'm sorry, I shouldn't have come, but—"

"Is all to your likin', sir?" the giant said, with a distinctly Scottish accent. This must be Geordie, who had helped rescue her from the highwaymen.

"Yes, everything looks fine, Geordie. As to the other thing," Philip fixed him with a stare, "we'll talk more on that later."

"Aye, sir. I'll be in the stables, be ye needin' me. Good day, miss." He tugged at his forelock as he passed by Sarah and then went out, closing the door and leaving them, for the moment, alone in a well of silence.

"I—you told me not to come here, but I had to," Sarah said, when she could handle the silence no longer. "But I thought, since we are friends—"

"This is rather extraordinary of you." Philip, who had been looking at the book, straightened again, closing the volume with a thud. "What of your reputation?"

"Oh, hang my reputation! Everyone in the neighborhood will be talking about me by this evening, anyway."

The corners of Philip's mouth twitched. "Have you managed, then, to get yourself in that much trouble since we've seen each other?"

"Oh, yes." Sarah sank down on a stool, hooking her heels on the bottom rung. "Give me an hour and I can cause all sorts of havoc."

Philip consulted his watch. "Forty-five minutes, actually."

He walked around the table toward her. "Come, then, as long as you're here, you might as well tell me about it."

"You'll think I'm an absolute fool." Sarah's voice was rueful as he sat facing her. "What is that?"

Philip didn't even glance toward the book. "Nothing of importance. Now, come, Sarah, what is it?"

"I don't know where to start! What is wrong with you men, anyway? First Mr. Ramsay and now this and God knows I'm not even pretty—"

"Whoa." He held up his hand. "I don't know what you're going on about. Who is Mr. Ramsay?"

"My employer in Norfolk. Why he chose to make advances to me—"

"Did he molest you?" Philip said sharply.

"No. Not for lack of trying, but—"

"Good God. Is that why you left your position?"

"I didn't choose to leave. I was dismissed. Mrs. Ramsay believed I encouraged him, if you can believe that. And look at me!" She flung her arms open wide. "I'm fat and plain! What does anyone see in me? First Mr. Ramsay and then Basil Abbott and now Sir Edwin!"

"Sir Edwin? What in the world has he done?"

"Asked me to marry him, that's all."

Philip's fingers, until then toying with the pages of the book, went very still. "To marry him? How extraordinary," he said, in a reasonably normal tone. "Isn't he your uncle?"

Sarah shook her head. "No. I call him that because he was my father's business partner and my godfather. I'm fond of him, of course, but to *marry* him! Good heavens!"

"What are you going to do?"

"You could at least pretend to be interested."

"Oh, I am," Philip said, but he kept his eye on the book, flipping the pages back and forth with his restless, long fingers. "Are you going to marry him?"

"Good heavens, no! At least, I don't think so. At least—I thought if I came here and talked with you I could figure something out."

"Such as?"

"I don't know! You're the only friend I have here; I can talk to you. Tell me what to do, Philip!"

"For God's sake, Sarah!" Philip rose abruptly, pushing the book away so hard it skidded across the table and fell off. "What do you expect me to tell you? I am a man, and yet you come to me and tell me that another man has proposed to you. How am I supposed to react to that?"

"I—don't know." Sarah's voice was very small as she watched him standing at one of the arched windows, his back to her, his shoulders tensed. "I suppose I thought you might . . . *care*." He didn't turn. "I'm sorry. I've made a mistake, I'll go."

"No." He turned, his hand outstretched. "No, I can help you, I think."

"Can you? Oh, how? Please, tell me what to do!"

"Marry me instead."

Good heavens! Two proposals within one hour! Sarah began to laugh. "Oh, my heavens, but—"

"For God's sake, Sarah!" he said savagely. "What do you think I am? Yes, I am your friend, but I am also a man. This," he pointed at his eye patch, "this doesn't matter. I am still a man."

"Oh, Philip." Sarah's laughter had died, to be replaced by tenderness. "I know that."

"Do you?"

"Yes. And it wasn't you I was laughing at, but me! Plain, fat Sarah Chadwick, with not a penny to her name, receiving proposals from the two most eligible men in the neighborhood. Good heavens, Philip, why in the world would you want to marry me?"

"You make me laugh."

She stared at him blankly. "Well! I'm glad I'm good for something!"

"Sarah, no, I didn't mean it that way." He caught her hand in his as she was about to rise. His long-fingered grip was strong and cool, quite unlike Sir Edwin's. "You, Sarah Chadwick, are a beautiful woman."

"Oh, nonsense." Sarah's cheeks turned pink, and she averted her eyes. "I'm plain."

"You're beautiful," he interrupted. "Inside, where it matters." Sarah's head came up at that. "And though you don't believe me, on the outside, too. I'm not totally blind, you know. This eye sees very well, indeed."

"You're funning me," she said, her voice uncertain.

"No. I don't lie, Sarah. I've done many things in my life which I regret, but I don't lie." He looked down at their linked hands. "I know you can do better for yourself—"

"Better! Heavens, no! If circumstances were different, I think I might marry you at that. But as they are . . ."

"I see." He withdrew his hand. "I can understand you'd want someone who is whole."

"Philip!"

"Nevertheless, my offer still stands."

"Philip, that isn't it at all." She held her hand out to him, but he had turned away and didn't see. "It's not you. It's me. You're a marquess. You could have your choice of brides. While I—I'm the daughter of a thief."

"A thief?" Philip looked up in astonishment.

"Yes." Sarah's head was held high. "My father, much to my surprise, had gambling debts. Huge gambling debts, and to cover them he took money from the mill he owned with Sir Edwin. He not only died in debt, he died a thief."

"My God. I'm sorry."

"Thank you. Though sometimes I've wondered—"

"What?"

"Nothing. I've worked since to pay back the money he owed, though Uncle Edwin offered to forgive the debt."

"I see," Philip said thoughtfully. "So? What has that to do with me?"

"Oh, really! My debts would become yours, should we marry. And it would do you little good. All that old business would be raked up." She shuddered. "I don't want to face it again. I'd rather go to Yorkshire."

"Sarah. I am sorry." He placed his hand on her shoulder. "Of course I'd do what I could to protect you. As to the debts, I'm not exactly poor, you know."

Sarah turned to smile at him. *My white knight.* "Somehow

71

you're always there when I need rescuing."

"Mind you, I'm not such a good bargain myself. A man who makes contrivances of the devil."

Sarah laughed, as he had intended her to. "And a balloon to fly to the moon."

"Perhaps. Someday. Sarah." He turned her to face him, taking her hands in his. "I'm serious about this. Will you marry me?"

Sarah searched his face. The eye patch usually made him look inscrutable, even sinister, but today she looked closer. There was pain in his face and vulnerability. For some reason, if she refused him, she would hurt him. And herself. She could think of worse fates than to be this man's wife. "Yes. Yes, I think I will," she said. He smiled, a smile of such sweet warmth that it made her wonder, for the first time, how he had looked before the fire that had taken part of his sight. "I know I'm no beauty like your first wife —"

"It's of no moment. We'll deal well together, Sarah. We're already friends."

She looked down at their linked hands. "I'd want children," she said, feeling herself color.

"Well, of course." His voice was so matter-of-fact that she looked up again. "Well. We'll have to be making plans."

"Yes. Oh!"

"What?"

"Uncle Edwin! How can I ever tell him —"

"I'll deal with Sir Edwin." There was a curious note in Philip's voice, almost as if he anticipated the encounter. "Go on home now." He bent and brushed a kiss over her lips quickly, too quickly.

"I — yes," she said, her hand to her lips. They were tingling in an odd, alarming, and altogether pleasant way. "Why?"

"Before your reputation is completely ruined."

"Oh. Of course." Still she made no move, and at last Philip took her by the shoulders, walking her to the door. If she didn't leave soon, he would give her more than just chaste kisses, God help him.

"I'll pay a call on Sir Edwin this afternoon. Will you be all right getting home?"

"Oh, yes, perfectly," Sarah said, her voice abstracted, and at last drifted out, hardly aware of her surroundings. Good heavens. She, Sarah Chadwick, was engaged to, of all people, a marquess! A man she didn't love, she thought, coming down to earth as she ran down the stairs of the house which would soon be hers. Somehow, though, that didn't matter. He was kind, intelligent, and extraordinarily attractive, even with the eye patch. In fact, the patch added a kind of allure. And he needed her. She'd realized that just now when she'd looked at him though she doubted he knew it. It wasn't, she reflected cheerfully as she set off toward home, the something wonderful she had anticipated on her fateful journey here from Norfolk, but it would do. Oh, yes. It would do marvelously.

Sir Edwin looked with surprise at the card his butler, Mackie, handed him. "He wishes to see me?"

"Yes, sir." Mackie's eyes glittered at having actually seen such an astonishing person with his own eyes.

"Well, bring him in then. Though what he wants with me, I don't know." Sir Edwin rose and had his hand outstretched as his unexpected guest, the Marquess of Pembroke, was shown in.

"Good morning, good morning," Sir Edwin said, with more exuberance than was warranted for a simple visit. "A pleasure to see you, my lord. Sit, sit. Can I offer you coffee? Or brandy, perhaps, seeing as there's a nip in the air today."

"Coffee would be fine, thank you." Philip sat in the comfortable red leather armchair his host indicated, his fine long fingers folded into a steeple, his eye regarding Sir Edwin. Under that steady, unblinking regard, Sir Edwin could only look away.

"Good, good. Coffee it will be, then, Mackie. Now, my lord." He sat, pretending not to be affected by the presence of his guest, the stern austerity of his clothing, black and white, the absolute stillness of his posture, and, of course, that eye patch. "What can I do for you this morning?"

"It would perhaps be best if we waited until coffee is served."

"Of course, of course." Sir Edwin frantically cast about in his mind for a reason for this visit, but could think of none. He'd had little contact with the marquess beyond the first, formal visit to welcome him to the neighborhood. "Ah, you've had luck with your crops, I hear? Been a good year, a good year."

"Yes."

The monosyllable was daunting. "Ah, yes, of course. Tell me, I hear you've been following Coke's experiments in agriculture. Do you find they work?"

For the first time, Philip shifted, and a gleam of what might even have been amusement appeared in his eye. "Yes. I think it's time for a change in the way things are done in farming. Of course, my tenants didn't agree at first. But it looks to be a good harvest this year."

"Very good, very good. Of course, I've always found that the old ways work best. Thank you, Mackie, there's nothing more we need."

"Sir." Mackie bowed and, after one last fascinated look at the marquess, went out.

"Now," Sir Edwin said, as the door closed behind his butler, "you didn't come here to talk farming, I'll warrant. What is it I can do for you, my lord?"

"You are a blunt man. Good. I shall be equally blunt. I have asked your ward to marry me and she has done me the honor of accepting."

"What?"

"And as you are her guardian, we would of course like your consent, even if she is of age."

"There must be some mistake," Sir Edwin spluttered. "Sarah is engaged to me."

"She doesn't believe so. I believe she looks on you more as an uncle."

"As indeed she should, after all I've done for her! Who else could she turn to when she was in need? No, my lord, you must be mistaken."

"Shall we call Sarah in and hear her opinion?" Philip said.

There was a little smile on his face that, for some reason, made Sir Edwin profoundly uneasy.

"Ah, no. No. We can settle this between ourselves. Frankly, my lord, I don't know why you'd want Sarah. I didn't even know you knew her."

"Oh, I know her quite well. Do you remember the highwaymen who attacked a carriage a few weeks ago? She was the passenger."

Sir Edwin started up from his chair. "The devil she was! But . . ." He eyed Philip speculatively. "She didn't come here until a week later."

"She was at Havenwood."

"The devil she was!" Sir Edwin exclaimed again. "Good God, man, do you know what this means? You've compromised her."

"No harm came to her at my house, and I took good care no news of her would get out," Philip said sharply. "If you wish to broadcast it about, that's your business."

"Good God." Sir Edwin stared at him. "So I am to believe that you, of all people, want to do the honorable thing?"

There was a little smile on Philip's face. "Believe what you wish."

Sir Edwin's eyes narrowed. "By God, but this explains much. Why a man of your stature would want to marry a girl with no dowry."

"No dowry. Yes. She told me about that. How much money did you take from her father, sir?"

Sir Edwin paled. "I beg your pardon! That is an outrageous accusation to make—"

"I've spent time looking into Benjamin Chadwick's affairs—"

"Why, you—"

"—and everything I've seen convinces me he was a man of probity. He would not have left his daughter penniless."

"No, he left her to my care! Damme, I'll not listen to such rubbish in my own house!"

"Won't you?" Philip said quietly, and fixed him with an unwavering regard. "How much were you into the cent-percenters for?"

Under that steady, hostile gaze, Sir Edwin collapsed. If Pembroke knew of his indebtedness to the money lenders, then he did, indeed, know everything. "I didn't mean Sarah to suffer, I swear it," he babbled, suddenly scared. "Nor Benjamin, neither. I thought I could repay the money, but then Benjamin had to go and die." He pulled a capacious handkerchief from his pocket and mopped at his face. "It was the devil of a coil, sir. Especially when Sarah turned proud and wouldn't take any money from me, and I'm the one that beggared her." He tucked the handkerchief away, his eyes averted. "I've not told anyone of this. How did you know?"

"It matters not." Philip had no intention of telling him that his suspicions had started with a lucky surmise, nor that he hadn't known the depth of Sir Edwin's involvement until now. "What does matter is what we're going to do about it."

Sir Edwin looked up. Eye patch or not, he was not going to let himself be intimidated. "I can't see where that's any of your affair, my lord."

"Oh, but it is. You see, I will marry Sarah whether you approve or not. And then I shall have to decide what to do about your part in this."

Sir Edwin stared at him and then rose. "The devil blast it!" He pounded his hands on the back of his chair and then leaned against it. "Damme, I suppose you're going to take me to court."

"No. It would only cause a scandal, and Sarah's been through enough. I believe there is another way to settle this."

"I'd be glad to hear it. I don't mind telling you, my lord, this has been preying on my mind."

"Has it?" Philip allowed the merest trace of skepticism to color his voice as Sir Edwin sat down again. "Then you may ease your mind, sir. It is not my intention to bankrupt you. However, I think we agree that amends should be made."

"Of course, of course." Sir Edwin leaned forward, feeling hope rise within him. Perhaps he'd get off easy, after all. "What would you suggest?"

"Several things. First, your approval of my marriage to Sarah."

That one was hard to take, but Sir Edwin nodded. "Done. And may I tell you, sir, that you are a lucky man."

"More than you know." Philip fixed him with that gaze again, and Sir Edwin's eyes dropped. "Second, that any debts outstanding be taken care of . . ."

"Of course, of course. I've always wanted to."

"And finally, that you provide Sarah with a dowry. I wish her to have her own money, so she need never governess again."

"Of course, of course, but if you knew how stubborn she can be—"

"I've an idea of it. In return for this, I promise I will take no legal action for your misdeeds and that no one will know of them through me."

Sir Edwin eyed him a moment and then held out his hand. "I'd say we have a bargain, my lord. Shall we drink a toast to celebrate?"

"Thank you, no, I don't drink so early in the day. Shall you let Sarah know of our agreement?"

"Of course, of course." Sir Edwin tugged on the bellpull to summon Mackie and then sat back, his face impassive. He could hide his feelings quite as well as the marquess, aye, that he could, and he had no intention of allowing what he really felt to show. Relief, of course, that his long nightmare was over, but also a festering resentment against this man for knowing so much of his affairs and for forcing him to take action. He, too, had his pride. He'd never forgive Lord Pembroke, no, that he wouldn't. He only hoped he hadn't made matters worse for Sarah, pledging her to this man. He only hoped it would not end in disaster.

Philip met Sarah in the hall, her stricken, pale face telling him all he needed to know. "You heard," he said, taking her arm and leading her toward the door, away from Mackie's curious eyes.

77

"Yes, I fear I eavesdropped. Oh, Philip—"

"Not here, my dear." Firmly he closed the door of the house behind them, and they dropped onto the stairs, Sarah's shoulders slumped.

"I always wondered," she said, after a moment. "Papa just didn't seem the type to steal. But the proof was there."

"It's easy enough to change account books, Sarah. And, to be fair, I think Sir Edwin tried to make it up to you."

"But to let me go all this time thinking—and what it did to Papa's reputation!" Her hands clenched into fists. "I shall never forgive him for this. Never."

"It's past, Sarah." He put his arm around her shoulders, drawing her against him. "I could take him to court over this, but 'twould only create more of a scandal."

Sarah burrowed her head into his shoulder, glad for his support. "There's nothing I can do about it, is there?"

"No, I fear not. And he's offered you a handsome dowry."

"But he can't give me back the past two years. Or Papa's reputation."

Philip's temper, which had flared when he'd learned the full extent of Sir Edwin's crimes, had cooled. "There's nothing you can do about it. You told me that once."

"I've wasted two years of my life repaying debts that weren't mine. I think I've a right to be angry." She turned to look at him. "I realize this doesn't concern you directly, but it does me. Doesn't anything get you angry enough to fight for?"

He regarded her steadily and under that gaze her own eyes dropped. "Some things are worth fighting for, Sarah. This is not. And there are other ways of fighting."

"Meaning?"

"Meaning that I'm the one marrying you, not him."

Sarah's mouth opened to speak, leaving her gaping at him. "You mean you really do wish to marry me? It's not just to rescue me?"

"I'm hardly a knight in shining armor, Sarah."

"Perhaps slightly tarnished." She leaned her head against his shoulder again, her mind whirling with the implications of his words. He wanted to marry her, Sarah Chadwick. "Well."

She got to her feet and dusted off her skirts. "It seems I've a wedding to plan."

"Now that sounds more like my Sarah." He stood gazing down at her, a little smile on his face. He was going to kiss her again, she could sense it, and this time perhaps it would be more than a brief brushing of lips against lips. She raised her face, and at that moment a groom came around the side of the house, leading Philip's horse.

"Your horse, my lord," he said, looking curiously from Philip to Sarah.

Philip turned. "Thank you. Sarah." He turned back to her. "You're all right?"

"Of course I am. We Chadwicks are made of stern stuff."

"So are the Thorntons." He mounted his horse, sketching a salute to her in farewell and then was gone.

Sarah stood on the porch a moment, thinking. Sarah Thornton, Lady Pembroke. She rather liked the sound of that. Philip was right. The past was past. What counted was the future. Smiling to herself, she turned and went inside to face Sir Edwin.

Chapter Seven

The banns announcing the marriage of the Marquess of Pembroke to Miss Sarah Chadwick were read at the little Norman church in Bibury the following Sunday to the astonishment of all. Heads craned to see the mysterious marquess, seated in the black leather-lined pew that had once belonged to the Granthams, his wife's family, and which he had inherited when Havenwood came to him. With him were Miss Chadwick and Sir Edwin. The marquess, to be married! It almost caused a spate of whispering throughout the church, except for the look that the Reverend Crabbe sent his congregation. Any gossip would have to wait until services were completed.

The vicar himself, standing at the door to the church, was the first to congratulate the happy couple, shaking Philip's hand and smiling as if they were on the best of terms. It was then the turn of the rest of the parishioners. Philip received the well-wishers and the curious with a cool nod and smile, Sarah with more effusiveness, as if she actually believed people did wish her happy. At last, though, the ordeal was over and the party from Havenwood was safely ensconced in the marquess's barouche, Sir Edwin freely mopping at his brow.

"There," Sarah said, reaching over and patting Philip's hand as if he were a small boy. "That wasn't so bad, was it?"

"Madam, I'd rather return to the fighting on the Peninsula than go through that again," Philip said, and she laughed.

"It will get easier. You'll see. You have to expect people to be curious, Philip, since you never go out."

"Is she always like this?" Philip addressed his words to Sir Edwin, his voice almost plaintive. "So managing?"

"It comes of being a governess, I expect." Sarah sounded cheerful. "But it will get better, I promise."

"Am I to assume, then, that I'll be attending services each week?"

"Why, of course. At least, I intend to, and I hope you'll accompany me."

Philip muttered something under his breath. "What other plans do you have in store for me, madam?"

Sarah merely smiled. Three days after her engagement to this extraordinary man, and she was well content. She had seen past the eye patch, seen through the forbidding facade he had erected to the man beneath, intelligent, curious, knowledgeable, and very, very lonely. She intended to do something about that, no matter what he might think. She had even come to terms with Sir Edwin's dishonesty, which he had confessed to her in a most embarrassing apology. The past was past, and without Sir Edwin's actions, she might never have met Philip. "Have you family, Philip, that should be invited?"

"I thought this was to be a small wedding."

"Of course, but a girl only marries once, and she wants it to be a day to be remembered. I have Uncle Edwin, of course, and some relatives on my mother's side. But what of your family, sir?"

"I have a sister in London, Lady Rebecca Lawrence. And will she be pleased about this," he added darkly. "Her only disappointment will be that she didn't play the matchmaker."

Sarah laughed. "Poor Philip. We ladies do make your life a trial, do we not? I'm sure she and I will like each other immensely."

"I think you will. There is also my cousin Richard." For the first time, his face relaxed into a smile. "Richard Thornton. He's my heir. For now." Sarah blushed, making his smile widen. "I've thought of asking him to stand up for me."

"Then you must. You sound very fond of him."

"I am. His father and mine were twins, and we grew up together, went to school together. If his father had been born first, he'd be the marquess now, but he doesn't seem to mind. He's more a friend than a cousin, really. When things went bad . . ." His voice trailed off, and his face darkened in a way already familiar to Sarah.

"I'm sure I'll like him, too. Oh, this is so exciting."

"I'll be glad when all the fuss is over," he muttered.

"Yes, and you can go back to your experiments." *Or so you think.* She had other plans for her future husband.

Leaning back, Sarah pretended to look out the window, while instead covertly studying Philip. With a wife by his side to prod him along, a wife, moreover, who had no intention of immuring herself in Havenwood, splendid though it was, he might find that life outside was not as bad as he thought. In the meantime, there was a wedding to plan, and thank heavens it wasn't to Uncle Edwin. She could never have contemplated marriage to him. Pembroke, however, was another story. He was very much a man. In the warmth of the day, she shivered.

Across from her, Philip sent Sarah a quick glance. It hadn't been so much of an ordeal as he'd feared, hearing the banns read. Oh, there'd been the whispers, the stares, but that was nothing new to him. What had been new was the genuine pleasure that had been mixed with the curiosity. Sarah, it seemed, had managed to make herself well-liked in the few weeks of her stay. He felt oddly proud of her for that and pleased that others didn't see her as she persisted in seeing herself. For she was beautiful. Not the way Anne had been, all pink and gold and white, but in her own way, with a glow that came from within and that stirred him as few things had done in the last years. Well, perhaps the odd experiment or two, but not another person. He hadn't planned on ever marrying again. He didn't love her, nor did he expect he ever would. Perhaps, though, that was just as well, considering his past. If nothing else, he had found a friend, someone he could live with, someone, he had found to his great surprise, that he wanted very much. Underneath Sarah's governess's gowns was a lush figure waiting to be discovered, he was certain of that. The man who could awaken the woman in her would be very lucky indeed, and he intended to be that man. It was enough. He was content.

"You are a toad, Richard," Lady Rebecca said, setting down the teapot with a decided thump.

"Why?" The Honorable Richard Thornton lounged back in the blue brocade chair in Lady Rebecca's London drawing room, idly stirring his tea. He was dressed, as always, in the height of fashion, fawn-colored pantaloons neatly tucked into glistening Hessian boots and a coat of blue superfine, tailored by Weston, of course, sitting well upon his broad shoulders. He was a handsome man, with his curly, chestnut hair brushed forward *á la Brutus,* if one ignored the eyes that were a little too small, the lips a little too full and red. A dandy, a true Corinthian; a catch on the marriage mart, and he knew it.

"I merely said that she must be after him for his money," he went on, sipping at his tea. "Well, think of it, Becky. A girl of her background—"

"With a wealthy father," Lady Rebecca retorted.

"Who died penniless. And in trade, too. Quite a catch she's made for herself, this Miss Chadwick. Whoever she is."

Lady Rebecca eyed her cousin over the rim of her teacup. She, too, had her doubts about this marriage. Philip had been through so much in his life. She wanted only the best for him and had, in fact, tried to present him with suitable girls on the rare occasions when he visited London. None had taken, of course. He had chosen to lock himself up in that extraordinary house in the Cotswolds, until this unknown girl had come along.

"I do agree she may not be quite suitable," Rebecca said finally. "However, since Philip isn't at all sociable that may not matter."

"Ha." Richard set his cup down on the low sofa table. "You want him back in London, and you're as worried about this unknown girl as I am. Admit it, Becky." His eyes met hers. "I

83

know we don't always agree on everything, but I don't think either of us wants to see Philip trapped in an unhappy marriage."

"No, of course not. But what can we do?" She shrugged. "Philip's a grown man. He can make his own decisions."

"And you haven't tried to meddle, Becky? You surprise me."

His tone was sardonic, making her look at him quickly. She had her reasons for not being pleased about this marriage, but they were concerned with Philip's happiness. What, though, were Richard's? Unlike Philip, she had never completely trusted him. "So what is it you think to do? Buy her off?"

"So blunt, Becky? However, that is a thought. But, no, I may be able to think of something else."

And he smiled, a charming smile that Rebecca didn't quite like. What, though, could she do? Until they traveled to Gloucestershire and met the girl, they were powerless. And Philip could be stubborn when he wanted to be. She would not meddle, Rebecca vowed. At least, not yet.

"Richard! Becky!" His face alight with pleasure, Philip hurried down the steps of Havenwood to greet his guests. "And Lawrence," he said less effusively, shaking his brother-in-law's hand. "Good to see you again."

Rebecca wasn't satisfied with merely grasping the hands Philip held out to her; instead she threw her arms around his neck in a stranglehold and then pulled away to scan his face. "You look good."

"Must you sound so surprised? Richard." He clasped his cousin's hand warmly. "Good of you to come."

"Wouldn't miss it for the world," Richard drawled, as they strolled into the house. "You getting leg-shackled again — an occasion not to be missed. Quite unexpected of you, you know."

"I know." Philip was smiling as he led his guests into the drawing room, sparing not even a glance for the portrait of his first wife. "Rather took me by surprise, too. But it's the right decision, I think."

84

Rebecca carefully tugged off her gloves. She had missed neither Philip's smile nor his avoidance of Anne's portrait. "When will we meet Miss Chadwick?"

"Yes, when?" Richard echoed. "Must be a beauty like Anne."

"In a different way." Philip's geniality remained unimpaired. "Sarah is an original." At that, Rebecca exchanged glances with the others. "She and her guardian will be here for dinner tonight."

"I quite look forward to meeting her. But tell me, Philip, is she at all suitable?" Becky said.

"I think so." Philip was too accustomed to his sister's bluntness to take offense. "Her family was good — yes, I know her father was in trade — but it's an old family, particularly on her mother's side. I knew you'd want to know."

"That's all right, then." Rebecca ignored his teasing grin. "All that matters is that you're happy with her."

"Oh, I am. I think you will be, too."

"She must be brave, to take you on," Richard said.

"Richard! That is a perfectly odious thing to say!" Rebecca said, glaring at him.

"No, no, you misunderstand. I meant because of the rumors, and the way society has reacted. I apologize, cousin, if it sounded otherwise."

Philip smiled faintly, though for a moment his confidence had been shaken. Sarah was brave, indeed, to marry such as he. "It is of no moment. By the bye, Richard."

"Yes?"

"I made you something." With some diffidence, Philip picked up a small, highly lacquered box. Atop the box was a strange metal fitting. "For lighting those endless cigars of yours." He pressed a catch on the metal and instantly a small flame shot up.

"How ingenious." Richard took the box, playing with the catch, staring fixedly at the flame. "What things you do think of."

"Yes, a contrivance of the devil," Philip said, smiling.

"I wouldn't quite call it that, cousin." Richard flicked the catch again. "How does it work?"

"When you press the catch, it strikes the flint, and that ignites the wick. Let up on the catch, and it snuffs the flame. Be careful with it, by the way. There's paraffin inside."

"I will be. Thank you. I'll use it often."

"I thought you might. Now." He rose. "You must want to wash the dirt of the road off you. Mrs. Stevenson will show you to your rooms."

"I confess I'll be glad of a rest," Rebecca said. "The roads are in such horrid condition."

"Tell me, old boy," Sir Lawrence said, taking Philip's arm as they walked out to the Great Hall. "This gel of yours. She hunt?"

"No. She barely even rides."

"Barely rides?" Sir Lawrence drew back in horror. "But she is pretty."

"Oh, yes." Philip kept his face straight with an effort. "I believe you'll think so."

"Very good, old boy. Very happy for you, and all that."

"Thank you," Philip said and stood on the marble floor watching his guests ascend the stairs. Sir Lawrence he tolerated, but Rebecca and Richard were the only people he loved in the world. He turned away, feeling more in charity with the world than he had for years. He had made the right decision.

Oh, dear, *what* was she going to wear? Sarah gazed into the depths of her wardrobe with dismay. What did one wear to meet a leader of London society, as well as a pink of the *ton?* When she had accepted Philip's proposal, she'd given not a thought to his family. It had been a mistake. The family of a marquess was likely to be starchy and dignified, puffed up in their importance. And here was she, a poor country mouse, as it were. What would she do if they didn't like her?

The contents of her wardrobe weren't reassuring. There were her gray, governess's gowns, the most lively of which was silk, trimmed with lilac twill. There were also the gowns left from her disastrous season, all pink and white and girlish, and not at all her style, even when she had been young. Besides, they no longer fitted her; to her surprise, they were much too big. She hadn't realized how much she had slimmed down over the past few years.

She sighed. The gray silk it would have to be. What other choice did she have? She only hoped she wouldn't disgrace Philip.

Sometime later she stepped into the drawing room at Havenwood on Sir Edwin's arm to face a frightening array of people. The tall man with the chestnut hair leaning against the mantel and slowly, carefully scanning her from head to toe had to be Philip's cousin Richard. Flushing from the almost tactile quality of that look, she turned away to encounter the frankly interested gaze of another man, this one stout and bluff and beaming. Heavens! What was it about men? she wondered yet again. In her high-necked gown with her hair pinned into a neat knot at her neck, she knew she looked impossibly dowdy, impossibly plain. She doubted that Philip's sister would look upon her so kindly. To her surprise, however, the woman seated on the straw-colored sofa was looking at her with the same frank, friendly interest. Lady Rebecca. Sarah felt herself tensing, but, to her surprise, the other woman's smile was kind, and her eyes sparkled with curiosity.

"Miss Chadwick," Rebecca said, extending her hand. "How lovely to meet you at last. Come, sit by me. I am Philip's sister. Don't let's stand on ceremony, shall we? The family calls me Becky."

"Thank you," Sarah murmured, her curiosity rising at this unexpectedly warm welcome. There were undercurrents here; she could sense it in the way they looked at her, the way they looked at each other. Sarah raised her head and smiled. After all, she was no young miss making her debut. She was not going to let these people intimidate her. "It's nice to meet everyone at last."

Philip performed the remaining introductions. Richard Lawrence merely bowed, making her wonder if she had imagined that earlier look, but Sir Lawrence beamed. Sir Lawrence. In her nervous state, it was nearly enough to overset her, but she controlled her giggles with a great effort. This might not be so bad, after all.

They talked of generalities for a while, rising when the bell for dinner sounded. As Sarah passed Sir Lawrence, he winked at her, making her look at him in surprise. "Lawrence, really! Behave yourself," Rebecca scolded, but the corners of her mouth twitched the same way Philip's did.

"Sorry, my love," Sir Lawrence murmured, looking abashed as he crossed to take her arm. "Afraid I lost control for a moment."

"Well, don't let it happen again. I am sorry, Sarah."

"Lawrence is harmless," Philip said. "He winks at every woman."

"Every beautiful woman," Richard said at her other side, taking her elbow. "Come, let me escort you in to dinner. It's obvious nobody else here really appreciates you."

"Thank you," she stammered, and glanced back at Philip. Heavens! And why hadn't he defended her honor? *My white knight. Huh.*

Dinner went smoothly, starting with two soups, a clear bouillon, the other a mock turtle. They were accompanied by the latest London gossip, and followed by several fish dishes, trout served with a wedge of lemon, and turbot in lobster sauce. Sarah struggled to keep up with both the conversation and the meal. Because she followed current events, she was able to join in the discussion of politics and the war in the Peninsula, which was going well, but when the talk turned to the latest *on-dits,* she fell silent. What did she know of London? She glanced back and forth from Rebecca, poised, elegantly gowned, to Richard, handsome, enigmatic, and sophisticated, and wondered just what they thought of her. Thank heavens she wouldn't have to go to London and face the scrutiny of other stylish people.

Or would she? She glanced at Philip, sitting at ease, a little smile on his face as his fingers toyed with his water glass. He looked the most relaxed she had ever seen. Obviously he enjoyed the company of these people; why then did he keep himself hidden in the country? Sarah had no great desire to see London, or, at least, she hadn't since childhood, but suddenly a longing to go there rose up in her. Not for herself, though. For Philip, who had so much to give and was instead locked away in a prison of his own making, no matter how luxurious and comfortable it might be.

He looked up and caught her gaze. His smile faded as their eyes held, and Sarah had the odd sense that he was seeing more than was on the surface, that, eye patch or no, he could see to her very soul. It was exhilarating and exciting and also just the slightest bit frightening. She was the first to turn away, her cheeks reddening. Something of importance had just occurred between them, and she hadn't the slightest idea what it was.

The entrées were served then, and Sarah's attention was distracted. In a long, bewildering procession came a baron of beef, a roast of veal, larded pheasants, julienne potatoes, and green beans with almonds. These were followed by the sweets, stewed apples, a confusing array of cheeses, a rice pudding, and a thick, dark chocolate gâteau. There was also a different wine for every course, more wine than she had ever seen consumed at one sitting. After her first glass she had been careful to take only small portions, but even so she was somewhat lightheaded when, after dinner, she and Rebecca left the gentlemen to their port and went to the drawing room, Sarah sinking onto one of the straw satin sofas. She felt not at all up to dealing with her future sister-in-law.

Rebecca chose to sit in a matching armchair, the folds of her sapphire silk gown settling attractively about her, looking quite self-assured and sophisticated as she asked the footman to serve them coffee. She was much like her brother, in looks, at least, though the dark hair, bright blue eyes, and chiseled features that looked so well on Philip made her a handsome woman rather than a beautiful one. There was, however, an air of assurance about her that Sarah feared she herself quite lacked. What must the woman be thinking of her?

At that moment, Rebecca looked up and smiled. "You come as quite a surprise to me, Sarah. I may call you Sarah? Philip told me nothing about you until he wrote announcing the engagement. But then, that's just like Philip. As you must know."

"I know he tends to be reserved," Sarah said cautiously.

"Reserved! A hermit is more to the point. But I have hopes of him yet." Rebecca's shrewd eyes evaluated Sarah, but somehow she didn't mind. There was friendliness in that look, rather than hostility. "After all, I never thought he'd marry again. Thank you." This was to the footman, serving their coffee. When he had retired, Rebecca fired her first salvo. "How did you meet Philip?"

Sarah had been expecting it, of course. She had a story ready, of trespassing on Havenwood lands and meeting Philip that way, thus concealing the fact that she had spent a week in this house. Looking now at Rebecca, though, she knew it wouldn't work. Besides, she didn't know how much Philip had told her. "He rescued me from highwaymen."

"Gracious! How romantic."

"Yes, perhaps. But I was unconscious, you see, and didn't know it until I woke up, here. I," she took a deep breath, "spent a week here recovering."

"Even better!"

"But I was unchaperoned—"

"It doesn't matter. I know Philip is a man of honor. So that's it. He always did enjoy playing the white knight."

Sarah looked startled at this echo of her own thoughts. This woman was altogether too perceptive. "I'm not marrying him because of that, of course," she said, her governess manner settling about her like a cloak. "Ours is not a love match. But we are fond of each other."

"Oh, I don't doubt it." Rebecca's eyes gleamed with mirth at a joke only she seemed to understand. "Are you a managing sort of female?"

"I fear so, yes."

"Good. He needs that."

"But—"

"He's spent entirely too much time by himself these last years. It's high time he got out and about again, and I think you are the person to help him do it."

"But, why me? Heavens knows I'm nothing like his first wife."

For a moment, each regarded the portrait. "Anne was lovely," Rebecca said finally. "But you, my dear, have made him smile again, and I find that far more important. Not that you couldn't be pretty, if you tried."

"Nonsense, I'm fat and plain."

"Oh, gracious, no, I wouldn't say that. But that dress, my dear, is a disaster."

Sarah's eyelids lowered. "Yes, I know. Unfortunately, it's the best I have."

"Oh, dear. What of your wedding dress?"

"Miss Austin, the seamstress in the village, is making it up for me. I decided on blue. It's practical and serviceable and—"

"Dull. Oh, my dear, please don't take insult." Rebecca leaned over and laid her hand on Sarah's. "But you needn't dress like a governess anymore."

"Why, no, I don't intend to." Sarah slipped her hand free. "But you must agree that putting fine feathers on me would be something of a waste."

"No, I'm not sure I agree with you at all." Rebecca studied her a moment, and a slow smile spread across her face. Sarah was already beginning to mistrust that smile. "I've some fabric I brought with me from Town. May I give it to you? As a wedding present, of course."

"Why, yes, I suppose so."

"Good. And then tomorrow we shall go to Bibury and see what this Miss Austin of yours can do with it."

Sarah gave her a long look. "You're something of a managing female yourself, aren't you?"

Rebecca smiled. "Of course. I think we'll get along just fine, my dear."

Sarah was about to answer when the door from the hall opened and the men came in, their voices loud and jovial. Richard was smiling easily, and Sir Lawrence, still beaming, headed straight for the sofa next to her. Hastily she rose and crossed to a chair, and only when she was seated did she look up to see Richard, one arm propped on the mantel, smiling sardonically at her. She glanced away and met Philip's gaze, steady, reassuring. Suddenly all her nerves relaxed. It didn't really matter what these people thought of her. All she cared about was Philip.

The evening sped by. Sarah, accustomed to being ill at ease in groups or to being the authority in a nursery, was startled by how much she enjoyed everything: the conversation; the silly songs played on the pianoforte by both Rebecca and Philip, songs they'd sung in childhood; even Richard's flirting. For the first time she felt she might actually belong in this family and that her future was, indeed, as bright as she had hoped.

The tea tray was brought in at ten o'clock and then it was over. Philip ordered his carriage brought 'round and rose with the express purpose of escorting Sarah home. To Sarah's surprise, Sir Edwin made no protest at that, and no one else seemed shocked, either at the thought of her being alone with a man, fiancé or not. Not that Philip was likely to do anything, of course. After all, he was a gentleman. *More's the pity,* she thought to her surprise. *Behave yourself, Sarah!*

Sarah smiled as she rose, even allowing Sir Lawrence, still beaming, to take her hand. He was probably harmless, she decided. And then it was Richard's turn. He crossed to her from the mantel where he had watched the evening's entertainments with a languid, somehow superior eye and took her hand, fixing his eyes on her. Sarah suddenly didn't know where to look. She didn't want to glance away; that would be impolite. Something in his eyes, though, a smoldering, possessive look, made her extremely uneasy. It took every ounce of courage she possessed for her to raise her own eyes and meet them.

"Philip is a very lucky man," Richard said, his voice husky as he took the hand Sarah held out to him. She expected him to raise it to his lips, but she didn't expect at the last moment that he would turn her hand over and kiss her wrist. It was unexpectedly warm and hard, and she distinctly felt the tip of his tongue touch her skin, making her jerk back. "Yes. Very lucky, indeed."

"Th-thank you, sir." Sarah at last managed to free her hand, and this time she didn't care about politeness. She couldn't meet that burning, somehow mocking gaze any longer. Heavens! So this was what it was like to be courted by a London dandy. She wasn't altogether certain she liked it.

"Come, my dear." A hand was laid reassuringly on her back, and she turned to see Philip. "I'll see you home."

"Thank you," she murmured. It was with vast relief that she allowed him to lead her out of the room and to his carriage. She wasn't certain she could support Mr. Thornton's dalliance much longer. Thank heavens he lived in London.

"That went well, I think," Philip said, as the carriage set off.

"Yes. I do like your sister, and I think she liked me."

"Of course she did." Philip leaned over and laid his hand on Sarah's. The brief touch sent a curious warmth through her. So much of her life she had had to be the strong one, supporting her father through his long widowerhood, bearing up as a governess to other peoples' children. Now someone was telling her, without words, that he would be there for her. It meant more than all the languishing gazes or burning kisses on the wrist ever could.

Philip settled back. "I dread to think, though, what you and Becky were planning while we men were at port."

Sarah smiled, a secret, feminine smile. Goodness, she possessed wiles she hadn't even realized. "You'll see."

"I'm not sure I like the sound of that." Philip rose as the carriage came to a stop and jumped nimbly out to assist Sarah down. For the first time in quite a long time, Sarah was aware of his eye patch and what it meant, simply because of his agility. Any disability he might have certainly hadn't hampered him. He was, as he had stated quite definitely, a man, and the thought thrilled her.

"Well." They stood at the door of her uncle's house, and a curious awkwardness fell between them. "I shall see you tomorrow?" Philip said.

"Yes, of course." She watched as if from a distance as Philip seemed to hesitate and then took her hand. A courtly gesture, of course, kissing a woman's hand, she told herself, but somehow this kiss, too, landed on her wrist, and somehow Philip's gaze was holding hers in such a way that she couldn't look away. Then he lowered her hand and stepped away, and it was over.

"Good night, my dear."

"Good night," she whispered, aware that the door to the house had opened, but focused only on her betrothed.

Philip cleared his throat. "Tomorrow, then?"

"What? Oh, yes, of course. Tomorrow." She smiled at him and at last turned to go in, bemused. It certainly wasn't Richard's kiss that made her feel as if she were floating. No, not at all. She was barely aware of Mackie's deferential greeting, barely aware later of Sir Edwin's comments on the evening. All her memory, all her being, were focused on that one moment when the world had narrowed to just two people: herself and Philip. Heavens! Was she falling in love with her fiancé?

Chapter Eight

It was her wedding day.

Sarah stood in the back of the little Norman church in Bibury, its stone walls cool even in the unseasonable September warmth, and waited, her hand resting on Sir Edwin's arm, for the processional to begin. Butterflies danced in her stomach, and she had to force herself not to fidget. Now that the time was here, she wasn't at all certain she was doing the right thing. The self-confidence she usually drew around herself like a cloak had deserted her, leaving her feeling much as she had as a young girl, awkward and plain and very unsure of herself. She was marrying a man who, in spite of his secret-enshrouded past, in spite of his reclusiveness and isolation from the neighborhood, was nevertheless handsome, talented, intelligent. A catch, in other words, something she had never expected. And what had she to give him? Only herself.

Her heart beat faster as the processional began to play and she stepped down the aisle. The tiny church was crowded with well-wishers and villagers, and as the rays of the sun, streaming through the tiny-paned windows, touched upon her, there was an audible gasp. Sarah could feel herself turning red. It was the gown, of course. She had expected muslin, perhaps even silk from Rebecca, in white or ivory; what she'd got instead was cloth of gold. Of course she had tried to refuse the gift, it was so extravagant, and of course Rebecca had been adamant. Even dowdy Miss Austin had been thrilled at the thought of working with such beautiful fabric. All Sarah's protests had been in vain. The only argument she had won had been over the neckline. It was, quite properly, high, and that was the only thing that made her comfortable wearing the gown. It was not at all her style; it was cut closer to her body, for one thing, and it flowed sinuously almost to the floor. Rarely did she call attention to herself in such a way, but there was no denying that she loved the gown or that it suited her. And so, embarrassed and just a little proud, Sarah continued down the aisle toward her groom.

Another ray of sunlight touched upon her, and Philip blinked. She was dazzling, radiant, a creature of sunlight and life, a magic presence that had somehow been granted to him and that, for a time, wiped away the darkness. Sarah's hair was softly looped up instead of being pulled into its usual tight knot, and a circle of white roses crowned her head. She was beautiful, he realized for the first time, beautiful in a way he had never expected, and in a few moments she would be his wife. And what did he have to give her? Only money and a dubious reputation.

At last Sarah reached the altar, handing her bouquet of white roses to Rebecca, standing as her matron of honor. Taking her place at Philip's side, she stole a quick glance up at him to see his face looking set and pale. That did nothing for her confidence, and again she felt nervous giggles rising inside her. No, she would not disgrace herself! This was her wedding day, something she'd thought she'd never have. She wanted it to be perfect.

The ceremony passed in a daze of words and suddenly she was married. Philip bent to place a brief kiss on her lips, and for a moment their gazes met. Then they had to sign the register and receive the congratulations of their guests and the moment passed. Somehow they found themselves in Philip's barouche, being driven to Havenwood.

"Phew!" Philip took out his handkerchief and wiped his brow. "Thank God that's over."

"Well, thank you very much!" Sarah exclaimed. "It isn't every day a girl gets married —"

"And you were as nervous as I was."

"Nervous?" She stared at him and then a smile spread across her face. "Oh, poor Pembroke." She laid her hand on his. "Were you nervous?"

"Philip." He brought her hand to his lips. "Not Pembroke. Philip."

"Of course."

"Say it."

"Philip," she said, gazing up at him just as she had in church. There it was again, the magic, as if a spell had been cast over them, and neither could look away. She saw his lips soften, part, and let her eyes drift closed for the kiss she was certain would come.

The carriage came to a stop. "We're here." Philip looked away, and Sarah's eyes flew open.

"What? Oh, of course. Havenwood."

"I'm rather sorry now we invited so many people." He jumped down and turned to assist her, helping her loop the train of her gown over her arm.

"But they're your tenants, Philip, and our neighbors. We couldn't very well ignore them."

"No, I suppose we couldn't. Worse luck," he added, as the door opened. Inside the hall, the staff was assembled, all smiling with pleasure, even Mrs. Stevenson. At least, Sarah assumed that was what her stiff little grimace was.

"Welcome, my lady," Mrs. Stevenson said, curtsying, and Sarah heard her new title for the first time.

"Heavens! I'm a marchioness," she said to Philip as he escorted her into the drawing room.

"Yes, of course. Didn't you realize that?"

"No. I never thought of it. Gracious, if my father were only here, he'd be so proud."

"I think he'd be proud of you anyway."

Sarah looked up at him and was unable to look away. Philip's hands rested on her shoulders, her face tilted up, and at last, finally, he was kissing her, all too briefly.

A noise behind them broke the spell, and Philip looked up. The first of their guests had arrived for the wedding breakfast. He muttered something that Sarah didn't catch and then turned, taking her arm. After that, there was no chance for any private conversation as each was caught up in the festivities. Sarah drank sparingly of the wines used to toast her and her new husband, and ate even less of the sumptuous meal. Hearing her title had brought home to her exactly what she had done and what kind of world she had entered. She was a marchioness, lower in rank only to a duchess and royalty. Good heavens! *If the Ramsays could only see me now,* she thought, and bit down another hysterical desire to giggle.

It was a long afternoon and a somewhat tense one. Philip was not well-known to his neighbors, beyond the tales that had spread about him, and it was with some relief that the guests turned to the libations he had so generously supplied. Soon everyone was talking and laughing, except for Philip, who remained rather quiet. Sarah glanced at him, talking with a tenant and looking serious and then saw, beyond them, Sir Edwin deep in conversation with Richard. Now what could they find in common? she was wondering, when an arm suddenly clamped about her waist. Startled, she looked up just as Sir Lawrence planted a moist kiss on her cheek. "Must kiss the bride, you know," he said genially, and his head bent again, though Sarah tried to pull away.

Damn Lawrence, Philip thought, and was about to make his way through the crowd to Sarah's side when a hand clamped down on his shoulder. He turned to see Geordie. "Damn, what is it, Geordie?"

"Just thought ye should know, sir. Charles Grantham was at church, and looking none too happy, neither."

"Damn the man." Philip put his hand to his eye patch, and then snatched it away. "All right, Geordie, keep watch for him, though I doubt he'll do anything. Now, if you'll excuse me, I have to rescue Sarah from Lawrence."

"Aye, sir." Geordie watched him go, frowning. Not all wished the marquess well this day. No, not all.

"Only one kiss allowed, Lawrence," Philip said. Lawrence looked up, startled, and that gave Sarah the chance to step free, going to Philip's side and taking his arm. He had rescued her again, thank heavens.

"Of course," Lawrence said. "You're a lucky man, and so —"

"And so keep your hands to yourself." Philip's voice was pleasant, but his gaze was hard.

"Sorry," Lawrence muttered finally. "Must go find my wife. Must be here somewhere."

Philip again muttered something under his breath. "Excuse me?" Sarah said.

"I said I can't stand this any longer. Come." He grasped her hand and began pulling her toward the door.

"But, Philip, we have guests!"

"They won't even notice we've gone. Come," he said again, and this time she willingly obeyed.

He was only partly right. From across the room a pair of cool gray eyes watched as they made their escape. So, Richard thought, sipping carefully at the excellent champagne, the plain little bride wasn't quite so plain as he'd thought. If nothing else, that would make his task easier. A bit too plump for his taste, she was, a bit too gauche and naive, but at least she wasn't ugly. In short, she was ripe for seduction by the right man. Not Philip; he obviously still hadn't learned how to treat a woman. Probably he'd dragged her off to see one of his inventions, Richard thought with derision. Fine marquess he made, and a fine husband; Richard could do much better at both, if he only had the chance. If Philip weren't careful, he'd make the same mistakes he had with Anne, and look where that had landed him. Not that he'd married Miss Chadwick for love, not if what Sir Edwin, who bore Philip little love, had told him was true. Interesting, that, that Philip had compromised her and had married her out of honor. Interesting, and encouraging. There were many possibilities here for an enterprising man like himself.

Richard drained his glass and snapped his fingers at a footman for another. This was going to be easy. This time, his plans would succeed.

Sarah emerged onto the roof of the turret, gasping slightly for breath from the long climb and from laughter at the impetuous way Philip had pulled her away. "I still can't believe you—oh!" She stopped still in wonder, staring at the early evening sky. In the west, a hint of pink remained from the sunset; overhead, the first stars were beginning to appear. "Oh, how beautiful."

"Yes," Philip said, coming up behind her and laying a hand on her shoulder.

Sarah started. *Steady on, girl*, she cautioned herself. "This is such an unexpected house. Whyever did you build it?"

"I've always liked castles."

"But what do you need with turrets and battlements and—"

"I've found uses. Come." He took her hand and led her across the flagstoned floor. "Have you ever looked through one of these?"

"A telescope? No. What do you use it for? To spy on your neighbors?"

Philip's teeth gleamed briefly in the darkness. "Hardly. No, I study the stars."

"Heavens," she said, bending to the eyepiece.

"Exactly," he answered, laying his hands lightly on her shoulders to guide her. "Here, we'll turn it this way."

"This is exciting." Her voice was slightly breathless. She was very aware of the warmth spreading through her at his touch, very aware of his presence, so close behind her.

"Yes," he said, in such a way that she suspected he wasn't thinking of the stars, either. "Not many to see yet, though. Later on there'll be enough." And he named some of the stars of late September, Andromeda, Cassiopeia, Perseus, Vega, pointing out to her where they would be.

"Heavens," Sarah said again, at last straightening. "An inventor, a farmer, and now an astronomer. Is there anything you can't do?"

It was nearly the same question he had asked himself when he had seen her, shimmering and shining with happiness, walking down the church aisle toward him. He could do a great deal, except the one thing he suspected she needed the most. He could not give all of himself to her. "Yes." His voice was clipped, making her look up at him in surprise. "Sarah.

He laid his hands on her shoulders again, turning her to face him. "Are you sorry you married me?"

"Why, what a question! Of course not, silly. You—you're not, are you?"

"Oh, no, no. But . . ."

"But?"

"I'm not the easiest man in the world to get along with. What do you see in me, Sarah?"

In the darkness, Sarah tried to see his face. "More than I think you realize," she said softly. "It's I who isn't really a proper wife for you."

"We'll have no more of that nonsense." He laid his finger on her lips, and she stilled. The magic, the tension that had been between them earlier stretched, grew, as they continued to peer at each other through the darkness, and Sarah moved her lips lightly against his finger.

That seemed to rouse him. Letting his hands drop, Philip turned away. "It's been a long day. You must be tired."

"No, not terribly, but I admit I would like to just sit for a while."

"Why don't you go downstairs then, and—?"

His final word and what it implied hung for a moment in the silence. "Our guests," Sarah finally managed to get out.

"Will all have left by now. Geordie had his orders."

"Oh. Oh, I see." The impulse to go to him, to throw herself into his arms, was very strong, but Sarah held back. There was a new awareness between them and a constraint that hadn't been there before. They were suddenly much more than merely friends. "Then I think I'll get ready for bed."

"A good idea. I'll just take a turn or two around here and then come down."

"I'll be waiting," she whispered, and whisked herself down the stairs.

She was nervous again as she prepared for bed, startled to find that Mrs. Stevenson had assigned her a maid, the same one she had had during her unexpected visit. She was mistress of this unique house, but that amazing fact seemed very unimportant just now. In a little while, her husband would come

101

to her and make her his own. Clad in a white silk nightrail with a matching wrapper, something Rebecca had insisted she must have, Sarah sat before her dressing table, her hands twisting in her lap as Millie brushed out her hair and chatted cheerfully about the wedding. Sarah's answers were absent, automatic, and at last she had had enough. Rising abruptly, she smiled at the girl and sent her away. "Oh, and please don't wake me until I ring for you," Sarah called after her, and Millie gave her a feminine smile of complicity.

Goodness! Sarah twisted her hands together again as she turned to examine her new bedroom. The marchioness's room. Philip had told her she might decorate it anyway she liked, but for now she was pleased with it: the mahogany bed with its delicately turned posts, ruffled canopy, and chintz curtains; the matching wardrobe and dressing table; the chaise longue of rose velvet; the thick carpet of rose and cream and soft green. Colors she might not have chosen herself but which she liked. For the first time in a very long time she felt feminine, pretty. Her days of governessing were past.

Now. What should she do? She could sit in the rose velvet chair and pick up a book — no, she was much too nervous for that! Well, there was always the chaise longue. Sarah stretched out on it, arranging her wrapper attractively around her, reclining as she had once seen in a book, a picture of a lady — well, a woman, anyway — in a harem. That made her giggle, and she jumped to her feet again. She certainly wasn't the type to recline languidly! But what was she to do? She didn't want Philip to come in and catch her simply standing in the middle of the floor like a ninny. That left only the bed.

Sarah regarded it for a moment. If she climbed in, she would appear eager, but then, that was what this night was about, wasn't it? She was not naive, nor was she ignorant. She knew what happened between a man and a woman in marriage, though the reason for it, beyond producing children, mystified her. Why be so missish over it, then? With a nod of decision, she took off her wrapper, laying it across the bottom of the bed, and climbed in, drawing the covers up to her chest, though the night was warm. There she sat and waited.

And waited. When what seemed like an hour had passed, she heard movement in the next room, her husband's room, and she tensed. Well! It had taken him long enough, she thought with a burst of wifely indignation. Any moment now, there would be a tap on the door adjoining their rooms, and he would come in. Any moment .

The candle on the bedstand burned lower and lower still and at last guttered, abruptly plunging the room into darkness. He wasn't coming. Sarah sat with her arms wrapped around her knees and admitted the stark truth to herself. Her new husband, apparently not finding her attractive enough, would not be coming to her that night.

Philip waited for a long time, looking up at the stars and counting them, as was his habit, until they became too numerous and he lost track. Only then did he leave the roof, descending the turret's circular staircase carefully because the narrow end of the stairs was on his blind side. He hadn't been with a woman in three years, not since Anne's death, not since he'd been forced to wear an eye patch. At first it had been because of the lingering grief that had robbed all color from his days and left everything a uniform gray. The return of life and desire had come slowly, startling him, but by then he was accustomed to people shying away from him or avoiding him altogether. What woman would possibly want him? He was scarred. Alive, capable, but scarred, and with rumors that swirled about him persistently enough to frighten away most women.

Except Sarah. Entering his room, he smiled at the thought, and at her fierce partisanship of him. Sarah. A remarkable woman, cheerful, curious, headstrong, true, but beautiful, so beautiful it made him ache. He hadn't wanted any woman so much in a very long time, and yet, what did he have to give her? For the third time that day, he asked himself the question, and he didn't like the answer.

Waving his hand in dismissal, he sent his valet away and then went to stand in front of his mirror. He untied the eye patch and studied his scars. There was his legacy to his new wife: a shrouded past, an uncertain future. And yet . . .

He glanced toward the door separating their rooms and tied the patch again. She had chosen to marry him. No one had forced her, not even when her reputation had been compromised. No, she had come to him freely, fully, aware of what life with him would entail. Certainly she hadn't seemed aware of the advantages of marriage to him; he smiled, remembering her ingenuous surprise of this morning when she had realized she had a title. For whatever reason, she had chosen him, and he was suddenly eager to begin his life with her.

There was no answer when he tapped lightly at her door, and her room was in darkness, making him bring his candle with him. From the bed came the sound of even, measured breathing. Sarah, asleep. He stood and watched her for a long time, saw her glossy hair spread across the pillow, watched the rise and fall of her chest with her breathing, and wanted her. Wanted her more than he had ever wanted anyone, even Anne, and knowing that he couldn't have her. She deserved better than he.

Quietly, Philip turned and went back into his own room where he sat, head in hands, for a very long time.

Chapter Nine

Little had changed at Havenwood. Philip still took his early morning rides, alone, still spent much of his day in his workroom, alone, still went to bed, alone. The servants still scurried quietly about their rounds with the dour face of Mrs. Stevenson to hurry them along. There was no noise, no laughter, no music, and that was as it always had been. The only difference now was that the master was married, and his wife was, as yet, an unknown quantity.

Sarah was bewildered, unprepared for the role she had been thrust into, that of virgin bride. No matter what else had happened in her life, she had always managed to have some involvement in it, whether as her father's companion or in her work as governess. Now there was nothing. She saw her husband only at dinner, seated far down the long table from her. Under such circumstances conversation was desultory and formal at best. Sarah didn't know what to do, even had they had the chance to talk intimately. Why he hadn't yet come to her bed was a mystery to her, one she felt shy about probing. It just wasn't done, for one thing, but beyond that she feared she knew the answer. She simply wasn't attractive enough.

She sat at breakfast alone one morning, a week after her wedding, mulling over the matter. How did one go about seducing one's husband? Long used to relying on herself, Sarah was not one to wait upon events, but Philip's coldness baffled her. In the past, men had pursued her, though she hadn't always known why. Now the man she wished would pay her some attention was avoiding her. It was all most frustrating and annoying.

At least she was decently clothed again. Sir Edwin's dowry had allowed her to order an adequate trousseau, and she was rather pleased with what Miss Austin had made. Nothing could compare with her wedding gown, of course, but Sarah liked the dress she was wearing, a round gown of rose muslin with a white ruff at her throat and long full sleeves tied at three places with ribbons. She liked wearing colors again after so many years of black and gray; if she could she would garb herself in even brighter tones, scarlet and purple and azure. With her figure, though, she'd only look ridiculous.

The door behind her opened. "Excuse me, my lady." Sommers the butler stood there, holding out a silver salver. "There is a guest."

"This early?" Sarah took the card from the tray. "Who in the world—Oh, do show him in, Sommers!"

"Very good, my lady." Sommers bowed and left the dining room, and Sarah rose, feeling flustered and excited and happy. This might be just what Philip needed to chase away the blue-deviled mood he appeared to be in.

"Richard!" She held out her hands, and he paused in the doorway at the unexpected effusiveness of her greeting. "How wonderful to see you! I didn't expect we'd be seeing you so soon."

"I had business in the neighborhood." He took Sarah's hands, smiling down at her. Well. The new marchioness looked rather attractive, with a better figure than he'd realized, and rather desperate. His dolt of a cousin was at it again apparently, treating his wife poorly. Marvelous luck for his own cause, Richard thought. If husband and wife were estranged, there was little chance there'd someday be another heir to the Pembroke title and estates. "A matter of a pair of grays. You wouldn't know anything about them, would you?"

"Oh, no, I know nothing about horses. You'll have to ask

Philip. Please, sit. Sommers, more coffee."

"Thank you." Richard took the chair at right angles to her, flipping back the tails of his morning coat. He looked rugged and handsome and very much alive, and Sarah's spirits picked up immeasurably. "I hope you don't mind my imposing on you like this, but as I was in the neighborhood . . ."

"We'd have been insulted if you hadn't stopped in! Can you stay a few days?"

"Well, I'm putting up at the Bell and George—"

"That's nonsense, staying at an inn when we've all this room. You must stay here. I insist."

"Coming from such a beautiful lady as yourself, how can I resist such an invitation?"

"You must tell me all that is happening in London," she said, leaning toward him, and it was in this attitude that both of them were sitting when Philip came into the room.

For a moment he stopped, looking at the two dark heads bent together, hearing the animated conversation, and he felt as if someone were squeezing his heart. His wife. Yes, and what had he done to make her feel that way? Precious little. He was driving her away from him, and he hadn't the slightest idea how to stop.

"Richard!" he said, aware his voice sounded overhearty, and Richard looked up.

"Cousin." Richard rose, holding out his hand. "Good to see you."

"And you. Rusticating, Richard?"

Richard smiled. "Devil a bit. I won't deny I'm in low water, but I'll come about. I was just telling Sarah about the pair of grays I came to see."

"Ah, yes, those would be Mr. Bolton's, over by Ablington. A good team, but not much stamina, I understand." He was amazed at how normal his voice sounded as he took the chair across from his cousin.

"Richard is going to stay with us a few days," Sarah said, her face beaming. "Isn't that wonderful?"

"Yes, indeed," Philip said, though to him the words rang

hollow. For once he was not happy to see his cousin. "Have a good journey?"

"Yes," Richard answered, and the conversation turned to generalities. Philip was acutely aware of his wife, sitting to his right, close enough to touch, if he only dared. With her hair plaited and wrapped around her head, she looked queenly, magnificent, and yet the glow on her face was that of a young girl. She was so beautiful he ached with it. Why did she never look at him like that?

"Well." Philip placed his cup back on its saucer and rose. "I must be returning to my workroom."

"Oh. What are you working on, Philip?" Sarah asked, smiling up at him.

"Nothing of importance, my dear." He smiled impartially at each of them. "I shall see you at luncheon."

"Of course." Sarah's bright smile faded, and she gazed into space. Before their marriage, she and Philip had been able to talk about anything. Why was he now shutting her out?

"Is he still doing that?" Richard said, and she came out of her daze.

"Excuse me? Doing what?"

"Closeting himself in his workroom."

"Yes." Sarah set down her cup with a definite thump. "Every day, and I don't know what to do about it!"

"He is a fool." Richard's fingers brushed lightly across her hand, and she drew back, startled. "He did the same thing after Anne died. That, I could understand. But, this . . ."

"I am not Anne, sir." She rose, tossing her napkin down.

"No, of course not."

"And I'm rather tired of people mentioning her. I feel as if I'm competing with a ghost!"

"Poor Sarah," he said, his voice so sympathetic that she felt absurd tears starting to her eyes. "Has it been so hard for you?"

"No, of course not." She turned away. Not even to Richard would she reveal how difficult the past week had been. "I'm sure that in any marriage there must be adjustments."

"But my dolt of a cousin isn't making it easy for you. Ah, well, never mind, this must be better than governessing."

"Much," Sarah said stiffly, uncertain whether to be insulted on her own behalf or her husband's.

"Come, don't poker up so. I meant no harm." Richard gave her a smile so warm and winning that she found herself smiling back. "Tactless of me, I know. But I had hoped you could bring my cousin out of his shell."

"So had I. But it's early days yet, sir."

"Of course, and I am deeply sorry if I offended you." He caught at her hand and raised it to his lips. "Let me make it up to you."

"That—that isn't necessary, sir."

"Of course it is. I know. Come with me to see Bolton's grays."

"But I know little of horses, sir."

"No matter. It will do you good to get out for a time, I think.

Sarah gazed up at him, and some of her old feistiness returned. Of course she could go out if she wanted to. Why, then, had she been mooning about like a silly female? If Philip chose to close himself away from her that was his problem. "I'd be pleased to go with you, sir," she said, smiling. And maybe, just maybe, Philip would be annoyed enough by her desertion to do something about it.

The expedition proved to be a great success, though Richard had to agree with Philip's assessment of the grays and decided not to purchase them. Instead, he set himself to amuse his companion and succeeded so well that she was laughing when she again entered the dining room, this time for luncheon. Philip, who had been waiting for them for quite some time, rose at their approach, and Sarah stopped in the doorway.

"Oh! Philip!" she said, her hand to her heart. "Is it that late, then? We went to inspect Mr. Bolton's team, and I fear the time just got away from us."

"Ah. So that is where you were." Philip's face stayed stern.

109

Flushed with laughter, Sarah looked amazingly pretty, and the glance she sent Richard was filled with mingled mirth and complicity. It was happening again. His wife preferred someone else. "Did you decide to buy them?"

"No, cousin." Richard seated Sarah and then crossed to his own chair. "I agree with you that they lack stamina. But the morning wasn't wasted."

"Yes, I do wish you had come with us, Philip," Sarah said, impulsively laying her hand on his arm. "Much better than being cooped up in your workroom."

"That depends," he said, stiffly, withdrawing his hand.

"Cross patch. Did your work at least go well?"

Philip gazed at her with some surprise. With Richard, handsome, charming, and above all, whole, sitting across from her, Sarah was actually looking at him instead. "Yes, it did," he said, relaxing. "And how did you find the Boltons?"

"Oh, Mrs. Bolton was very kind. And curious." Again she exchanged that look of complicity with Richard. "The questions she asked, Philip, about you and this house!"

"Which you parried very neatly, Sarah," Richard said.

Sarah, is it? No need for Sarah and Richard not to be on first name terms, Philip thought, but it rankled. "I'm sure Sarah can hold her own with anyone."

"Oh, and Philip. She mentioned the Harvest Home festival. It's coming up soon, you know."

"Such rustic entertainment, though," Richard said.

"I think it sounds quite fun. I'd like to go, wouldn't you, Philip?"

"We'll see," he answered.

"But it would be good for you to get out and meet your tenants more—"

"I said we'll see." His voice was clipped, and Sarah's face fell.

"Good show, old man," Richard muttered.

"I beg your pardon?"

"Nothing, cousin. Tell me, what are you working on now?"

And so luncheon proceeded with Philip giving a rather tedious account of his latest project. Richard appeared to listen with great interest while Sarah sat unnaturally quiet, pushing her food about her plate. At last the meal was over, and they rose.

Sarah gave both men a brief smile. "I must speak with Mrs. Stevenson about tonight's menu," she said by way of excusing herself, and whisked through the green baize door that divided the main part of the house from the kitchens and storerooms. Philip turned, his mouth open as if to protest, and then turned away to meet his cousin's keen gaze.

"Trouble, cousin?" Richard said, his voice sympathetic.

"Of course not."

"She's a remarkable woman."

"I know."

"And you're a lucky man who's going to lose her, if you're not mindful."

"Be careful, cousin."

"After all, remember Anne. You never did find out who she was seeing, did you?"

"No." Philip's voice was clipped again. "If you'll excuse me, I've things to do."

"Of course," Richard said, as Philip stalked off, and smiled to himself. A good morning's work. All was going splendidly.

All was going terribly, and the reminder of Anne's treachery didn't help, Philip thought, climbing the stairs toward his workroom, his refuge. There he removed the drop cloth from the easel and stared at it without seeing it, though just this morning this painting had absorbed all his interest. God! His wife was falling in love with another man. Not that he blamed her, or Richard either, for that matter. Richard couldn't help being as charming as he was, while he—well, any charm he might have possessed had been burned away by the fire. No wonder if Sarah turned to someone else. What had he done to attract her? What *could* he do? It had been a very long time since he had courted a woman, and then he had been whole. Now was a different matter.

His fingers went involuntarily to his eye patch, and then, with sudden revulsion, he untied it and flung it across the room. Damn the thing! It set up a barrier between him and the world, between him and Sarah. An invisible one, true, but effective, all the same. In the past it had protected him, but now he wanted to breach it and he didn't know how. Somehow, though, he felt his very life depended upon it.

There was no blinking it, he thought, smiling grimly at the unintentional irony. He was scarred, and though he thought he'd come to grips with that long ago, apparently he hadn't. It had been before he'd met Sarah, though, and his whole world had changed. And she cared for someone else.

He crossed the room and retrieved the eye patch, tying it securely in place. Perhaps he couldn't win his wife away from another man, but he could certainly do something to improve his own life. Without another look at his work, he turned and strode out of the room, heading, unusual for him at this time of day, for the stables and a ride about his estate. It was time to let down the barriers, no matter how much the prospect terrified him. It was time to start living again.

"Philip?" Sarah paused in the doorway of her husband's workroom, peering in. After speaking with Mrs. Stevenson (and failing, yet again, to get that lady to smile), Sarah had realized she had more unfinished business to see to. The look on Philip's face when he had seen her with Richard! Well, it served him right, and yet — and yet she hated seeing him look that way, all closed-up and stern. It was worse even than the way he'd been since their marriage, as if he had shut himself off from her entirely. And that she couldn't allow. Inexperienced though she might be in affairs of the heart, she knew she couldn't let this estrangement between them go on much longer. What had caused it, she didn't know, but she was determined that they could deal together better than they had.

"Philip?" she called again, edging the door forward. When there was still no answer, she stepped hesitantly over the threshold and stopped for a moment, looking around. She half expected him to stand up and order her out, but instead there was silence, deep and profound. Dust motes danced in the sunlight coming through the window, touching on the books and papers scattered across the marble-topped tables. Across the room the great printing press was still, and under the skylight in the north wall that easel that had tantalized her during her previous visits stood shrouded by a drop cloth. Philip was not here. Where he might be, she had no idea.

She stood in the middle of the flagstoned floor, turning slowly around, taking everything in. So far, the room had yielded few clues to her husband's character. That he had many and varied interests, she already knew, and she was beginning to suspect that he used them as a shield against the world. Why else would he need to spend so much time in this room? It was all very interesting, Sarah supposed, but far removed from what she knew of life: people, activities, children. Though she still didn't understand her husband, she feared she knew too well what he thought of life. Well! It was high time he came out of it, she thought, crossing the room to the easel. After all, she wasn't a managing female for nothing. If she were to have a happy, or at least satisfactory marriage, she needed to learn all she could about her husband.

Her fingers twitched toward the canvas shroud and then pulled back. Somehow this object was the most private in the entire room, though she wasn't sure why. Perhaps it was merely because she hadn't realized her husband painted. And what he had likely painted, she thought, was some sort of vegetable, a rutabaga, perhaps, or some equally obscure thing. Nothing private in that, she thought, salving a suddenly queasy conscience, reaching for the cloth, and pulling it away. And then she merely stood and gaped. For it was no mere picture of an inanimate object, no depiction of some-

113

thing scientific. It was, instead, a portrait of a living, breathing person. It was a portrait of her.

The drop cloth fell from her nerveless fingers, as she continued to stare. The portrait was not yet finished, yet Philip's intent was very clear. It was she, clad in her gown of cloth of gold, her face filled with such happiness and life that it outshone the gown. She looked — good heavens, she looked beautiful, when she knew quite well she wasn't. Oh, Papa had always told her she was, but that had come from love, and —

Love. Was it possible? No, of course not. Philip didn't love her, his actions of the past week showed that. And yet, here was proof that she meant something more to him than someone to run his home. Why couldn't he show it to her?

Because he's scared, she answered herself, bending to pick up the drop cloth and briskly draping it over the easel again. Because life and his injury had taught him to be scared. And here she was, invading the most private realms of his existence. She'd gone a bit too far, looking at the portrait, but she was glad she had. From that single glance she'd learned more about her husband than she might have in a year. She'd learned that behind the eye patch hid a man of great feeling, feelings he kept to himself. Well, no longer, she thought, crossing the room and leaving the door ajar as she had found it. Philip was right to be scared of her. Somehow, she would make him show his feelings. They would have a real marriage at last.

"How long will Richard be staying with us?" Sarah asked at breakfast the following morning, and Philip looked up from his newspaper in surprise. So far, this day was not starting as most days did. Usually he breakfasted early, and alone. Having Sarah sitting next to him at table was not a totally pleasant experience. Exquisite torture, in fact, knowing she could be his if he but said the word, if he could but take the chance. If she weren't in love with his cousin.

114

"As long as he wishes," he replied finally, and picked up the paper with a rattle.

"Oh."

Philip slowly let the paper drop. " 'Oh'? I thought you liked Richard."

"I do. He's very charming."

"Very."

"But since he's been here I've seen little of you."

"And whose fault is that?" He set his coffee cup down with a thump. "The two of you are as thick as thieves."

"You blame me when all you do is hide in that workroom of yours?"

"Madam, I do not hide," he said icily.

"Oh, Philip." Sarah laid her hand on his, which he quickly withdrew. "I am sorry. But if you are forever in your workroom, doing heaven knows what, who am I to turn to for companionship?"

Philip stared at his plate. Companionship. If he could be certain that was all Sarah and Richard shared, perhaps he wouldn't mind so. Instead, a raging jealousy gnawed at him, a feeling he'd never had for Richard before. In truth, he wished his cousin would leave, too, but some perverse impulse kept him from saying so. Why, he wondered, was he allowing this to happen?

He looked up at his wife. Lord, she was so beautiful. There was something different about her today, and though he couldn't pinpoint what it was, it made her even more attractive. It was no wonder Richard couldn't resist her. "What would you have me do?" he asked, biting off the words.

"Send him away. He'll understand, I'm sure. After all, we're newly wed."

"So we are." Philip rose abruptly, his chair scraping on the fine parquet floor. "For all the difference it makes," he said, and stalked out of the room.

"Philip!" Sarah half-rose from her chair, but he was already gone. "Oh, drat," she said, pounding her fist on the table. This seduction business was trickier than she'd expected. Here she'd donned her prettiest frock and dressed her hair as she had for her wedding, and all for naught. What ailed the man? She had practically told him she wanted to be alone with him and, instead of eagerly taking her up, he had chosen to pick a quarrel. It would all be very lowering to one's spirits if it weren't so maddening.

Tossing her napkin onto the table, she rose and wandered into the hall, at loose ends. Lord knew when she'd see Philip again that day, and she had little desire to encounter Richard. With his burning glances and fulsome compliments, he was making her increasingly uneasy. Perhaps she should have stayed a governess. At least then, she'd have known where she was.

Almost at random, she opened a door and found herself in the drawing room. Anne's portrait beckoned to her from across the room, and she went to stand before it. Had Philip painted this, too? Perhaps that explained the obvious love that had gone into it.

"What did you do?" she addressed the painting. "When Philip acted like this, how did you get him out of it?" There was no answer, of course, though she could swear that the blue eyes twinkled. "Oh, of course, you probably didn't have to do anything, you were so beautiful. How I ever thought I could compete with you . . ."

But Anne was gone. Sarah looked up at the portrait sharply, almost believing for a moment that the words had been spoken aloud. Anne was gone. Sarah was Philip's wife now, and it was up to her to do something. And since beauty had never been her strong point, it would have to be something more than wearing a pretty frock and dressing her hair attractively. The time had come to take more direct action. Since when had she sat back awaiting events? She'd always gone out and made her own life. No matter that this was a new situation or that someone else was involved. She had made a promise to herself that she would not let Philip hide himself away. It was high time he stopped doing so, even from her.

The quick autumn dusk fell early. Richard, Philip, and Sarah dined together, talking of inconsequentials, and then Sarah excused herself. She'd long since given up expecting Philip to come to her room. Nervous though the prospect made her, she was going to go to him. They would have a real marriage at last.

A little while later, Sarah stood at the door that joined her room to Philip's, her hand poised to knock. She had donned the silk nightrail and wrapper worn on her wedding night and never since, and on the whole she thought she looked acceptable. Now, if only Philip would think so.

There was only one way to find out. Taking a deep breath, Sarah knocked on the door.

Chapter Ten

"Enter," Philip said, sounding slightly surprised. Biting her lips, Sarah opened the door. Philip was sitting in a chair across the room, a book on his lap. At the sight of her, he scrambled to his feet, turning his back, but not before Sarah caught a quick glimpse of his face. He wasn't wearing his eye patch! She stayed by the door as he slowly and methodically tied the patch on. Only when it was back in place did he turn to face her.

Oh, Lord, she was so beautiful, it made his heart stop. There she stood, her eyes as wide and as deep as a startled fawn's, with her glorious hair falling over her shoulders, and her ensemble — Philip nearly groaned aloud. Why had she chosen to come in dressed only in thin silk? With the light of her room at her back, every line of her soft, rounded body was clear to him. Oh, God, he wanted her, wanted her with every fiber of his being, and he couldn't have her. Thank God the chair was between them, hiding the extent of his desire.

"Philip?" she said after a moment, her voice questioning and uncertain, not at all like his Sarah. For a moment he regretted doing this to her, making her come to him, but what else could he do? It had been a mistake, marrying her. If she knew the whole man, the real man, she'd want nothing to do with him. And to think she'd caught him without his eye patch.

"What do you want?" he said, his voice harsher than he'd intended.

"I — merely to talk," she said, progressing farther into the room. Her movements were unconsciously seductive, and his grip on the chair tightened.

"Talk?"

"Well, no." She flushed. "Philip, do I have to come out and say it?"

In spite of himself, he felt a smile twitch at his lips. "You're usually straightforward, Sarah."

"And you're not about to make this easy for me, are you?" she snapped. "Good heavens, Philip, I am your wife! What kind of man are you?"

Philip went very still. "I bid you good evening, madam."

"Oh, gracious, I didn't mean —"

"Good night, Sarah."

Sarah stared at him, and her shoulders slumped. She knew well by now that cool gaze, that rigid pose. She had offended him, the very last thing she had meant to do, and underneath that lay hurt. If he would only let her comfort him . . . "Good night," she whispered, and fled. The silk of her wrapper caught on the doorknob, and she fumbled with it for a moment before freeing herself. Then she was back in the safety, and the loneliness, of her own room. What was she going to do now?

Philip stood like a statue long after the door had closed behind her, long after the candle on the stand next to his chair had guttered. Only then did he move stiffly to sit down again, his face in his hands. God! For a moment he had almost given into his urges, almost crossed to her and caught her up in his arms, kissing her senseless and making love to her until they both forgot the past, the future. Too late now to wish he'd done so; he'd sent her away and he wouldn't go after her though he ached for her. Oh, how he ached. In her pristine silk wrapper with her hair tumbling about her shoulders, she had looked innocent and uncertain, and yet far more seductive than the most experienced courtesan. And she was his wife. Why, in God's name, had he sent her away?

Philip lifted his head. He knew quite well the answer to that question. Fear, pure and simple. Oh, he was a coward — not physically, but when he needed to expose himself, the whole person. People had shrank from him for years, so that it had become second nature for him to protect himself. Would Sarah scorn him? No, not likely. Nor did he really fear to see rejection on her face. What he most dreaded and fully expected was the pity that would come into her eyes if he let her get too close. And that he couldn't bear.

Oh, God, he thought, putting his head in his hands again. What was he going to do?

Sarah arose later than usual the following morning and went down to breakfast later, thus running little risk of seeing Philip. How she would ever be able to face him after last evening, she didn't know, though at some point she would have to. He didn't want her. He had made that quite clear last night.

She pounded on the table. "Damned infuriating, aggravating *man!*" She would not let this defeat her, she thought, rising and tossing her napkin on the table. In fact, she was more determined than ever to succeed. Philip had best watch out. She had yet to give up.

"Cousin?" Richard stood in the doorway, watching her quizzically, and she wondered how much of her outburst he had witnessed. "Is all well?"

"Oh, quite," she muttered, though she felt herself going red. "If you'll excuse me—"

"No, stay. I hate eating alone. You're up early," he commented, as he sat at the table.

"Not as early as usual." Sarah reluctantly sat across from him; to do otherwise would be bad manners. "When you're a governess you haven't the luxury of sleeping in."

"Ah, yes. A governess."

"Do you think Philip married beneath him?" she said swiftly.

"Not at all, Sarah. I think you are quality. And beautiful as well. "

"Thank you," she mumbled, looking down at the table, unnerved by the intense way he was gazing at her, like a hungry tiger. Heavens knew she wasn't beautiful. If she were, Philip would want her. "Richard. You and Philip have been friends for a long time?"

"All our lives. Come, won't you at least have some coffee? There, that's better. Why do you ask?"

Sarah sipped at the coffee she hadn't wanted, not looking at him. "What was Anne like?"

"Anne?" He sounded surprised and then smiled. "She was an angel. Philip was lucky to have her, and he knew it."

"Did he love her?" The words caught at her throat.

"Very much."

"Oh."

"But he was as hopeless then as he is now."

"Excuse me?"

"About treating women. Imagine neglecting someone so lovely as you."

Sarah flushed uncomfortably as memories of last night intruded. "He doesn't neglect me. At least, not precisely."

"Come, come, Sarah, he isn't the most romantic of men, is he? Even Anne had to do something from time to time to remind him she was there."

"Such as?"

"I don't know. Whatever it was, it would wake him up."

"Wake him up," Sarah murmured, in dawning realization. Philip needed to be awakened to her presence. It was what she had tried to do this past week, but maybe, just maybe, something else was needed, something more startling but, at the same time, less obvious than last night's ploy. Something that would make him take the initiative. She thought she knew just what it was. "Of course. That's it."

"What is?"

"I think I know what I'll do." She bounced up from her chair. "Thank you, Richard," she said, placing a quick kiss on his cheek.

"For what?" he called after her.

"Never mind. I must go talk with Mrs. Stevenson." Smiling, she went through the green baize door that led to the kitchens.

121

Thus she didn't see the shadow move at the other doorway, though Richard, glancing up quickly, did, in time to see Philip draw away. Ah. So he had witnessed his wife's behavior most likely without knowing the reasons for it. "Ah, cousin," Richard murmured, and tucked into his breakfast with relish. Events couldn't have happened better had he planned them.

"Ye're sure ye know what yer doing, my lady?" the groom said, eyeing Sarah askance as she sat her horse early the next morning. "Ye don't look none too steady."

I don't feel very steady, Sarah thought, clinging to the reins, but she was determined to go through with this. "I shall be fine, Wilkins. After all, you've assured me this mare is placid. And I have ridden before." *Once.*

"At least let me escort ye, my lady."

"No," she said firmly. "I shall only be gone for a short time, and I'm sure I shall manage fine."

"Very good, my lady." The groom tugged at his forelock, and Sarah at last left the stables. The first golden rays of the sun were just shining through the trees, and the air had a dewy freshness. No wonder Philip enjoyed riding at this time of day. Today, however, his quiet ride would be interrupted. Sarah had other plans for him.

By now she was quite familiar with the route Philip took on his morning ride, and she had calculated to a nicety just where she should go into action. Fortunately her mount was calm; fortunately she herself had courage and determination. Otherwise she might have returned back home. Somehow she knew this was a crucial moment in her life. If she failed today, she might as well give up.

She turned into the lane where she and Philip had met many times before their marriage. The foliage was thinner now, and far ahead she could see a lone rider on a white horse. She took a deep breath. There he was. The moment was now.

"Go!" she exclaimed, slapping the horse on its forequarters. The horse shied and then, to her surprise, went absolutely still. "Oh, for heaven's sake! Go, you old nag!" The horse tossed her head and snorted, but didn't move. "Oh, really! I don't want to hit you again. Go. Please?" Carefully, considering she was riding sidesaddle, she kicked up her heel. The horse snorted again, moved a few paces sideways, and then stopped, more dug in than ever.

Down the lane, Philip rode farther from view. For a moment Sarah considered calling out to him and then the ludicrousness of the situation caught her. She had come out on horseback with the idea of having Philip rescue her from a runaway horse, but what would he think of one that wouldn't budge? Ridiculous.

She laughed. "Well, girl," she said to the mare, whose ears pricked back, "it seems I wasn't meant to be a temptress. I'll just have to think of something else." The horse snorted again. "Oh, never mind, we'll go back. I suppose I'll have to lead you." She swung her leg over the high pommel of the saddle, and at that moment the horse bolted.

Sarah shrieked, digging her foot into the stirrup, clinging to the reins that a moment before she had held loosely, scrabbling with her other leg to regain her seat. It was as if the mare had released all the pent-up energy of her many years and was determined to give Sarah the ride of her life. *Philip will have to rescue me,* she thought, and might have smiled if she hadn't been so frightened.

From ahead of her, she heard a shout. *Philip. Thank God.* And then the horse came to a dead stop, and Sarah, not expecting it, was tossed ignominiously to the ground.

"Sarah!" Philip tossed his reins down with little care as he jumped off his horse and ran to his fallen wife. Her mount was standing by the side of the lane, contentedly munching grass, while Sarah — Sarah lay much too still, her eyes closed, her limbs flung out at all angles. Oh, God. Was he going to lose her? God, why hadn't he let her come close the other night? Now it might be too late.

"Sarah!" Panic lent a note of urgency to his voice. It seemed to reach Sarah. She opened her eyes, staring up at him so blankly that for a moment he feared for her mind. Then, to his immense surprise, she began to laugh. He knelt back, certain her mind was gone. "Sarah, for God's sake."

"I'm all right, Philip." She sat up, though he would have restrained her. "Though I'll probably ache for weeks. But if you could only have seen — Oh, you did, of course, but it was so funny . . ."

"Sarah, for God's sake, it's not funny. What the hell are you doing out on a horse when you can't ride?"

That made her look up at him, her eyes sparkling with amusement and something else. So. He had rescued her after all. "But it was funny. First she wouldn't go when I wanted her to and then when I didn't, she did."

"And I thought you were dead, damn it."

"Oh, Philip." Sarah's face softened. "I'm sorry. I never meant —"

"I am so angry with you I could, I could —"

"What?"

"Oh, for God's sake. This." And he caught her in his arms and brought his mouth down hard on hers.

Sarah made a muffled noise of surprise that changed quickly to acquiescence. Her arms crept about Philip's neck of their own accord, and she pressed up against him. Oh, this was glorious, the feeling of a man's mouth pressed to hers, of his hard body close, so close. She felt no inclination to swoon, as the ladies in the novels she read did; instead, she felt alive, tingling and vital and yet curiously languid. In that moment, she knew the real reason she had married Philip.

Abruptly, she was released. Without the support of his arms around her she fell backwards, lying among the fallen leaves and the tussocked grass, watching Philip as he rose and paced away from her. "Philip?" she said, after a moment.

"That was unpardonable of me," he said, sounding surprisingly normal and very distant. "Forgive me."

"Don't be silly. You're my husband. Philip, please."

He turned. She had propped herself up on her hands, and she looked attractively disheveled, her hat gone, her bosom heaving with exertion, the skirts of her riding habit tucked up to display shapely ankles. He wanted her so much it hurt, and she loved another man.

124

"Go home," he said flatly. "You have no business being on the back of a horse."

"No, I haven't, have I?" Her voice was cheerful as she rose, though her hand flew for a moment to her head. "In fact, Richard offered to teach me to ride, and—"

"Damn Richard!" In two paces he had crossed the space between them and caught at her arms. "Madam, remember whose wife you are."

"Philip, for heaven's sake."

"Understand me, Sarah. I will not be cuckolded again."

"Philip!" Pity, inspired by what he had said, by what he must have gone through, warred for a moment with outrage, and lost. "Oh, you stupid, stupid—man!"

"A most unoriginal insult, madam."

"I can't believe that's what you think of me. As if I would." She squirmed free. "And Richard, of all people, your own cousin. You should be ashamed of yourself. Stop laughing! This isn't funny."

"Oh, Sarah." He held a conciliatory hand out to her. With her hair coming down about her shoulders, she looked like nothing so much as an angry kitten. With every right to be angry. His accusation had been absurd. Sarah, of all people, had no duplicity in her. And he wanted to hold her again; he wanted to kiss her again to make up for the unpardonable way he had treated her the other evening. Perhaps there was hope for him. "Forgive me, I had no right."

"You certainly did not! And to laugh at me—ooh!" With an angry flounce of her skirts Sarah turned away, striding toward the house and leaving both Philip and her mount behind. Philip watched, a little smile on his face. Sarah. Who would have though that desire would return to his life for a woman so unlike his first wife? Perhaps he had misjudged her, he mused, picking up the reins of the now-obedient mare and mounting his own horse. He knew not why she had married him, but he did know that she had never seemed to care about his eye patch or the deformity it concealed. Perhaps he was wrong, perhaps he shouldn't have married her, but he was going to try to woo his

125

wife. The devil of it was, he hadn't the slightest idea of how to do so.

Sarah was in high dudgeon as she stomped into her room, and Millie stared at her in surprise. "My lady? Your habit, it's all over mud—"

"Damned irritating, aggravating man!" Sarah exclaimed, stomping over to her wardrobe. "Help me out of this infernal thing—ouch!"

"Ma'am, are you hurt? Oh, my lady."

Sarah looked ruefully at the bruises on her arms, knowing she had them in other, less obvious places as well. She would pay for this morning's folly. "Well, I won't be able to wear short sleeves for a time," she said, laughing a bit. "No, Millie, I have not gone mad, but I have been incomparably foolish."

"Yes, my lady. I mean, no, my lady."

"Never mind. Help me out of this and then I'll need a bath, I think. Have you ever tried to ride a horse, Millie?"

"No, ma'am," Millie said, her nimble fingers working at the complicated fastenings of the habit.

"Take my advice. Don't. The things I do for that man . . ."

"Ma'am?"

Sarah looked up to see Millie's eyes, confused and yet curious, in the mirror. She had little doubt this escapade would soon become servants' hall gossip. Served her right, too, she admitted when Millie had gone off to draw her bath and she was alone. She had been remarkably foolish. Why she had ever thought she could be a temptress, a seductress, she didn't know.

With a little moan, she sank down at her dressing table, her face in her hands. It was one thing pursuing a man; it was quite another to look the fool doing so. No wonder he had laughed. The sound of it rang in her ears even now, hurting so much more now that she had finally realized what she felt for him. Perhaps Anne could have succeeded with such tactics, but not her. Philip, at this moment, must be wondering what he had done to deserve someone like her.

126

"My lady?" Millie said from the doorway of Sarah's dressing room, and Sarah rose. One of the delights of Havenwood was its plumbing, another of Philip's contrivances. With water tanks on the roof and an ingenious heater, there was no need for maids to carry heavy cans of steaming water from the kitchen, nor to set up a hip bath before the fire. Luxury of luxuries, Sarah had her own room for bathing.

A good thing, too, she thought when Millie had left her to soak in peace, and she was surveying her bruises. Ah, well, their ache would soon go away, but she was not so certain about the pain in her heart. She had failed miserably in her attempts to seduce her husband. But she hadn't given up. Sitting up and reaching for the bath sponge, she began to lather herself vigorously. Hadn't she always told her charges to keep optimistic and to keep trying for their goal? And hadn't she tried to do the same herself? No matter how insurmountable her task seemed, no matter how little she was like Anne, she was not giving up.

The sponge dropped into the water, and she stared straight ahead. Easy to say, but not so easy to do. For the stakes now were higher than they had been. She loved her husband, and she hadn't the slightest idea what to do next.

"Philip!" Richard called as Philip rode into the stable yard, leading Sarah's mare. "That's not Sarah's mount, is it?"

"As it happens, it is. She decided to forgo riding for this morning."

"She's not hurt!"

"No. Angry. Mostly at me," he added ruefully.

"At you, cousin? Have you quarreled? I am sorry."

Philip waved his hand in dismissal. "It is of no moment. I made the mistake of laughing at her."

"Never a wise thing to do to a woman, cousin." The two men fell into step as they walked back toward the house. "I was thinking, old man, of teaching Sarah how to ride."

"No, old man." Something in Philip's voice made Richard turn to look at him. "If anyone is to do that, it will be me."

"Cousin, I meant no harm."

"She is my wife, Richard."

Richard stared at him for a moment and then a smile overspread his face. "But we are the merest friends! Surely you're not jealous, cousin."

"Of course not." Of course he was. "But I think you've overstayed your welcome, Richard. I trust we're good enough friends that you won't take offense if I ask you to leave."

"Oh, no, no. To tell you the truth, I've been finding it rather dull here in the country. Don't know how you stand it."

"I like it. Well?"

"Oh, very well. I'll have my valet pack my bags and we'll be gone this forenoon."

"Thank you."

"But, cousin." They strolled into the great hall, and crimson light, from the stained glass high above, fell onto his face, giving it a diabolical look. "Let me give you some advice about Sarah."

"There's no need," Philip interrupted, his voice steely again. "I can handle my own affairs, cousin."

"Can you?" Richard stared at him for a few moments and then shrugged. "As you wish." He held out his hand. "Thank you for letting me stay, cousin. It's been enlightening."

"Has it?" Philip shook Richard's hand. "I wish you Godspeed, cousin."

"Thank you," Richard said, and turned toward the stairs.

Philip watched him go and then turned away himself, toward the dining room and the breakfast that awaited him. A smile flickered briefly on his face. He was at last taking his life into his own hands, and it felt good. No more drifting along with the current of events as he had for the past few years. From now on, he would run his own life and be damned to what Richard, or anyone else, thought. From now on, he would try to make a life with Sarah.

First, though, he would have to give her time to cool down. Women often baffled Philip, but one thing he knew. He knew enough to stay away when one was in such a state as Sarah had been. Let her calm down, let him think of a way to apologize

4 FREE BOOKS

TO GET YOUR 4 FREE BOOKS WORTH $18.00 — MAIL IN THE FREE BOOK CERTIFICATE T O D A Y

Fill in the Free Book Certificate below, and we'll send your FREE BOOKS to you as soon as we receive it.

If the certificate is missing below, write to: Zebra Home Subscription Service, Inc., P.O. Box 5214, 120 Brighton Road, Clifton, New Jersey 07015-5214.

FREE BOOK CERTIFICATE

4 FREE BOOKS
ZEBRA HOME SUBSCRIPTION SERVICE, INC.

YES! Please start my subscription to Zebra Historical Romances and send me my first 4 books absolutely FREE. I understand that each month I may preview four new Zebra Historical Romances free for 10 days. If I'm not satisfied with them, I may return the four books within 10 days and owe nothing. Otherwise, I will pay the low preferred subscriber's price of just $3.75 each; a total of $15.00, *a savings off the publisher's price of $3.00.* I may return any shipment and I may cancel this subscription at any time. There is no obligation to buy any shipment and there are no shipping, handling or other hidden charges. Regardless of what I decide, the four free books are mine to keep.

NAME _____

ADDRESS _____ APT _____

CITY _____ STATE _____ ZIP _____

TELEPHONE (   ) _____

SIGNATURE _____ (if under 18, parent or guardian must sign)

Terms, offer and prices subject to change without notice. Subscription subject to acceptance by Zebra Books. Zebra Books reserves the right to reject any order or cancel any subscription.

for this morning before approaching her. In the meantime, there was work to be done.

True to his word, Richard left a little later. After seeing him off, Philip went up to his workroom, taking the stairs two at a time in his excitement. Here, where no one disturbed him, he felt alive, vital, needed. Contrivances of the devil, Sarah might teasingly call his innovations, but he knew he'd made real contributions toward progress on his estate. Coke's modern agricultural methods, which he had adopted first on an experimental basis on the Home Farm and then estate-wide, brought in incredible yields each year. In a time when the poor suffered from increased food prices due to the war, none of his tenants went hungry. Nor did they have to go without an education, which was his current interest.

The printing press stood silently against the wall until he would pull the lever to bring it to life. It was what he should do, but the shrouded easel at the north end of the room beckoned to him, drew him, almost against his will. Slowly, he removed the canvas, folding it meticulously until at last he had no excuse. At last, he faced the portrait. Sarah, garbed in her wedding gown, looking beautiful, so beautiful. He gazed at it for a long time and then reluctantly draped the canvas over it, turning away. First things first. He had all the time in the world to woo his wife.

He strode across to the printing press. The primers he had written and set in type had proven to be a great success in the village school, and his man of business in London had spoken with a publisher about distributing them in other places. He was really quite pleased with that, more pleased, even, than he had been about his agricultural improvements. People needed food, certainly, but they also needed education if they wanted to better themselves. And Philip was, in his own quiet way, a man who wanted to better the world.

He checked the plates to make certain the correct type was set and then stepped across to the window to inspect the cords that ran from the press. Quite ingenious, this, if he said so himself. Having dammed a small stream on his property, he had used the resulting water power to generate electricity on the principles laid down by the American, Benjamin Franklin. It was this which ran the press. Satisfied with the condition of the cords, Philip walked across to the lever that, when pulled down, would start the press, and slipped.

Cursing, Philip recovered his balance, reaching out for the lever and landing against the wall instead. Clumsy. Sometimes his blind eye made him miss things, but what had he slipped on? He looked down and went still. Then, very carefully, he stepped away from the wall, away from the press, away from the lever. Water. A large pool of it, reaching from an overturned beaker on one of the tables, almost to the printing press. Good God, how had that happened, and how had he missed seeing it? Innocuous looking though it was, that pool of water was deadly. Had he touched the lever while standing in it, the electric current would have gone through him, rather than to the press. Another in the long string of accidents that had bedeviled him, and this one would have killed him.

Who else knew about electricity? he wondered, and instantly dismissed the thought. No one, and everyone. In his eagerness and pride, he had talked about the printing press to anyone who would listen when he'd first installed it. He doubted, though, that anyone had really understood him. Most people thought of electricity as magic. God! His fingers went to his eye patch, his habit when he was upset. He had nearly been killed again, and this time, it would have been his own fault. It had to be. No one came into this room without invitation, except for Geordie, and he allowed maids in to clean only when he was here. Who else but he could have spilled the water, though he had no memory of doing so. Clumsy, clumsy. The eye patch was a constant reminder of that.

Of a sudden, he had had enough, and anger, which he rarely allowed himself to feel, surged through him. He had had enough of his arid life, of the projects and experiments that had so absorbed him before, of the responsibility of running Havenwood, gratifying though it usually was. Most of all, though, he had had enough of the eye patch, and all that it represented.

He slammed the workroom door shut behind him and strode off toward his own room. There he dismissed his startled valet and began muttering to himself. Stupid, stupid. Because of him, people had been hurt. Sarah, caught in an attack that surely had not been meant for her, and Anne—

Anne. He stopped his pacing and stared at himself in the mirror. Damn the thing! He scrabbled frantically at the strings that held the eye patch on and flung it across the room, not caring what was revealed, not, for once, flinching from it. Damn it, he was a man with feelings and needs and desires, but the eye patch did more than hold people at arm's length. It reminded them all of his own part in his life's tragedies, and it scared them away. Even Sarah, his own wife.

Sarah. Tiredly he sank into a chair, running his hands over his face. What was he to do about her? She had married him, true, but there was one essential thing she didn't know about him. She had never seen him without the eye patch. God knew how she'd react if she did, if she'd scream, as had the doxy he had one night taken to his bed when he was desperate. No. Sarah had more compassion and sense than that. But seeing him like this, what could she feel for him but pity and disgust? Those were the very last things he wanted from her.

He was tired, deep in his body, deep in his soul from the fight he had put up over the past years. Very rarely did he allow himself to relax his vigilance, and so he was somewhat surprised to feel himself drifting off to sleep. It didn't matter. Havenwood would go on without him. Sarah would go on without him. Stretching out his legs, he let his head fall to his chest, and he slept.

It was thus that Sarah found him.

She had done some hard thinking in the hours since her disastrous ride. Subtlety and seduction hadn't worked; she didn't know why she had thought they would. After all, it had never before been in her makeup to be subtle, and as for seductiveness—well! Yet, for better or worse, Philip had married her. It was up to her to find a way to approach him, and she thought she knew what it was.

131

She stood patiently in front of her dressing table mirror while Millie draped the round gown of soft aqua muslin about her and tied the lacings at the back. Sarah herself adjusted the white frill of the chemisette at her throat, noting almost dispassionately that the gown was flattering. It made her cheeks pink and her eyes sparkle. She also allowed Millie to dress her hair in the softer, more relaxed style she had adopted since her marriage. Seductiveness might not be in her, but she might as well look her best when she faced Philip again.

At last she was ready, and she rose, dismissing Millie and heading toward her husband's workroom. It was time to try something different. It was time to be herself, straightforward and honest. Philip had seemed to like her that way before their marriage.

There was no answer to her knock on the workroom door, though, and when she opened it, she saw the room was empty. Resisting the impulse to look just once more at her portrait, she turned away, gnawing her lip. Now, where could he be? Sommers had informed her that the marquess was still within, but in this great castle of a house he could be anywhere. He was not, however, in any of the places she'd expected to find him as she searched, the conservatory or the book room or even the drawing room. He was apparently nowhere to be found.

Frowning, Sarah wandered back into the great hall. The day had turned overcast, and the huge space was cold and bleak. How quiet the house was, how still. How empty and lonely. Suddenly, she had had enough of it all. If she had to search him down in his own rooms, then she would.

Courage and determination carried her as far as the door that joined her room to his, but there she faltered. Except for the other evening, she'd never been beyond this point. To proceed past it now, without invitation, was an unforgivable breach of propriety. Since when had propriety stopped her, however? Certainly not when there were more important matters at stake.

Still, her knock on his door was tentative, and she was both relieved and chagrined when there was no answer. Where in the world could he be? She was about to turn away when curiosity got the better of her. She hadn't got much of a look at this room the other night, and perhaps it would give her some clues about Philip. She was mistress of this house now. Why shouldn't she go where she wished?

Quietly, she pushed open the door. Philip's room was comfortable looking, furnished with a mahogany tester bed and decorated in rich, masculine colors, burgundy and dark green and just a touch of gold. It wasn't that that caught her attention, however. Across from her in a burgundy leather armchair facing the fireplace, Philip slept, the soft, regular sound of his breathing the only noise in the room. Sarah's heart stopped for just a moment and then started again. She should leave, she knew, but something drew her inexorably across the room, her footsteps noiseless on the fine Turkish carpet until she at last stood at his side.

Still he slept, and for a moment she stood there, irresolute. But she hadn't come all this way for nothing, she told herself. Carefully she edged over to settle herself on the footstool. Only then did she look up at him.

Only then, for the first time, did she see his scar.

Chapter Eleven

Sarah's knees suddenly lost all strength, and she dropped onto the stool. Quickly she controlled her first impulse to gasp in horror; she didn't want him awakening and seeing her staring at him so. No wonder he allowed few people close. And yet, she thought, her curious, practical side taking over as she studied his scars, it wasn't really so bad. That he had lost his eye was obvious, but other than that the damage appeared slight. His eyelid was puckered and red. Now, so close to him, she could see fine white lines radiating out to his temple. Poor Philip. Sarah wanted nothing so much just then as to pull his head down upon her breast and comfort him.

At that moment, though she had made no sound, he awoke and stared at her, defenseless, vulnerable in those first few moments of awakening. Not quite knowing why, Sarah reached out and traced the scars with gentle fingertips. Philip flinched and then relaxed, his gaze wary.

"It's not so bad, Philip," she murmured, after a moment.

"Bad enough." He should get up; he should find his eye patch and cover his shame, but something about Sarah's touch, something about the way she was looking at him, held him there. There was no fear, no revulsion in her eyes; there wasn't even pity. Instead, there was something else: compassion and an emotion he couldn't name. "You can see why I keep it covered."

"Of course. But not from me, Philip."

"It doesn't revolt you? Make you want to run in fear?"

"No." Her fingers continued their gentle stroking, and he had to resist the urge to lean against them. "You must have been badly burned."

"Bad enough."

"Just here?"

"No." He moved his head, and her fingers dropped. "This was where I was hurt the worst. But I also was burned along the side of my face and into my hair. My hands, too."

He held out his hands to her. For the first time, she noticed that they, too, were crossed with fine white lines. Before she could stop herself, she grasped his strong, brown hand, bringing it to her mouth and kissing it, making him gasp in surprise. "You're lucky your hair grew back."

"I don't know. Sometimes I think I didn't do enough to save her."

"Oh, no, Philip!"

"You see, Sarah, I seem to have this habit of getting into accidents where people I care about are hurt."

"Then we'll just have to watch out for each other, won't we?"

Philip stared at her and then hauled her into his arms, onto his lap. Sarah had time only for a muffled squeak of surprise before his lips came down on hers, hard, passionate, demanding. In his kiss were all the years of frustration, of hurt, and all the complex emotions he felt toward this remarkable woman. Gratitude was part of it, but not all. Not all.

"Well!" Sarah said when he had released her and she was leaning back against his shoulder. "I think we can safely say you like me."

Philip laughed. "Yes, I think we can."

She reached up and feathered her fingers through his hair, over his face. "Even though I'm not like Anne?"

"Anne is gone, Sarah." His hand stroked her hair. "We have the chance to start a new life." And how would Anne, who had been so concerned with physical beauty, have reacted to his scars? Not as well as Sarah, he suspected.

"I'd like that." Sarah snuggled her head against his shoulder. "As long as you don't shut me out."

135

Philip didn't answer for a moment. "You scare me sometimes."

"What?" She raised her head. "How in the world could I scare you?"

"You're so positive, so sure of yourself."

"Not always."

"You make me feel things I thought I'd never feel again."

"And you're afraid I'm going to leave you," she said softly. She reached up to touch his mouth, which had opened to protest. "We married very quickly, Philip. Perhaps we need time."

"Time?"

"To get to know each other. To learn how to deal with each other. We have time Philip. Just please don't shut me out."

He grinned, the first time she'd seen him truly do so. "My life is an open book."

"Ha. Then why won't you let me in your workroom?"

"Sarah." He turned serious. "Were you in there today?"

"Today? No," she said, her eyes avoiding his. "I went there looking for you, but otherwise, no."

"Not this morning?"

"No. Why do you ask?"

"No reason." He gazed off into space again. The water had fallen onto the floor by accident. That was the only explanation. It didn't matter now when he had his wife in his arms, warm and sweet and willing. Even if she had just lied to him. "You are so beautiful," he murmured, stroking her cheek with the back of his fingers.

"I'm not," she began, but the rest of her protest was cut short by his mouth coming down on hers. This time his tongue pressed against her lips and, though startled, she opened to him, giving herself freely, fully. When at last they parted, both were gasping for breath.

"I think," Philip began, his forehead resting against hers, "I think — Sarah, do you know where this leads?"

She nestled against him. "Yes."

Yes. Just like that, with no artifice or teasing. His Sarah. Sometimes she did scare him with her openness and forthrightness. The thought of opening himself to her in the same

136

way, of being vulnerable, was frightening after all the years spent protecting himself. "We have time."

"All the time you need," she agreed, running her fingers through his hair again. He grunted in surprise at her answer and instinctively tried to hold onto her as she slipped from his lap. "Come." She held out her hand. "Show me this workroom of yours."

What he chiefly wanted to do was to catch her up in his arms and carry her over to his bed. Lord, it had been so long since he had had a woman, and he couldn't remember ever wanting one so much. Something held him back, though. Though she had seen him without his patch and knew the worst, in some ways they were strangers. Rather odd to have the courtship after the marriage, but Sarah was right. They had time.

In his workroom Philip went straight over to the printing press, staring down at the pool of water that had only partially evaporated. "Now, how did that get there?" Sarah said, not noticing his frown. "Is there a mop in here?"

"Hmm?" Philip looked up, distracted from his thoughts. "I'll ring for someone to clean it up."

"Nonsense, I'm perfectly capable. Now if this isn't just like a man!" She stood in the middle of the floor, her hands on her hips. "All this equipment in here and not one lowly mop or broom! And I understand you don't like anyone coming in here to clean."

Philip looked sheepish. "They might disturb things."

"Yes, like the dust."

"It isn't that bad."

"Well, no," she relented. "You certainly are one of the tidiest people I know. Do you at least have a rag?"

"I'll do it." Philip pulled a rag from a drawer and wiped up the water. There. That took care of that, though he still wondered how it had gotten there.

"What are you working on?" Sarah hoisted herself onto one of the tables, reaching for an apple from the bowl of fruit he kept handy should he miss luncheon. "No, let me guess. A scientific paper of great importance on sailing a balloon to the moon. No? Oh, I know. You've turned alchemist and have finally discovered the process of turning lead into gold."

"Hardly." Philip smiled as he checked his electrical cords and plates again; all seemed in working order. He tried to imagine Anne sitting on a table with her legs swinging back and forth, contentedly munching on an apple, and failed. "No, something much duller. Primers."

"Primers?" Sarah shouted over the noise of the press as he pulled the lever to start it working. "How do you do that?"

Pulling the first printed sheet off the press, he walked over to her. "Electricity. The village school needed new primers, and I didn't like the ones they'd been using."

"Electricity?"

"Yes. I'd like to extend it to the entire house, but I haven't figured out how yet."

"Good heavens!"

"Yes, well." He felt just the slightest bit embarrassed by the pride and wonder in her eyes, and inordinately pleased. "As I was saying, the school needed new primers. So I—"

"'A New Reader, by Anonymous,'" Sarah read, and looked up. "Did you write this?"

"Yes. As I said—"

"Yes, yes, they needed new primers."

"And I didn't like the ones they'd been using. I have these bound in London and sent directly to the school. From an anonymous donor, of course."

"But why? I should think you'd want them to know what you've done."

Philip turned away, and his voice when he spoke was so soft Sarah had to strain to hear it. "I doubt they'd want them then."

"Oh, Philip." For a moment she was so filled with pity for him that she wanted to go to him and comfort him, but she steeled herself against it. Pity was the last thing he needed, particularly when he already had so much for himself. "Well, I don't care what they think. I'm impressed, Philip."

"What?"

"Does the school need someone to teach, do you know?"

"No, Reverend Crabbe handles matters pretty well, though

he isn't quite so good with the younger children."

"I'm not surprised! What would you think if I taught them?"

He turned from the press. "You?"

"Yes. I do know how to teach, you know, and it would give me something to do."

"I thought you'd be busy running this house."

"No, Mrs. Stevenson takes care of everything. Does she ever smile, by the way?" she asked, tossing her apple core into the wastebasket.

"Not that I've ever seen." He came to stand next to her, leaning his elbows on the table, so that they could hear each other over the thump, thump of the press. "You're not bored, are you?"

"Well, actually, yes, I am. I'm used to being busy, Philip, even before Papa died. And I don't even know how to ride. Could you teach me?"

"I thought Richard was going to do that," he said, prompted by some inner demon.

"He was, but even if he were still here, I'd rather have you. I'm surprised he left so quickly."

"He had business in Town."

"So you don't mind, then?"

"Teaching you to ride? No, of course not."

"No, silly, I meant my teaching reading."

"Are you always like this?" he demanded. "Talking all the time and changing subject in midstream?"

"Oh, no." Sarah popped a grape into her mouth. "Usually I'm much worse."

"God help me."

"Yes, I'm afraid you're in for it."

"So it seems," he said, but he was smiling as he walked over to check the press. "You'd really want to?"

"Teach? Yes. I need something to do, Philip. And I haven't really had the chance to get to know any of your tenants or the villagers."

"I see."

Sarah regarded his back as he raised the plate and began setting new type. "Philip, why do you stay hidden away?"

Philip looked up. "You know quite well."

"The eye patch, you mean."

"No. What the eye patch means."

"But surely no one really believes the rumors."

He shrugged and turned away. "They appear to."

"I see." Sarah munched thoughtfully on another grape. "You're scared, aren't you?"

"No."

"Oh, come, Philip, there's no blinking it," she said, and he laughed at her unintentional pun. "Sorry. What I mean is, this is something you need to face."

Philip lowered the cover of the press. "And do you always face your fears?"

Sarah looked away. "No. But I've been glad when I did. They never bother me so, afterwards."

He stood for a moment with his hands on the press. "You may teach, if you really wish to. But don't expect more of me than I can give, Sarah."

"We'll see," Sarah said over the noise of the press, and reached for another grape. So, she would teach and come to know their neighbors and then they would indeed see. Philip's talents were too broad, his heart too big for him to keep himself confined. Somehow, some way, she was going to get him out of this house.

"Will say, the master's good with horses," Wilkins the groom said, leaning against the stable doorjamb and looking out into the stable yard.

"Aye. Losin' the eye hasn't hurt him any," Geordie replied, though more absently. In the stable yard, Philip was leading Sarah about on the same mare that had several days ago been her downfall in his attempts to teach her how to ride. So far he hadn't seemed to have much success, but they were enjoying themselves, judging by the laughter. That was due to the mistress. Laughed at everything, she did, including herself when she took the inevitable fall. Wonder of it was, the master laughed right along with her. Glad to see that, Geordie was,

140

and yet he couldn't forget recent incidents. Sometimes he thought they'd been safer on the Peninsula than in England.

There were just too many accidents for Geordie's liking: the fire that had taken Mistress Anne's life and could just as easily have taken the master's; the attack upon Mistress Sarah's carriage; the water spilled near the printing press, which Geordie had learned of by accident. Aye, too many accidents, even for one who claimed to be prone to them. Geordie was beginning to get suspicious. Someone was out to hurt the master, and whoever it was didn't seem about to give up.

The question was, who could it be? He knew the master wasn't well-liked, but Havenwood had always been safe enough. Not like Thornhill, where Mistress Anne had died and the master was ostracized. No, Havenwood was just what its name implied. Or, rather, it had been. Now Geordie wasn't so certain.

Philip and Sarah came into the stable laughing, Sarah ruefully rubbing her hip. "I'll be bruised all over before this is done," she said.

"You're getting the hang of it." Philip handed the mare's reins to Wilkins. "Here, Wilkins, rub her down."

"Oh, can't I do it? I've time before I go to the village and I'd like to learn. Besides, Polly's a good old girl." She patted the mare's flank. "Stubborn, like me."

Geordie, about to follow Philip toward the house, glanced over at Sarah. Stubborn? Aye. But cheerful as well and competent, in an outgoing, feminine way. No question she'd made a change in the master's life already, even if servants' hall gossip had it they still slept apart. But the master smiled more these days, and he spent less time in his workroom. Just might be that Mistress Sarah was good for him.

"Ye like working in the village, mistress?" he asked.

Sarah looked up in surprise from rubbing down the mare. Geordie intimidated her, so large and fierce-looking was he. She had the feeling he didn't entirely approve of her. "Very much. I enjoy teaching, and the new primers are far superior to anything else I've used. I'm not certain the children are as appreciative," she added candidly. "Such a lovely autumn as

141

it's been, I'm certain they'd rather be out of doors. And then, of course, so many have to help with the harvest."

"Aye. A good one this year."

"Yes. People will eat well. Though no one at Havenwood looks hungry to me."

"No, mistress."

Sarah picked up a brush and a currycomb. "Pembroke takes good care of his people. I wish they'd realize it."

"What d'ye expect of them, mistress? After all they've heard about the master—"

"Rumors, Geordie, vicious rumors!" she exclaimed, brushing the horse with such vigor that the mare snorted and sidestepped. "You, of all people, should know that!"

"Aye, mistress," Geordie said, looking at her, startled.

Sarah abandoned all pretense of currying the horse. "So what do we do about it, Geordie?"

"What can we do about it, mistress? If the master chooses to keep himself to himself . . ."

"Nonsense! Oh, you'd best take her away, Wilkins. I'm not in the best mood to care for her, I fear." Giving the groom a quick smile, she stepped out into the sunshine, and Geordie followed. "He's scared, Geordie. He's scared to go out among people."

"Aye, that he is. And I can't say I blame him, mistress."

"No, nor do I, the way they look at him, but there has to come a time when it ends! When is he going to stop mourning Anne?"

Geordie stopped and turned to her, his face softening. "Ye can cease worrying about her, mistress. She's not what the master misses."

"But he loved her."

"Aye. But she wasn't the easiest of women, mistress."

"No?" Sarah caught up with him, her eyes bright. "Tell me about her."

"Not my place, mistress. Ye'll have to ask the master."

"He won't tell me. Oh, never mind. But I don't like competing with a ghost, Geordie."

"I doubt ye are, mistress."

"No?" Sarah looked up at him and smiled. Geordie didn't smile back, but something about his entire demeanor toward her had changed during their conversation. "Well. That's all very well, but what do we do about Philip, Geordie? We just can't let him languish in his tower."

"So ye'll rescue him, mistress?"

"Yes."

For some reason, that made him grin. "And how do ye propose to do it?"

"Get him out in the world, of course. I've heard in the village of the Harvest Home festival—"

"Ye'll never get him to that, mistress."

"I can try." She rushed on, in spite of Geordie's skeptical look. "If they only knew, Geordie, the tenants and the villagers, all that he's done for them! But now all they see is a cold, aloof man who has made them change their old ways for reasons they can't guess. Not one of them realize the changes Philip's made in the farming have helped increase the harvest. No one knows he wrote the primers or that it was his money that rebuilt the church steeple two years ago when it was hit by lightning."

"And you think telling them will make a difference?"

"No, of course not. But if they could only see him as we do, Geordie."

"Aye," Geordie said slowly. "But that's up to him, mistress."

"No, it isn't. Are you going to stand there, Geordie MacLeod, and tell me that with that red hair you're not as stubborn as I?"

"No, mistress." For the first time, Geordie smiled at her. "What are ye thinkin' of doin'?"

"Getting him to the Harvest Home, of course."

Chapter Twelve

"I don't want to go to this," Philip stated, as he climbed into the barouche.

"I know you don't." Sarah carefully spread the skirts of her azure silk gown about her. With it she wore an evening cloak of black velvet and her mother's pearls, the only legacy remaining to her from her parents. She didn't know when she'd last worn anything so pretty. "But you wouldn't want me to waste this beautiful gown, would you?"

Philip gave her a look that said clearly that he saw through her subterfuge. "This once, Sarah. That's all."

"That's all I ask."

Philip shifted in his seat, annoyed by her serenity. He hadn't attended a social event since Anne's death. To be going now to the village's celebration of its abundant harvest after his long, self-imposed exile, was both exhilarating and frightening. "They won't want me there, you know."

"You're the owner of this estate, Philip. They owe their livelihoods to you."

"Yes, yes, but—"

"All you need do is put in an appearance. After that, you needn't stay."

"I needn't? You speak as if you plan to."

"Well, I might," Sarah said. "I like these people since I've got to know them. You might, too, if you gave them a chance."

"It's not I who scorns them."

144

"What do you think they're going to do? At worst, they might cut you. At best . . . well, who knows. Give them a chance to know you."

"They knew me at Thornhill."

"Where?"

"My estate in Kent. Where Anne died." His voice was remote as he gazed out the window. "Geordie and I were returning from there when we came across your carriage being attacked." He paused. "The villagers at Thornhill threw stones at my carriage."

"Oh, Philip!" Sarah reached a hand across to him and quickly withdrew it at the look he gave her. "But surely they won't do that here!"

"No, likely not," he admitted. "But there is no love for me here, madam. I'm glad they like you, but they'll never accept me." He looked out again as their carriage trundled over the narrow stone bridge into Bibury past the dormered cottages of Arlington Row. "This is a fool's errand."

"Perhaps. It may work out better than you expect. Will you promise me one thing?"

"What?"

"Will you dance with me? Once, anyway."

He regarded her for a long moment. "Very well. If I haven't been chased away."

"You won't be," Sarah said, with serene self-confidence as the barouche came to a stop. "We're here. Courage, sir!"

Courage! As if he'd ever lacked for that! Philip's mouth set in an angry line as he jumped nimbly from the carriage. No, it wasn't lack of courage that made him want to run from this situation, it was—

Fear. You're scared. As Sarah laid her hand on his arm, he forced himself to face the fact. He *was* scared. But, damn it, he'd never run from a battle before! He wasn't about to start now.

"Very well," he said, giving Sarah a smile of such cold brilliance that it startled her. "Into the fray, then, madam."

The villagers of Bibury were already milling about the

green where a bonfire had been laid, waiting for the last sheaves of wheat to be brought in from the fields. Sarah looked around, bright-eyed with interest. She'd never been to a harvest celebration before, though she'd heard of them. In fact, Reverend Crabbe's diatribe about it and its pagan origins, when she had mentioned it to him last week, had served only to pique her interest. Though this year's harvest owed more to modern farming methods than ancient ritual, what harm was there in paying some sort of token to the old gods? Especially since it had proven to be a successful ruse to get Philip out of the house.

The last rays of the sun were streaming across the green when a large cart trundled down the street and a great shout went up. Sarah unconsciously squeezed Philip's arm harder in her excitement, standing on tiptoe to see. There it was, the cart bearing the very last grain. Riding atop the grain was the Harvest Queen, a girl from the village garbed in white, her unbound hair crowned with woven sheaves of grain. As the cart was surrounded by villagers, the vicar in his black silk gown stepped forward and intoned a long, solemn prayer while people shuffled their feet and whispered to each other. At last, though, he finished and handed Philip a lighted torch. It was Philip's task, as lord of the manor, to light the bonfire.

He stepped forward, setting the flame to the kindling and the dried wheat stalks. Instantly the bonfire went up, and a cheer erupted from the crowd. The light bathed Philip's face, the flickering shadows giving almost a sinister aspect to his lean face and accentuating his eye patch. Several people nearby gasped and backed away, and Sarah stepped forward.

"It's splendid, isn't it?" she said, taking his arm, and he turned to her with a smile, dispelling the diabolical effect of a moment before.

"Rather. Though I dislike fire," he said.

Sarah hugged his arm. She wondered if anyone else realized what this was costing him. "But a bonfire is special. Oh,

146

this is such fun!" She turned away from the fire, bringing him with her. "Have you seen how they've decorated the barn? No, of course you haven't. The children made figures of corn. Fertility symbols, you know."

"Yes, I know. You're not by any chance nervous, Sarah?"

"No, of course not. Why?"

"You're chattering," he said, but he smiled.

"Because this is such fun." And because she was nervous, for him. No one had cut him yet, but no one had welcomed him either. She'd have to do something about that.

They continued on through the crowd, Sarah nodding and speaking to people she knew. Philip realized with surprise that his wife was well-known and well-liked in the village. People's reactions to him were different, but he had expected that: the fascinated, curious stare; the instinctive shrinking away of the ladies; the cool civility of the men. Somehow, though, with Sarah on his arm, those things didn't matter quite so much as they had. He began to relax and to smile.

"They've a feast laid on for us," Sarah was saying. "Well, for everybody, I mean. The dancing will be after that. Don't forget your promise."

"I haven't forgotten, Sarah."

"Oh, I'm Sarah again, rather than 'madam'? That's a good sign."

He gave her a look, but before he could say anything, they had reached a small group of people. "You know the Abbotts, don't you, Philip? Of course, they're your neighbors. And Uncle Edwin, how good to see you."

"Good to see you, child," Sir Edwin said, hugging her. "Pembroke."

"Staples," Philip replied, equally terse.

"And this is Mr. Fellowes, you must know him, he rents Woodbury Farm from you."

"Of course I know him." Philip held out his hand, though he was feeling increasingly hemmed in by people. "Good to see you again."

Mr. Fellowes bobbed his head, and his wife dropped into a curtsy. "An honor to have you here, my lord."

"Your crops did well this year, I understand."

"Yes, my lord."

"Mr. Fellowes had some thoughts about the new crop rotation system," Sarah put in.

"Have you? But I thought it worked quite well for you," Philip said, forgetting any awkwardness for the moment in his enthusiasm for the subject.

"Yes, my lord, but I'm not that sure of it. Makes it difficult to plan the planting each year," Mr. Fellowes said.

"But that's the beauty of it — Sarah?"

Sarah turned, smiling. "Since you men are going to be busy talking farming, Lady Amanda and Mrs. Fellowes and I thought we'd see if we can help with supper."

"But —" Philip watched helplessly as Sarah, laughing at something one of the other women had said, walked away. He had come tonight only for her sake, and he had not expected to have to deal with anyone on his own. He felt curiously abandoned, but he was not about to make a fool of himself by running after her. He would stand his ground, though he had faced less threatening situations in Spain. "Now," he said, turning back to Mr. Fellowes with a brisk air that belied his discomfort. "Let's see what we can do to solve this problem of yours."

"Thank you, my lord." Mr. Fellowes looked uncomfortable, too. Except for when the new house was built — and he liked Havenwood; he didn't care what anyone else thought — he'd never talked with his landlord. He wished his wife hadn't left him alone to deal with the man. But as Philip listened with interest and concern to his problems, he gradually relaxed. Maybe his lordship wasn't quite the monster rumor had painted him. After all, the harvest had been good this year with the new system.

For a time, the crowd eddied about the two men, so deep in their discussion that they weren't aware of the small space that separated them from the other villagers. Eventually, though, another tenant joined in the conversation and then another and soon it became more general. At its center stood Philip, enthusiastically explaining the theories behind the new agricultural techniques being put into effect at Havenwood and parrying all arguments for the old ways. Sarah, watching from across the green, smiled. In the past days she had done her work well, mentioning some of the things he had done for both tenants and villagers. And now the men, at least, were starting to realize he was human. Sarah's heart swelled with pride.

"He's a fine-looking man, if you don't mind me saying so, ma'am," Mrs. Fellowes said at her side. "The marquess, I mean, begging your pardon."

Sarah's smile was warm. "Oh, I quite agree with you."

"Funny, but after awhile you don't even notice the eye patch." Mrs. Fellowes shook her head. "And to think all this time we were all so scared of him. Not that the men would admit it, of course, but the rumors—"

"They're not true," Sarah said swiftly.

"Now, of course they're not, or a smart girl like you would never have married him. Lucky day for him when you did."

"Lucky for me, too. Oh, is that the bell for supper?"

"Yes, ma'am. You are staying?"

"Of course. We wouldn't miss this for the world." Smiling at Mrs. Fellowes, Sarah worked her way through the crowd until she was again at her husband's side. He gave her an abstracted smile as she took his arm, and went on talking about, of all things, advances in plows. Sarah didn't mind. His face was as animated as it was in his workroom. She had been right. Bringing him here had been a good idea.

Supper was an informal, noisy feast with people jostling for space at benches set at long board tables in the barn behind the school. No one seemed to mind the hubbub as they reached for freshly baked bread or the fine baron of beef, the stewed venison or the vegetables that were arrayed on the tables in rainbow profusion. Ale and beer rather than fine wines were the beverages, but Philip didn't seem to mind.

149

Even Sarah took a sip of dark ale, making a face at the bitter taste and earning laughter from people nearby. And through it all, they talked: Sarah to the vicar, seated on her left, or the women across the table; Philip, beside her, moving on from agriculture to technology in his discussion with Mr. Fellowes. Sarah suspected he had found a friend there.

When the meal was over people set to work, the women removing the food, the men the tables, and a small band of musicians set up at the end of the barn, striking up a reel. Sarah grabbed Philip's hand, dragging him away at last from talk of the estate. By the end of the dance, she was flushed and laughing.

"You're having fun," Philip observed.

"Yes. Aren't you?"

"Yes." He sounded rather surprised, but this time, when the music began for a country dance, he was the one to pull her into the fray.

And so it went for the remainder of the evening, each dancing with different partners, but always finding each other again. When Philip claimed her hand for yet another dance, Sarah pulled back. "I do love dancing," she explained at his quizzical look, "but I'd like to rest for awhile. 'Tis rather warm in here."

"Oh. Do you want to leave?"

"No!" She hesitated. "Do you?"

"No. Let's step out for a moment."

They picked up glasses of the season's first cider, tart and tangy and cool, and went out into a night made brilliant by an orange moon and a star-studded sky. Leaning against the wall of the barn in the cool darkness, Philip draped his arm casually about Sarah's shoulders. She had to resist the impulse to snuggle against him for warmth, and more. *I love you.* The words sounded in her head, and she bit her lip to keep from saying them aloud. It was true, and it was almost time to say it. When had she started loving him? She suspected it had been when she had first seen him. There was no doubt, too, that being with him these last weeks had been exciting, exhilarating, and just a little frightening. Though she had never fallen in love before, Sarah had known what was happening to her. Tonight, though, it had somehow become very real. She was very much in love with her husband.

"Cold?" Philip said, his warm breath close to her ear, making her shiver.

"A bit. It feels good." She rested her head on his shoulder, and his arm tightened around her. "Which stars are those?"

"Stars for wishing on."

"Why, Philip, that's positively unscientific of you!"

Philip's teeth gleamed in the darkness. "I feel rather unscientific. This has been a remarkable evening, Sarah."

"Yes, it has been fun."

"More than that." He turned his head, and his lips grazed her hair, making her pulse speed up. "You have such life in you, Sarah. How did you ever end up as a governess?"

"You know how, Philip. My father—"

"Yes, yes, but how is it some man didn't come along and realize what a jewel you are? I find it hard to believe that your season was as disastrous as you've told me it was."

" 'Tis true. I was shy."

Philip burst out laughing. "Shy!"

"Don't laugh at me! I'm still shy in some ways."

"Sarah, there's not a shy bone in your body." Again his lips moved against her hair, lightly brushing against her forehead as well.

"Well, there was then. But . . ."

"But?"

"But I was engaged for a while."

"Good God!" Philip drew back and stared at her. "To whom?"

"It doesn't matter. It would have been a terrible marriage. I'm glad I found out about him in time."

"Why? What happened?"

"Well." Sarah moved away from the shelter of his arm toward the green where the bonfire still smoldered, and he fol-

151

lowed. "I'm not very pretty, I know, and when I was younger I was—well, there's no other way to say it! I was fat," she said, almost defiantly. "Fat and plain, and I didn't love him, but I liked him and I thought he liked me. And then one night at an assembly I overheard him telling a friend that yes, I was ugly, but there was all that money, and of course he'd have a mistress. So I broke the engage—"

"Who is he?" Philip grasped her arms with a ferocity that startled her. "Tell me who he is so I can knock his bloody teeth down his throat!"

"Philip!" She stared up at him. "It was long ago, and I'm quite over it, now. Thank heavens I learned in time."

"By God, if I ever meet up with him, I'll kill him, I swear I will."

"Oh, Philip." Tender amusement lit her eyes as she reached up to touch his cheek. "My white knight, always having to rescue me."

Philip turned his head and pressed a kiss into her palm, the tip of his tongue flicking briefly out. Sarah gasped and would have pulled her hand away had he not held onto it. "Madam, it has been my pleasure."

"H-has it?"

"Come here." His arm slipped about her waist, pulling her close against him, and his gaze caught hers. She was unable to look away. "You are a beautiful woman, Sarah Pembroke."

"Philip." Sarah pushed at his shoulders to no avail. "Someone will see."

His head bent; his lips slid along her jaw to her cheeks, her eyes. "No one will care."

Sarah's knees were growing decidedly weak. It was true that no one was paying them much notice. Some people still roistered around the bonfire, but most were inside the increasingly noisy barn. "But . . ."

"Beautiful." He kissed her quickly, once, twice, leaving her aching for more, her face upturned, her eyes half-closed. "Ah, Sarah." And his lips came down on hers, and he was at last kissing her as he had the day her horse had run away with her. There was no anger in this kiss, though, only passion, desire, and something more. Sarah twined her arms around his neck, mindlessly parting her lips as his tongue touched them. *I love you,* she thought exultantly. *I love you.*

Some young boys ran by, shouting. Sarah pulled back, startled. For a long moment she and Philip regarded each other with wonder and joy and awe. "I don't want to go back in," Philip said, after a moment. "Do you?"

"Only for my cloak." Her voice was so husky she barely recognized it.

"Then I'll have our carriage brought round."

"Yes," she agreed. Dazed, her body thrumming with feelings unknown to her and yet so right, she went in search of her cloak. So caught up was she in what was happening to her that she barely heard the greetings called out to her. Good heavens! When she had schemed to get Philip to attend the Harvest Home, she hadn't expected this!

In the carriage, Philip pulled her into his arms and his mouth sought hers again, his hands roving over her body under her cloak, making her squirm with the unfamiliar sensations. "You always wear high necklines," he murmured at one point, between the kisses he was planting on her throat. "Why?"

"I—" she began, but was cut off by his lips coming down on hers again. She gave herself up to his kiss willingly, wanting more, her hands moving over his chest, surprisingly hard-muscled, his shoulders, his back. She loved this man. Oh, she loved him, and she would do anything for him.

The ride to Havenwood was shorter than it had ever been, and yet it seemed impossibly long. It was only with reluctance that they parted as the carriage came to a stop, Sarah's hand going up to pat her hair into place. They were the very model of circumspection as they walked into the house, answering Sommers's greeting. They were equally dignified ascending the stairs together in silence. It was only at the top of the stairs that they stopped and looked at each other, searching each other's face, seeing equal measures of longing and desire, seeing vulnerability and drawing strength from each other. For just that moment, they saw all eternity before them.

And then Philip swept his wife into his arms and carried her to his bed.

Chapter Thirteen

The pale light of morning filtered through the drawn curtains. For a moment, Sarah lay still, not quite certain where she was until it came back to her in a rush. *Heavens!* she thought, and leaned up on her elbow to look down at her sleeping husband. In repose he looked younger, vulnerable, and yet the strength she knew was inside him shown through. It had shown last night in his tenderness with her, his patience, as he lovingly, gently, made her his own. They were truly husband and wife now.

Philip awoke and gave her a smile of such piercing sweetness that her heart swelled. "Good morning."

"Good morning."

"Come down here." He held out his arm, and she nestled against him, breathing in his rich aroma, feeling the rasp of his beard across her hair, luxuriating in the closeness of skin against skin. "Did you sleep well?"

"Mm. Did you?"

"Mm." His hand came up to stroke her hair. "You're beautiful."

Sarah turned her head into his shoulder. In the heat of passion last night she had believed the words he had whispered to her, the endearments, the praise. In the cold light of morning, however, it was a different story. "You are, too."

Philip chuckled, a rumble that started deep in his chest. "Ah, Sarah." He wrapped his arms around her and rocked her back and forth. "What did I ever do without you?"

"Made contrivances of the devil."

"Sarah—"

"Drew designs for a balloon to the moon. Made keys. And painted." She stopped, feeling him go still. "Philip, I saw the portrait you did of me."

Philip let out his breath. "It doesn't do you justice."

"Oh, nonsense!"

"I'd like to hang it in the drawing room when it's done."

"But Anne's portrait—"

"Anne is gone. By the way. . . ."

"What?" she said, wary at the note of mock sternness in his voice.

"Who told everybody in the village about the primers?"

"Oh, dear." Again she buried her head in his shoulder. "Are you mad?"

"I should have guessed what would happen when I married a managing, interfering woman," he said, but he was smiling.

" 'Twas for your own good." Sarah sat up, tossing her hair back over her shoulders and pulling the covers about her chest. "Come, now, admit it. Last night was fun."

Philip tugged at the sheets. "Which part of last night?"

"Philip—"

He drew a line across her breasts with his fingertip. "Why do you keep these pretty things so covered up?"

"Because I'd be arrested if I didn't," she said tartly, tugging the sheets back. "Admit it. You enjoyed the Harvest Home."

"Ah. The Harvest Home. That's what you're talking about."

"Yes."

"Very well. Yes. The Harvest Home was fun." He trailed his finger down her arm, making her shiver. "I suppose I shall just have to accustom myself to your managing my life."

"I suppose you shall," Sarah agreed, turning to him with an impish smile. "Do you mind?"

"Not very. Actually, Sarah, about those primers . . ."

"Oh, dear."

"No, I'm not angry at you. The man I had bind them in London wants me to write more, and publish them."

"Do you mean for the rest of the country?"

"Yes."

"Oh, Philip, that's wonderful! You're going to do it, of course."

"Of course. But I was thinking."

Something in his voice made her look at him more closely. "Yes?"

"Usually I have my man of affairs in London tend to such things. But, this time—Sarah, would you like to go to London?"

"What?" Sarah stared at him. She had wanted to get him out of his workroom, and she had succeeded with a vengeance. Harvest Home was one thing, though. London was quite another. "Philip, are you sure?"

"No. But I think it's time to lay old ghosts to rest. You've helped me see that."

She reached out to stroke his cheek. "The past is past, Philip."

"I know." He reached up his arm for her. "And the future is ours."

"Good heavens!" Sarah exclaimed, enthusiastically returning his kiss as he embraced her more fully. She was, at last, his wife, and the future was indeed theirs.

Richard's teacup stopped halfway to his mouth. "He's coming to London?"

"Yes, isn't it marvelous?" Rebecca poured her own tea and set the teapot down. "He's written and asked me to find a house to lease and possibly to buy. And I think I've found the perfect one, on South Audley Street."

Richard put his cup down, hard. "What could possibly possess him to come to London?"

"Richard, please, have a care! That was my mother's china."

"Doesn't he know what is likely to happen?"

"He knows. And I think it's high time."

"But, Becky, think of what will be said—"

"If the rumors bother you, Richard, you needn't stay. Oh, that's right, you've leased your country house."

Richard gritted his teeth at this reminder of his financial troubles. "Of course the rumors don't bother me, Becky."

"Don't they? How many people stood by him, Richard, after Anne died?"

"I did, Becky, so don't think to blame that on me. I know quite well he didn't kill Anne."

Rebecca sipped at her tea. "Then you'll be happy to stand by him now."

"Of course," he said hastily. "I just fear he's in for more hurt."

"Perhaps. But I think he's finally realized his own strength. I do like that girl."

"Who?"

"Sarah. I don't doubt that she's the one behind this."

"Yes, she is a managing female."

"Oh, do go away, Richard, if you plan on being so disagreeable! I think it's marvelous they're coming, even if it is only the Little Season. I must plan a reception for them."

Richard rose. "And I'll be prepared to support Philip when people cut him. They will, you know."

"Oh, pish! Go away, Richard, you are making me cross beyond all reason!"

Richard bowed, his face set. "Very well, madam."

"Richard!" He turned from the doorway. "You will come to my reception, won't you?"

He nodded. "Of course, Becky. I wouldn't miss it for the world." Bowing again, he left the room, and Rebecca settled back against the sofa with her tea, happily beginning to plan. Oh, this would be such fun!

* * *

"Oh, and Mrs. Stevenson," Sarah said, and that lady turned.

"Yes, my lady?"

"Never mind. I'm sure while we're gone you'll run the house in your usual excellent style."

"Yes, my lady." Mrs. Stevenson bobbed a curtsy and turned away, her face as dour as usual. Sarah watched her go, a little frown on her own face.

"I'll see that woman smile someday if it kills me," she muttered.

"I hardly think it's worth that, my dear," a voice said behind her. She turned as a hand was laid on her shoulder, and smiled up at Philip.

"What?"

"I believe that woman was born with a permanent frown."

"Now, Philip, everyone has a smile in them. You smile now."

"Yes." He tugged at her hand. "Come see something."

"What?" she asked as he dragged her through the hall into the drawing room.

"That," he said, and pointed. Across the room where Anne's portrait once had hung, the picture of Sarah now took pride of place.

Her breath drew in. "Oh, Philip. It's beautiful."

"Yes, it is, isn't it?" He rested his arm on her shoulder as they gazed at the portrait. "I rather hate to leave it behind."

"Well, you have the real thing!" She smiled up at him. "Philip, when we return, could we redecorate this room?"

He looked around. "What's wrong with it?"

"There's no color. All that straw-colored satin."

"It is rather dull, isn't it? Funny, I never noticed before."

"And you're the one who put stained glass in the dome."

"What colors were you thinking?"

"I don't know. Red, perhaps? Shall we think about it while we're in London?"

"We may as well." He gave her a quick kiss. "I'll just go see that everything's ready, so we can be on our way."

159

"Fine." Sarah stood for a moment in the drawing room gazing at the portrait, her heart so full she thought it might burst. Now that the time had come to leave Havenwood for London, she wasn't certain she wanted to go. She loved this house. It was turning into a home

Smiling, she gave her portrait one last look and wandered into the great hall. Havenwood was much changed these days. Philip no longer hid in his workroom so much, and she herself had gotten more involved in the actual running of the house, getting to know every servant by name. No longer did the staff scurry about in silence; instead, everyone was more cheerful, pleased to work for such a good man as the marquess. The quiet gloom that had pervaded every room had lifted, and everything seemed to sparkle more, from the stained glass in the hall to the gleaming woodwork. Even the weather was cooperating; beyond the open door she could see the sun shining on the barouche that would take them to London. Suddenly filled with happiness so great it threatened to overflow, she flung her arms wide and twirled around, exulting in the rainbow of colors that flashed in her eyes from the stained glass far above.

"My lady."

"What?" Sarah said, stopping, and turned to see the staff gathered in the inner hall, to see her and Philip off. Some of the maids were obviously holding back giggles, but what caught Sarah's attention was the odd look on Mrs. Stevenson's face. "Mrs. Stevenson! You're smiling."

Instantly, the smile disappeared. "I am not."

"You were. I saw you."

"It wouldn't be dignified in me, my lady."

"Dignified, my foot! There's nothing wrong with smiling."

This time, the maids did giggle, and Mrs. Stevenson turned, quelling them with a look. When she turned back, her face wore its usual somber look, but there was a suspicious twinkle in her eyes. "I must say, I like this hall. I thought the stained glass was a strange idea at first, I don't scruple to tell you that, but it brightens the place up like."

160

"So it does." Sarah beamed at her as Philip came to her side. "Take care of things while we're gone?"

"Of course. But it won't be the same without you, ma'am." Very dignified now, she curtsied as Sarah and Philip turned away toward the waiting carriage.

"What was that all about?" Philip asked, helping her into the barouche.

"She smiled!" Sarah smiled herself as she settled onto the seat. "Oh, Philip, I hate to leave."

"So do I."

"Are you sure about this?"

Across the carriage, Philip grinned and reached out to pat her hand. "I've told you. Don't be nervous."

"I'm not." Not for herself, anyway. She had succeeded beyond her wildest dreams in drawing Philip out of himself, but even she thought this was a bit much. Havenwood and Bibury were one thing. London was quite another. Sarah had never been to the city, but she had had her own experience of malicious gossip during her brief come-out. She was certain the capital would be ten times worse.

"Of course, once your business is completed, we needn't stay," she chattered. "I miss Havenwood already, don't you? And though I'm sure Rebecca has chosen a suitable house for us, I don't know anything about entertaining. Do you think—"

"Sarah." Philip's grip on her hand briefly tightened. "What happened to my brave, curious girl?"

"I've a secret to confess, Philip. I'm really a terrible coward. This is the first time you've been to London since Anne—"

"Do you think I won't be able to handle it if people snub me?"

"Well, actually, no."

Philip's face was inscrutable as he gazed at her. "I am happy to know that you hold such a high opinion of me, madam."

"Heavens, Philip, I know you're no coward!"

"Thank you."

"But I also know how cruel people can be."

"Come here." Philip reached out his arm to her, and she snuggled against him. "People we hardly know, Sarah. Why should we be concerned with them?"

"I don't know." The truth was, however, that they did concern her, and not, as she would have Philip believe, entirely for him. She suspected the *ton* would take one look at her and turn up their collective noses. In the past, it hadn't really mattered what people had thought of her; she had worked long and hard to rebuild her sense of self-esteem after her first, disastrous engagement. Now it did, though. She was a marchioness, and she felt woefully unsuited to the task. She was, after all, the daughter of a man who had been in trade, a former governess, a parvenu. She doubted they would be well-received, and all because of her background.

Philip absently stroked her cheek. Of course he wouldn't be happy if he were snubbed, he thought. He could handle it, though, even after the way life at Havenwood had changed; he'd grown used to rejection over the years. But, Sarah. Her first time in London, and she deserved to enjoy it, especially since her only season had been so dismal. If he were cut by society, she would be hurt. It didn't seem fair.

The house Rebecca had found for them was in a quiet neighborhood, but it was ideally suited to their needs. Narrow and high, it was built of brick, with black shutters and gleaming brass railings. Inside, it was furnished, rather surprisingly, in English Empire, the latest style, though the work of Robert Adam was evident in the strong, clear colors used and the plaster medallions on the walls. The dining room was gold and white; the drawing room, running the length of the house, was crimson damask, with several small tables with inlay work and brass trim scattered about the room. A crystal chandelier and several graceful Argand lamps provided ample illumination. The staff was well-trained and efficient, and the house even boasted indoor plumbing, to Philip's delight, though it wasn't as advanced a

162

system as at Havenwood. Best of all, he whispered into Sarah's ear, was the master bedroom, with its enormous four-poster bed. Sarah blushed. She was still a little astonished, and delighted, by that aspect of married life.

They had hardly had a chance to settle in when the door knocker sounded and Rebecca sailed in. "Oh, my dear," she said, holding her hands out to Sarah, "it is so good to see you! Welcome to London."

"Thank you, Rebecca," Sarah said, as they exchanged kisses on the cheek.

"The house is perfect, don't you think?" Rebecca went on, as they climbed the stairs to the drawing room. "Small, but I didn't think you'd want a great barn of a place. And I do hope the staff is satisfactory. Cooper used to be our butler, you know. I coaxed him out of retirement." She leaned forward. "He's a bit hard of hearing, I fear."

"Ahem." Cooper, a tall, spare man who carried his age well, stood in the doorway. "Would my lady wish tea to be served?"

"Yes, thank you, Cooper. He heard you!" Sarah said in a strangled voice as Cooper went out.

"Yes, well, I did always think he was selectively deaf. Philip, oh my." Rebecca gazed at her brother as he came into the room. "Do I actually see you wearing a gray waistcoat?"

Philip, leaning against the mantel, smiled. "My wife's idea."

"It suits you. Next thing we know, you'll be wearing colors. Now." She turned back to Sarah. "Town is rather thin of company these days, but I've been thinking of what we could do for your entertainment. There's the theater, of course, and the opera. Too bad Almack's isn't open, that's only in the spring, but we'll make do. I've been thinking of giving a reception for you. Just a small one, if you wish—"

"Oh, no, you needn't," Sarah interrupted, glancing at Philip. "I'm sure just being here will be exciting enough."

"Nonsense! You'll be expected to entertain, too, and this room is perfect. And if you're worried about people cutting

Philip, you needn't. I plan to invite only close friends."

"Well." Philip pushed himself away from the mantel. "If you ladies are going to discuss routs and such, I think I'll find something else to do."

"There's no workroom here for you to hide in," Rebecca called after him and then turned to Sarah with a worried frown. "You won't let him hide himself away again, will you?"

"I plan on letting him do whatever makes him happy." Sarah's voice was firm. "I think coming to London is enough, don't you?"

Rebecca studied her. "Who are you frightened for, Sarah? Philip or yourself?"

Sarah's smile was rueful. "Both, to be honest. I had a disastrous come-out."

"That's because you likely didn't have someone to manage it for you! Well, I plan to help you this time."

"Oh, dear."

"Now, none of that. We'll visit my modiste and the milliner's and—"

"Rebecca . . ."

"If you're thinking Philip can't afford it, he can."

"But I've enough new clothes."

Rebecca looked at her, her face stern. "A lady never has enough clothes. You wish Philip to be accepted, do you not?"

"Oh, yes, but—"

"Then you must look your best, and you must appear at the right places." Rebecca patted her hand. "Trust me, my dear. I know what I'm doing."

"That's what worries me." Sarah smiled. "Oh, very well, Rebecca, I'll put myself in your hands. Lord help me."

"Good." Rebecca rose. "I must fly; there's so much to be done! I'll come round tomorrow and we'll visit the shops, shall we?"

"Very well," Sarah said, seeing her guest to the front door. Only after Rebecca had left did she pick up her skirts, to

Cooper's astonishment, and run up the stairs in search of her husband.

She didn't have far to look. Within a few moments of Rebecca's departure, he had wandered into the drawing room. "She's gone, then?"

"Yes. I like your sister, Philip, but—"

"But she can be overpowering. I know."

"She told me I'm not to allow you to languish in your workroom."

"Oh, she did, did she?" He glanced about the room. "This would be perfect. All that northern light," he said wistfully.

"Oh, Philip." She crossed to him and looped her arms about his neck. "Set up a workroom, of course."

"You don't mind? After all, this visit is for you as much as for me."

"No, I don't mind. Just remember to come out now and then."

"Oh, I shall." He smiled down at her. "What has Becky in mind for you?"

"The worst," Sarah said gloomily. "New clothes."

"Not such a bad idea." Philip pulled back, studying her. "London is different from the country."

"But I don't want them!"

He grinned. "I fear you've met your match. Someone who is as managing as you are."

"Oh, dear. Am I that bad?"

"You? Managing? Whatever gave you that idea?"

"Oh, stop funning me! I'm only thinking of your good."

"Rather."

"Come to think of it, Philip, you could use some new clothes, too." Philip laughed. "Oh, dear. I am managing, aren't I?"

"In the very nicest way." He pulled her closer to him. "I'll visit a tailor if you'll visit Rebecca's modiste."

"I don't think I'll have much choice. And I'll look perfectly ridiculous."

"No, you won't. You'll look fine." He kissed her forehead

and then released her. "I think I'll find a room to set up my work. By the bye, I'll want to visit the British Museum."

"Fine."

"You'd go with me?"

"Of course. Why?"

"What about the museum of natural history at the Egyptian Hall?"

"I'd like that, too."

"Hmm."

"Philip, whatever in the world is it?"

"Nothing." He crossed the room and gave her a quick, hard kiss. "I shall see you at dinner."

"Yes," Sarah said dazedly, watching him leave the room. Now what had that been all about? she wondered, sinking down upon a settee upholstered in crimson and gold striped satin. Not that she minded. *I love him.* Her fingers drifted to her lips, still tingling from the kiss. The words had yet to be spoken between them, but they would be soon. She could sense it. What she felt for Philip was too strong, too intense to be one-sided. Good heavens, who would ever have believed that she would fall in love with a marquess?

"Ahem." Cooper stood in the doorway. "The Honorable Mr. Richard Thornton has called. Is my lady receiving?"

"What? Oh, yes, of course! Show him up, Cooper. And please, serve us tea." Sarah flew to the pier glass to smooth her hair and straighten her gown. Philip never seemed to care if her appearance were less than perfect, which was one of the things she loved about him. Richard was another matter. She disliked his searching gaze that seemed to find and catalogue every flaw. She disliked, even more, when his gaze lingered. It reminded her too much of Mr. Ramsay and other employers.

Richard paused in the doorway, looking across the room to where Sarah stood at the pier glass. Well. This was a surprise, and not a pleasant one. Bad enough Philip had actually ventured out of his house; worse that he had brought his wife, who glowed like a new bride. The first problem he could handle with a few rumors whispered in the right ears. The second, however, was a different matter. For Sarah had changed. Unsophisticated still, yes, but not quite the country bumpkin she had been. Leaving Havenwood had been a mistake, even if he'd had no choice. He only hoped he was in time to undo the damage to his plans.

"Welcome to London, Sarah," he said.

"Richard!" Sarah turned and went to him. On his face was nothing but simple friendliness. Perhaps she had only imagined those other looks? "How nice to see you again."

"I'm glad you've decided to come to town." Richard flipped back the tails of his coat before sitting on the settee next to Sarah. "You are looking as lovely as usual, Sarah."

"Oh, nonsense. But I am glad to see you. Rebecca has such plans for us, and I'm not certain how we'll bear up under them."

"I am persuaded you will be a success, cousin."

"Oh, not me." Sarah waved her hand in dismissal. "It's Philip I'm thinking of."

"Yes, that is a problem." From a pocket he withdrew a strange-looking device, a small cylinder of rosewood with metal fittings on the top. Idly he touched a catch, and flame spurted up, making Sarah start in surprise. "He hasn't been in London since Anne died. God knows what the rumor mongers will have to say. They were cruel enough before."

"What is that?" Sarah asked, as flame shot up again from the cylinder.

"What? Oh, this." Richard looked at the device in his hand as if he hadn't even realized he held it. "A cigar lighter. Philip made it for me. Do you know, I tinker with things myself. In a modest way, of course."

"No, I didn't."

"I would never have thought of anything like this, though. Ingenious, isn't it?"

Sarah shuddered. Anything to do with fire, in light of Philip's experience, scared her. "It looks dangerous to me."

"I doubt it, but if it bothers you, I shall put it away." He touched the catch one last time and then secreted the lighter in his pocket, patting it absently into place. "Now. How may I be of service to you, cousin?"

"Philip will need support, Richard. I know Rebecca says there are few people in Town, but I also know how people like to talk."

"I see. Rest assured, then, that I will stand by you both."

"Oh, thank you!" Sarah reached out an impulsive hand to him, and he slowly raised it to his lips. Again that look was in his eyes, making her want to pull away.

"I say, Sarah, I—" Philip said from the doorway, and stopped. A curious look passed over his face and then left. "Richard. When did you get here?"

Richard rose. "A few moments ago, cousin. Good to see you in Town at last."

"It's good to be here. I can see there's much I've missed."

"Indeed. While you are here, you should see everything. I'll be happy to escort Sarah for you."

Again that look passed over Philip's face. "Thank you, cousin. Sarah, do you know where the primers are?"

"We sent them on ahead, Philip, don't you remember?" Sarah said calmly, aware of a tension between the two men that hadn't been there before. "I believe Cooper said there's a large crate in the music room, of all places."

"Ah. That must be them. I'll go look. No, don't disturb yourself, Richard. I'm sure Sarah enjoys your company."

With that, he was gone, leaving Sarah to stare after him, frowning a bit. "Primers, cousin?" Richard said.

"Hmm?" Sarah turned. "Oh. Another of Philip's projects."

"Of which there are many. You don't plan to let him hide away, do you? Though it would be to my advantage."

Sarah drew back. "Philip and I will manage," she said, in her best governess voice. "I do appreciate your help, Richard, but—"

"Overstepped my bounds, have I? My apologies. But you could have worse guides, Sarah. With Philip you're likely to see only scholarly or scientific things."

"I don't mind."

"He is lucky to have you." His smile was charming again, dispelling any misgivings Sarah might have had. "Has Rebecca offered to take you to her modiste?"

Sarah wrinkled her nose. "Yes, though I doubt it will do any good."

"Now, cousin, if you truly want to help Philip, you don't want to look like a country cousin."

"Is that how I appear?"

"My apologies, cousin. I didn't mean to offend you."

A country cousin, indeed. She suspected Richard had meant exactly what he had said. A former governess, a girl who once would have been married for her money only. She was suddenly quite tired of it all. Perhaps she wasn't beautiful, but she resented the assumption that she couldn't be attractive. Philip, at least, seemed to think differently. "No offense," she said lightly. "I know you have Philip's best interests in mind."

Richard ignored the irony in her tone. "And yours, too, of course. Philip is a handsome man."

"Yes, I've always thought so."

"And he can be very charming when he wishes to be. You may have to watch for that."

Sarah set down her teacup. "Why, whatever do you mean?"

"Merely that women will flirt with a charming man."

"Well, of course they will."

"Yes, but—"

"What?" Sarah demanded. "I am tired of this shilly-shallying, Richard. If you've something to say, then say it."

"Very well. I don't want to hurt you, Sarah, but I feel you should know this."

"What, for heaven's sake?"

"When Philip was last in London, he had a mistress."

Chapter Fourteen

Sarah went very still. *"Had* a mistress?" she said at last, setting down the teapot without even a rattle.

"Sarah, I'm sorry. I shouldn't have said anything."

"Nonsense, Richard, of course you should. I think I have a right to know." She passed a cup over to him. "Besides, that's all in the past, isn't it?"

"Ye-es."

Sarah looked up sharply. Why was Richard telling her this? It was, at best, improper; at worst, certain to cause trouble between husband and wife. "Honestly, Richard, I didn't expect he'd lived like a monk! But I trust him."

"Of course you do," Richard said soothingly. "I am sorry, Sarah. I can see I've upset you."

"Upset me? Why, whatever gave you that idea?"

"I'm sure, as you said, it's all in the past."

Sarah sipped at her tea, not looking at him. "Of course."

"I'm sorry." He rose. "I think I'd best go, before I say something else to upset you."

"I can't imagine what."

Richard looked back from the doorway at her. So the little mouse had sharp teeth to speak with such angry sarcasm. He may have erred. Then, again, perhaps not. "Sarah," he said, and she raised her head. "I am sorry. If you ever need a friend, please don't hesitate to call on me."

"Thank you, Richard," she said, and he left at last, well-pleased with himself.

Left alone, Sarah gulped her tea furiously. A mistress. A mistress! Well, of course he'd have had one; he was a handsome and, as she well knew, virile man. But if Philip were to come into this room this minute, she thought she could cheerfully strangle him.

Or her. Sarah stood up suddenly, but Richard was gone. While he was here, why hadn't she learned more about this alleged mistress? Who she was, and if Sarah were likely to run into her in company? Suppose—no, she wouldn't think of that. She knew Philip held her in esteem. But love? The word had never been spoken between them. They had a good marriage that suited them both, and she'd given herself to him, heart and soul. She thought, too, that their lovemaking was special. Philip's feelings, however, were a mystery to her. What would he do were he to meet his former mistress, especially if she were beautiful?

"My lady?" Cooper came in. "May I take the tray?"

"What? Yes." Sarah paced to the window, looking out on South Audley Street without seeing anything. "Cooper," she said suddenly, turning, and the old man stopped at the door. "Where is his lordship? Do you know?"

"He's in the attics, my lady. He said something about needing northern light."

Cooper's mien was stiff and correct, but his tone was so puzzled that Sarah was hard-pressed not to laugh. "Ah. I see. Thank you, Cooper, you may go."

"Yes, my lady," Cooper said, and left, wondering, Sarah was certain, what kind of household this would be to serve.

Northern light. Sarah let out a giggle. Of course. She should have remembered that Philip, though very much a man, was not like other men. Her main competition was his tendency to absorb himself in his work, and she could deal with that. *A mistress, hmm? We'll just see about that, my lord!*

"Well," Sarah murmured, gazing at her reflection in the mirror in her room and turning so that she could see herself from all angles. "Well!"

"Well indeed, my lady," Millie said. "Now if you'd just let me adjust your headdress."

Sarah took a deep breath and then quickly exhaled it. No need to emphasize *that* part of her anatomy. Still . . . "Who would have thought?"

"You look a proper picture, my lady. Now, please, sit, so I can see to the headdress."

"Yes, Millie." Sarah sank down onto the tufted stool before her dressing table, carefully spreading the skirts of her gown around her. Good heavens, who would ever have expected such a transformation? She looked almost pretty. Certainly attractive enough to entice her husband away from a former mistress.

She frowned and then quickly stopped. If Philip had a mistress, he was showing no signs of it. They had been in London for two weeks, and when he had left the house, he had usually done so with her. They had gone to his publisher, who had been enthusiastic about the primers; to the Tower to view the animals in the menagerie; and to the British Museum to see the Egyptian antiquities there, having written a letter previously asking for admission, as was required. When Philip had gone out alone, it had mostly been to visit his tailor as he had promised. And she, of course, had gone shopping with Rebecca.

Their first stop had been at Madame Celeste's fashionable showrooms on Bond Street for Sarah's London wardrobe. There would be enough entertainments, even at this time of year, to make what she needed extensive: morning gowns in soft pastel muslins; afternoon gowns for when she was at home to guests; a new riding habit with epaulettes, in deference to the military mania gripping London; a red pelisse that she adored, with the new Prussian helmet to match; and, of course, evening gowns. Dozens and dozens of them, it seemed, and all cut down to *there*.

Clad only in her shift and stockings, Sarah had surveyed the first of these with dismay when it was brought to her in the dressing room. It was a lovely gown, a heavenly shade of emerald in watered silk that glistened as it moved. A far cry

172

from the fussy, fluffy white muslin gowns she had worn during her come-out and just as inappropriate. "Oh, dear," she said, when the gown had been draped over her head and Madame's assistant had hooked it up the back. "Oh, dear, this won't do."

"But it looks lovely." Rebecca, seated on a chair of blue velvet and leafing through the most recent issue of *La Belle Assemblée*, looked up. "It needs to be taken in at the waist, but otherwise, it's perfect."

"Oh, there's nothing wrong with the gown." Sarah put her hand to her chest. "It's me. My figure is so poor."

"Really? I don't think so."

"Oh, now, really, Becky! Of course you can say that, you're so slim. I look ridiculous with all these curves."

"Oh, stuff! You do not."

"I do so! And these gowns are just all wrong for me. I'm too . . . too . . ."

"What?"

"Top-heavy!" Sarah burst out, and Rebecca laughed. "It's not funny."

"Oh, Sarah, you are a dear." Signaling to the fascinated assistant to leave, Rebecca crossed the room to her. "I am fashionably thin, certainly but if you knew what I would give for a figure like yours."

Sarah gaped at her. "You're funning me."

"Not at all. If Lawrence saw you now, he'd wink at you for sure."

Sarah laughed. "Becky, he'd wink anyway. But look at me. I'm all hips and . . ." She gestured toward her bosom. "I am built like a cow."

"Oh, Sarah, now who told you that?"

"My aunt and my cousins and—"

"How wrong they were! I'd agree with you dear, if you were heavy, but you're not," Rebecca said, turning serious. "You have a lovely shape. It's all very well being slim, but I can assure you, most men would prefer someone like you."

"Really? Well, that explains that, then."

"What?"

"Well, I never really understood it before, why the husbands of my employers when I was a governess always seemed to want to—well, you know."

"No! They didn't."

" 'Tis how I lost my last post."

"Oh, Sarah. I'm sorry, I don't mean to laugh; I know it must have been terrible for you. But it should tell you something, don't you think? Has Philip complained?"

Sarah could feel herself growing red. "No."

"Well, all right, then!"

"Maybe." She looked at herself again and let her hand drop. The gown was revealing, but not immodestly so. No, Philip hadn't complained at all about her shape. Philip, in fact, called her beautiful. She'd almost believed him until she'd learned about his mistress . . .

"There," Millie said with satisfaction. "Now just you look at yourself, my lady. Look a proper treat, you do."

Sarah glanced up and then rose, walking across to the pier glass. She did, indeed, look a treat. Millie had worked her customary magic on Sarah's hair, sweeping it up and back into a cluster of curls and topping it with a headdress of ostrich feathers. Rebecca was right. There was nothing wrong with her figure, nor with her face. Why had she spent her life believing herself to be unattractive? Of course, she'd never had a gown like this, of crimson satin with short puffed sleeves and an even briefer bodice, the fabric draping about her curves, the color making her skin glow a creamy white. And there was a great deal of that creamy skin exposed. Usually she insisted on covering up her bosom, but that time was past. As she pulled on her elbow-length gloves of white kid, Sarah smiled. Let any mistress compete with this!

Head high, she sailed into the drawing room, and Philip, who had been staring into the fire, looked up. His eye grew wide and his mouth dropped and then he smiled, crossing the room to her. "Well," he said. "Well."

"Do you like it?" she asked, suddenly anxious.

"You might say so."

174

"You don't think it's too low? Perhaps I should tuck in a handkerchief."

He pretended to study her. "Well, my dear, I don't think you should keep your attributes hidden."

"Oh, dear." Sarah put her face in her hands. "You don't understand."

"No, love, I don't." Philip lightly drew a finger around the neckline, making her shiver, and then pulled her against him. "You look beautiful."

"I know." Her voice was muffled. "I'm not plain, am I?"

"I never thought so."

"Then why should I need a handkerchief?" She pulled back, smiling. "Madame Celeste would be horrified if I used a bosom friend."

"Quite. And we can't have that."

"Now you are funning me." She stepped back and, for the first time, took a good look at her husband. He was, again, in black, black coat and black pantaloons, but his waistcoat was silver gray, embroidered with silver threads and striped in the same shade of crimson as her gown. His shirt and neckcloth were a dazzling, snowy white. His dark hair was carefully cropped *coup de vent,* and he looked so handsome Sarah's heart ached with it. There was nothing she would change about him. Not even the eye patch.

"I've something for you." Philip's voice was husky as he stepped away and picked up a small velvet-covered box. "Can't have my wife going to her first reception without jewels."

"Philip, you didn't—oh . . ." Her words ended on a sigh. Against a bed of black velvet nestled the most exquisite things she had ever seen, a necklace, earbobs, and bracelet of diamonds and rubies, set in gold. "Oh. These are beautiful. Philip, you didn't buy them, did you?"

"And if I did? No, they're part of the Pembroke jewels."

"Part of?"

"I thought that would interest you. Here, turn around so I can fasten the necklace." His fingers brushed against the back of her neck, making her shiver. "My man of business has been keeping them for me. There's quite a collection. Every time my father came back to my mother he brought her jewelry."

Sarah looked up quickly at that. "Came back to?"

"They had a most fashionable marriage. They each had their amours." He stepped away. "I think that will do."

Sarah examined her reflection in the chimney glass, pondering on that piece of information, wondering about her husband's own past. "They're beautiful, Philip. Did Anne wear them?"

Philip hesitated for just a moment. "Anne wore some of them, yes. Sarah, I'm sorry." He turned her gently, his hands on her shoulders. "But she was my wife."

"Yes, I know. Well." She broke away from his grasp and went to pick up her shawl of white cashmere. "We should be going, else we'll be late."

"Yes." Philip took the shawl from her, his hands warm as he draped it on her shoulders. "It's you I'm with, Sarah," he said, his voice very close to her ear, making her shiver again.

"I know." She turned and gave him a brilliant smile. Anne was in the past, and so was his mistress. Sarah intended to see that things stayed that way.

Some of Sarah's apprehension returned as their carriage pulled up in front of the Lawrence house for the reception Rebecca was holding for them. After all, the last time she had really been in society, in Cheltenham, she'd been a miserable failure. And this was not Cheltenham. Peering out the carriage window, she could see a line of fine carriages ahead of them, their passengers all waiting to reach the Lawrence house, lit from top to bottom. Bewigged, gold-laced footmen lined the stairs on either side, and against the fence railings was pressed a mob of the common people staring with unabashed curiosity. No, this was not at all what she was used to. For the first time, she realized why people considered it so important to be accepted by London society.

She glanced across at Philip. In truth, she was more concerned about him than herself. Though he seemed calm enough, she wondered what he was really feeling. Sometimes she thought he hid behind his eye patch like a shield.

Their carriage at last reached the door, and they descended to the chatter and catcalls of the mob. Sarah's face was pink from the freely voiced comments, most of them complimentary, on her appearance by the time they were shown into the front hall. Ascending the stairs, they paused in the doorway of the drawing room, Philip's hand tightening on her elbow. She glanced up and gave him a quick smile.

"The Marquess and Marchioness of Pembroke," the butler intoned, and those assembled inside the drawing room turned to stare. Philip's hand clamped even tighter on her elbow as if he sensed her desire to flee or shared it. Again she looked up at him, but in the face of the looks directed their way, some cool, some malicious, all curious, he looked impassive. "When can we leave?" he whispered, bending to her.

"Why not now?" she whispered back, and at last he smiled.

"Courage, my dear," he said, and stepped into the room.

London may have been thin of company, but the Lawrences' drawing room wasn't. Decorated in pastel blue and white, a perfect foil for Rebecca's coloring, it shone, glittering with the reflection of light from crystal chandeliers and wall sconces, light that was refracted off the jewels worn by the women. So much for a small reception, Sarah thought wryly.

"Oh, my dears!" Rebecca came up to them, smiling. "Such a sad crush! Isn't it wonderful? Philip, you won't believe who is here, I can hardly believe it myself. Princess Esterhazy and the Duke of Rochester and Byron—"

"Lord Byron?" Sarah interrupted, delighted at the thought of meeting the famous poet.

"Yes, he actually condescended to come! Of course it meant I couldn't invite Lady Caroline Lamb, but then, she can be so tiresome."

"Of course." Sarah bit back a nervous giggle. Such elevated company as was here! How would she ever survive it?

A great bear of a man, broad of shoulder with thick, tousled hair, suddenly reared up before them. "Pembroke! For God's sake, man, where have you been hiding yourself?"

"Edward!" Philip grinned as his hand was wrung by a bear-like paw. "By all that's holy, what are you doing here?"

The other man grimaced. "Ran into a spot of bad luck at Vittoria. Damned leeches wanted to take my leg off, and I wouldn't let them. So I was invalided home. Spent a damnable time—sorry, ma'am—in that wreck they call a hospital, and damned if they wouldn't let me out until just last week."

"I didn't know. I would have visited. Oh, excuse me, Sarah. This is my wife Sarah. Captain Sir Edward Gregory."

"Major Sir Edward," he said, taking Sarah's hand in an amazingly gentle grip. "Heard you got leg-shackled again. High time, I'd say." He grinned at Sarah. "Picked yourself another beauty, too."

"I saw her first," Philip said, smiling. "Sarah, Edward and I served together on the Peninsula."

"But that's fascinating. What stories you must have to tell, sir," she said.

"Enough. But it's been hard." His face turned serious. "Lost a lot of good men, and a lot are still in hospital. Things aren't the same, Pembroke."

"No. Everything's changed."

"But tonight's not the night for such talk." He clapped Philip on the shoulder. "Come tell me what you've been doing. Hear you built a castle for yourself out in the country."

"Sarah?" Philip looked quizzically back at her.

"Go ahead. I'll find Rebecca," she said, and stood, smiling, as she watched the two men walk away. They were so unalike, the one tall, burly, walking, she could see now, with a limp; the other shorter, slender, yet with a wiry strength and grace of movement all his own. All the love she felt for her husband welled up within her. She knew this couldn't be easy for him, and yet no one would know it from looking at him. A brave man, her husband, and the most handsome one present. One glance around the room had told her that.

As for herself. She looked around, startled to realize that

178

she felt not the least bit shy or scared. Sir Edward's greeting and his obvious admiration for her had gone a long way towards reassuring her. After all, she was no longer the shy, plain debutante she had been. She was a married woman, a marchioness, wearing the most beautiful and daring gown she had ever owned, and she knew quite well how to handle people. No matter how exalted the company tonight might be, they were of little importance. Philip was all that really mattered to her. She would be here for him if he needed her, but in the meantime, she had every intention of enjoying herself, too.

"What, has he deserted you already?" Richard said.

"Richard!" Sarah turned, and instinctively snapped open her fan of ivory and silk, raising it to her face. "Such a pleasant surprise to see you."

"But surely you knew I'd be here, cousin." He gave her a long, leisurely look. "You are looking different tonight. Quite elegant."

"I know," Sarah said happily. "Amazing what the right clothing will do."

"You could never be less than beautiful, Sarah."

Sarah burst out laughing. "Oh, give over, Richard! You know I looked a perfect fright when first we met." And it had mattered to him. She'd known that in spite of the burning looks and fulsome compliments. It was Philip who had first truly seen her beauty.

"I'd be less than a gentleman to say so." He patted her hand as they both looked towards Philip in earnest conversation with Sir Edward. "He really isn't treating you right, leaving you like this."

"Nonsense, I can get along just fine! And I must say, it's good to see him like this."

"Mm. Nevertheless, London is not like the rustic society you're used to." Sarah opened her mouth to protest, but he rushed on. "And of course, people aren't really certain whether to accept you or not."

Sarah fanned herself harder. "Well, thank you very much!"

"I did not mean you, Sarah." He gave her his charming, totally self-deprecating smile, and in spite of herself, Sarah felt her indignation melting. He really was quite charming and handsome, if not so attractive to her as Philip. She could do worse than to have him as a friend. "I meant Philip, or you and Philip together. The rumors, you know."

"Surely no one will be rude enough to bring them up."

"Perhaps not, but it's on their minds." He looked down at her, and his gaze held only concern. "I would not see you hurt, Sarah."

"Thank you, Richard. But I'm stronger than you realize."

For a few moments, they stood together in silence, watching the crowd eddying about and absorbing the heady combination of many conversations, scents, and colors all mingled together. "You and Philip are getting on well, then?"

"Quite well."

"He hasn't shown any sign of dalliance with—"

"Sarah!" Sir Lawrence boomed, draping a heavy arm on her shoulders. "Must say you're looking good, gel."

"Thank you, Sir Lawrence," Sarah said distractedly. Dalliance with whom? Was Philip's mistress in this room?

"Can't keep her all to yourself, Richard. Got plenty of people want to meet her. Come, m'dear, let me introduce you to some of our guests."

A burst of laughter sometime later caught Philip's attention and momentarily distracted him from the tale Sir Edward was telling about the battle of Vittoria. A group of men had gathered around Sarah, who didn't seem to mind in the least. She sparkled, she glowed, and in all this exalted company she stood out because she was real. No pretenses with his Sarah. He wondered what she was saying that was so amusing.

". . . Well, of course I couldn't let him get away with putting toads in my bed!" Sarah was chattering, animated by the attention being paid her and the champagne she had drank. "Not that I'm afraid of toads, of course, I'm not such a poor honey! And he really was a dreadful little boy, the

worst I ever had in my charge. So that night I draped a
sheet over myself and clanked some chains in the nursery,
and so that is how the house got the reputation of being
haunted!"

Another burst of laughter. "They didn't make governesses
like you when I was a boy, ma'am," one man said, his smile
warm. "If they had, perhaps I would have stayed in the
school-room longer."

"Oh, nonsense," Sarah said cheerfully. "I am persuaded
you'd have found me a terrible cross to bear."

"But you are not a governess now, are you?" a silky voice
said, and Sarah's smile wavered a bit. She had been enjoying
this masculine attention, there was no denying that. After
her experience at her come-out, it was heady stuff, indeed.
Across from her now, though, stood the recently married
Duchess of Rochester, leaning on the arm of her elderly husband. She was not in the first bloom of youth, but Moira,
who had once been married to the equally elderly Duke of
Marshfield, was still an attractive woman. Her dark hair
was piled high atop a regal neck, pearl white teeth nipped
seductively at full lips so red they must have been rouged,
and long lashes flirted over her green cat's eyes. Worst of all,
though, was her gown, dark red like Sarah's, which at first
had caused the two women to eye each other. It, too, showed
a considerable amount of flesh and a figure far from sylphlike. *Running to fat,* Sarah thought, and felt immensely
cheered.

"No, thank heavens. I fear I wasn't a very good one," she
said. "But I do like my life now."

Moira glanced across the room. "Your husband is a most
mysterious man, Lady Pembroke."

"Mysterious?" Sarah said in surprise. Of all the people she
knew, Philip was the least mysterious—ah. The eye patch.
"Actually, I find him quite handsome."

"Oh, yes, that, too. But you must admit the eye patch
adds a certain quality of mystery."

There. It was out in the open, what had been unsaid all
night. Sarah wondered how many people had been discus-

sing the old rumors. "I think it makes him quite dashing. And now, Your Grace, gentlemen, if you'll excuse me, I think my husband wishes to speak with me." She smiled at their protests, but she was implacable. Philip, rather than having signaled to her, appeared to be quite taken with a young woman who was hanging on his arm and gazing at him adoringly. His former mistress? Perhaps not. Whoever she was, though, Sarah intended to put an end to it.

"Are you enjoying yourself?" Sarah purred, slipping her arm through Philip's.

"Sarah!" There was a distinct note of relief in Philip's voice. "Lady Bevin was just telling me about her life here."

"Was she?" Sarah smiled frankly at the girl, who, in contrast to the Duchess of Rochester's measuring look, didn't even glance at her.

"La, yes, living in Town is such fun!" Lady Bevin's dark curls danced about her face. "Bevin would have it we needs must go to his estate, but I convinced him to stay for the Little Season. And I'm so glad I did, else I might never have met you." And with that, she batted her eyelashes. Sarah didn't dare look at Philip for fear she'd burst out laughing.

"How kind of you to say so, Lady Bevin," she said, smiling, and Lady Bevin looked at her at last. She was very young, Sarah noted, and somewhat silly. It would do Philip good to receive such attention, so long as it didn't go to his head. "Philip, I believe Rebecca wishes to speak to us. You will excuse us, ma'am, won't you?"

Lady Bevin's hand slipped slowly from Philip's arm. "La, of course! Will you be at the opera tomorrow evening, Lord Pembroke?"

"I don't know. Come, Sarah, I believe I see Rebecca over there. Lady Bevin, a pleasure."

Lady Bevin dimpled. "Oh, the pleasure was all mine, sir," she said, and at last Sarah and Philip turned away.

"I can't turn my back on you for one moment without the ladies crowding around," Sarah teased, as they made their slow progress across the room.

"And what about you?"

182

"Me?"

"Yes, you. Standing there with all your court about you."

"My court?" Sarah laughed. "Heavens, that's hardly what it was! But it seems," she said, sounding mildly surprised, "that I am a success."

"So am I. I had more ladies tonight tell me how romantic my eye patch was. Once or twice I wanted to take it off."

"Oh, Philip." Sarah turned towards him, laughing. "We're a pair, you and I."

"Quite. Please don't turn into a fashionable lady on me, Sarah."

"Very well, so long as you don't turn into a dashing, mysterious man about town."

"Hardly likely."

Sarah glanced up at him, and again her heart swelled with love. She had known this would happen, once Philip got into company again. The rumors seemed only to add spice to his reputation. "Let's go home."

"I thought Rebecca wanted to see us."

"No, I made that up."

"Sarah. You lied?"

Sarah peeped at him over her fan. "Alas, sir, I must admit it. I lied to protect you from Lady Bevin."

Philip laughed, drawing the attention of those standing nearby. "Minx." His gaze swept the room; the crowd had thinned considerably and he doubted they'd be missed. And Sarah, in this playful mood, was delightful. "Very well." He looked down at her, and the warmth of his gaze made her color. "Let us find Rebecca and make our farewells, and then let's go home. And to bed," he whispered in her ear.

"Philip!" Sarah protested, but she was smiling.

Sarah and Philip were, indeed, a success. On her at-home days, the crimson drawing room on South Audley St. was filled with acquaintances and Sarah's admirers. She was still somewhat bemused by it all. Secure though she was now in her own attractiveness, she knew she was no match for the seductive charms of someone like the Duchess of Rochester or the bright youth of Viscountess Bevin. Whatever the reason, people kept calling, and the invitations poured in.

"We're becoming quite civilized," Sarah chatted happily one day to Richard as she poured him tea. Though it was not her normal at-home day, family was welcome anytime. "Goodness, the hours we're keeping! We're hardly ever home at night. We're either at someone's rout or at the opera—I do love it, don't you?—and we never get in early. So of course we're sleeping terribly late in the morning. Philip says he'll never be able to adjust to farmer's hours again."

Richard sipped at his tea. "Where is Philip? I expected to see him here."

"He's gone off with Sir Edward Gregory to inspect some hospital. They served together in the Peninsula."

"Ah, yes. Our glorious defeat and retreat from Corunna."

"Hardly Philip's fault," Sarah shot back, looking at Richard with some surprise. "I believe they also served at Talavera, and you can't deny that was a famous victory."

"I'm not saying it wasn't, cousin. Just that Philip never did strike me as a soldier."

"You never wished to go to war?"

"Hardly. There are other things I'd rather do." He went quickly on, at the way Sarah looked at him. "I'm the last of my family, Sarah, and at the time my mother was alive. I couldn't leave her."

"No. No, of course not," Sarah murmured, sipping at her tea. The earlier good humor of the visit had slipped away, and she wondered how to retrieve it.

"In any event, he's gone and left you alone again."

Sarah set her cup down hard on the piecrust table. "You talk as if he's constantly deserting me!"

"No such thing, cousin! I simply hate to see you left alone, when there is so much London offers."

"Actually, I'm rather glad to have a quiet day."

"If you say so."

"I do say so. Honestly, Richard, if you have come here with the idea of vexing me, you are succeeding admirably!"

"I am sorry, Sarah." Richard laid his hand on hers, and his smile was winning. "I hate to see him making the same mistakes with you as he did with Anne."

Sarah raised her cup to hide her face. "If he treated Anne as he treats me, then she had nothing to complain of."

"Yes."

"For heaven's sake, Richard, you are driving me to distraction! If you've something to say, say it."

"I would not have you hurt, Sarah." At her gesture of irritation, he set his cup down and took hers from her fingers, grasping her hands. "I've something unpleasant to tell you."

"Oh?" Sarah didn't look at him. At the moment all she could think of was that his fingers were cold and not nearly so well-shaped as Philip's.

"Yes. I'm afraid I've heard from Philip's mistress."

Sarah didn't raise her head. "Former mistress."

"Yes, of course," he said soothingly. "Forgive me, Sarah, but she asked me to talk to Philip for her."

"And are you?" she asked, her voice seeming to her to come from a great distance. *My, how civilized we are about this.*

"No, of course not. Or I wouldn't in the ordinary way. The thing is, the woman's causing trouble."

Sarah looked up. "How so?"

"Sarah." Richard's eyes were serious. "She claims she has proof that Philip killed Anne."

"What?" She clutched at his hand, and it was thus that Philip, striding into the room, found them.

her, Gently, Richard said, "I think it would be a good idea to understand each other a little better."

him face to face. "Why is it so urgent, and—"

Philip wanted everything clear. Philip inhaled deeply, harsh lines etched about his mouth. He finally—

Chapter Fifteen

Philip paused for just a moment and then strolled in. "Good afternoon, Richard. Is aught amiss?"

"Philip!" Sarah jumped up, pasting a smile on her face. "We didn't expect you so early."

"No doubt." There was an odd note in his voice. "I thought I'd spend some time with my wife."

"Nonsense, old man, you two are together constantly." Richard stood at ease, and Sarah glanced from him to Philip, puzzled by the tension emanating from them. "Not the fashion to live in each other's pocket, you know."

"But then, I've never been fashionable, have I?"

"By what I hear lately, you're all the rage. I understand the ladies find your eye patch mysterious."

Philip waved a hand in dismissal. "That's foolishness. Don't let us keep you, Richard, if you've things to do."

"Philip!" Sarah remonstrated.

"I do believe I'm being asked to leave," Richard said in a conversational tone. "Very well, cousin. Will I see you at the Stantons' do tonight?"

"Perhaps. Good day, Richard."

"Good day, cousin." Richard inclined his head, and at last was gone.

"Philip, really, that was terribly rude of you," Sarah said, sitting down again and smoothing down her skirts as if they were ruffled feathers.

"He didn't mind." Philip slouched in a chair across

from her. "Is something wrong, Sarah?"

"Wrong?" Sarah concentrated on pouring a cup of tea for him, her head bent. "Why no, of course not."

His wife wasn't a very good liar, Philip reflected. She was much too honest, too open. "Do you like Richard?"

"Like him? Of course. He is your cousin."

"Of course." Philip sipped his tea.

"Tell me about your day, Philip. Where did you go?"

"To London Hospital. Tell me, Sarah, do you think my eye patch is mysterious?"

"No, of course not, silly!" Sarah's smile quickly faded. "Philip, does it bother you that people say that? I thought you found it amusing."

"At first, but it does grow tiresome."

"If you must know," Sarah bent her head, "Richard was telling me he'd heard the rumors again."

"Ah, I see." But what was it Richard had really been saying? Something was very wrong. Dear God, was he losing Sarah as he had once lost Anne?

Abruptly he rose, setting his nearly full cup on the table. "I've things to do in my workroom. You'll excuse me?"

"Of course," Sarah said. He was closing her out again, and she didn't know why. Things had been so good between them that she had almost forgotten the bewildering way he had held her at a distance when first they were married. Oh, dear, and of all times! If he'd been his usual self, perhaps she wouldn't have hidden the news Richard had brought. Indeed, her first impulse had been to confide in him as she did with everything else. Except—what if the rumors were true?

"They're not!" she cried, jumping up and then falling back onto the sofa, her face in her hands. Oh, he couldn't have, he didn't have it in him to do such a horrible thing. But if he had . . . if he had, she was living with a murderer, and she didn't care. No matter what he might have done in the past, she loved him. She loved him, God help her, and because she did, she would have to protect him from this latest threat. Rumors, unsubstantiated and vague, were one thing. Proof was something else altogether. She wouldn't let him be hurt by it. She was going to have to do something about it.

Sarah nodded her head, feeling just a little better as her determination flooded back. As soon as she could, she would meet with Richard, and they would devise some strategy to outwit that woman. In the meantime, she had no intention of letting Philip withdraw from her.

He was sitting hunched at a table in the attic room he had claimed as his workroom, his hands idle, though a variety of materials were scattered in front of him. "Hello," Sarah said, putting her arms around his neck from behind and kissing his ear.

Philip started. "Sarah. I'm very busy."

"Oh, what a whisker. You're not doing a thing." Her voice and face were cheerful as she sat across the table from him, hooking her feet on the rungs of the high stool. "Philip, what is it? Was the hospital so very bad?"

"I don't want to talk about it," he said sharply, and Sarah drew back. "Bah. I'm sorry. But I really don't want to talk about it yet. What I saw was upsetting."

"I understand. But I'll listen when you're ready."

"I know you will." He toyed with a metal fitting of indeterminate origin. "Sarah, do you like Richard?"

"I've already told you I do, Philip."

"Yes, Sarah, but I mean, if I were to set you free—"

"Don't be ridiculous!" Sarah stared at him. "That's as bad as if I asked you if you had a mistress."

"Of course I don't have a mistress!"

"Well, I'm not in love with Richard."

A pause. "You're not?"

"No."

"He is a handsome devil."

"Yes, but you're much more mysterious," she said, and at last he smiled, the slow, warm smile she liked so much. "Shall we go to the Stantons' do, do you think?"

Philip was leaning over the table, his lips very close to hers. "Bugger the Stantons' do."

"Philip!" Sarah protested, but she was laughing as his

188

arms came around her and their lips met at last. It would be all right. She would find out what the so-called proof was the woman had and destroy it. And then everything would be all right. It would have to be.

They did, indeed, attend the Stantons' rout that evening, a little later than they had planned, with Sarah's color higher than usual. Negotiating the crowded stairs with some trouble, they stopped in the doorway to the drawing room. Lady Stanton had not been so selective in her guest list as had Rebecca, and the room was so crowded people could hardly move.

"I'll need both hands to get us through this," Philip commented.

Sarah clung to his arm. "That shouldn't give you any problem. I've never known anyone ambidextrous before."

"There are times it comes in handy," he said, looking at her so warmly that she flushed.

"If we weren't in company, I might slap you for that."

Philip leaned close to speak in her ear. "You look so beautiful tonight that if we weren't in company, I might—"

"Philip!"

"But, alas, we have our duties, my dear, you to your court and I to all the ladies who think me mysterious."

"What nonsense you speak," Sarah said, but she was smiling. "Oh, very well. Into the fray!"

It wasn't long before they were separated; it took even less time for the gentlemen whom Philip called her court to find her. There was nothing shy or restrained about Sarah tonight. She didn't flaunt herself, but she had a confidence that had before been lacking, making the men give her more admiring glances than usual. Sarah had been proclaimed an original. It was, she understood, the crowning compliment, and it puzzled her. She was only being herself.

Tonight she was wearing her wedding gown, though it was much changed. After her initial success with fashionable clothes, she had decided to have the gown altered with spec-

189

tacular results. Now boasting a low round neckline and short sleeves, with gold braid trimming the bodice and hem, the golden gown draped fluidly about her and shimmered when she moved. Topazes were about her neck and at her ears, and her hair was dressed upon her head in a coronet of braids with a slender fillet of gold resting upon her brow. She felt self-assured, almost queenly, and for the moment it seemed nothing could go wrong.

Lord Markham, one of her admirers, touched her on the shoulder. "Excuse me, Lady Pembroke, but I'd like to introduce you to an acquaintance of mine," he said.

"Of course," Sarah said, and turned to see Mr. Ramsay, her former employer.

She drew back, but it was too late. Her hand was already extended and Mr. Ramsay had taken it. "Charmed," he murmured as the introductions were made, his eyes admiring and puzzled.

"A pleasure, sir," Sarah said, withdrawing her hand as quickly as possible and fighting an insane desire to giggle. He didn't recognize her! He hadn't seen past her title. Mrs. Ramsay, however, was likely to be sharper of eye. "I don't believe we've met before."

"No, I am certain I'd remember it," he said, which made Sarah's desire to laugh even stronger. Surely he remembered assaulting her on the nursery stairs! "How could I ever forget meeting someone like you."

"Indeed, sir?"

"Harold," said a piercing voice, cutting through the conversation. Mrs. Ramsay, tightly corseted into a gown of brown silk with a great deal of gold lace trimming its formidable bodice, bustled up and took her husband's arm. "I have been looking all over for you, and—Miss Chadwick?" She stared. "What in the world are you doing here?"

"My dear, this is Lady Pembroke," Mr. Ramsay protested.

"Lady, my foot! Don't you recognize her, Harold? She was our governess, the one we had to let go."

Sarah couldn't help it. The giggle she'd been suppressing burst out. "Oh, dear. Mrs. Ramsay—"

"I say," said Lord Markham, coming to stand by Sarah's side, "did you really employ Lady Pembroke?"

"Oh, famous!" said another of Sarah's admirers. "She's told us the most wonderful stories about being a governess!"

Again, Sarah couldn't stop herself. She laughed, a golden peal of sound. "Mrs. Ramsay," she choked. "Oh, dear, I—"

"I fail to see anything amusing in this." Mrs. Ramsay stood ramrod straight. "To be insinuating yourself into proper society when you—"

"I say. Not the way to speak to a peeress, you know," Markham said.

"Has she bamboozled you all? Why, if you only knew!"

"What is so very amusing?" a voice said at Sarah's side, and a hand grasped her elbow.

"Oh, Philip!" she gasped, relief mingling with her mirth. "It really is the most amazing coincidence. Oh, dear, forgive me, but I'm quite undone by this. You see, this is Mr. and Mrs. Ramsay, my former employers. My husband, sir, ma'am. Lord Pembroke."

Philip looked at them, especially Mr. Ramsay, long and hard, before speaking. "The Ramsays? The ones you told me about, my dear?"

Mr. Ramsay took an involuntary step back at Philip's cold glare. "Quite a coincidence, what?" he said weakly.

"Quite. My wife has told me all about you, sir. She has happy memories of her employment with you. I trust they'll remain that way."

"Oh, quite, quite. Come along, Bella, we've stopped here too long as it is if we wish to make the opera in time."

"But, Harold, we're not going to the opera," Mrs. Ramsay protested, her voice high and querulous as Mr. Ramsay pulled her away, their rout complete. "Why are they all laughing? Harold, that wasn't funny!"

"Poor Harold," Markham commented into the laughter following the encounter, a twist to his lips. "My apologies, Lady Pembroke. My sister asked me to introduce them around. Mrs. Ramsay is an old school friend, I believe." He frowned. "I thought Catherine had better taste in friends."

"Hard to believe the Stantons invited 'em," someone else said. "Lady Pembroke, you're all right?"

Sarah's eyes were brimming with laughter as she looked up at Philip. "Yes, quite all right. But I think I could use some air."

"Quite." The corners of Philip's mouth twitched. "If you'll excuse us, gentlemen."

"Oh, dear," Sarah said again, as they leisurely made their way across the crowded room. "Of all people to meet."

"Shall I punch him in the nose for you?"

"Philip! Brawling in a drawing room? How scandalous!" Her eyes twinkled. "No, this was enough. I don't think Mrs. Ramsay will ever recover."

"I sincerely hope not. If he ever bothers you again . . ."

"I doubt he will." Her gaze softened as she looked up at him. She couldn't be wrong about him. She couldn't. "Thank you for coming to my rescue. Again."

"It was my pleasure, my dear." He lifted her hand to his mouth, and for one breathless moment, her heart stopped.

"Such public displays of attention are bad *ton*," a voice drawled, and they both looked up to see Richard.

"I never aspired to be a part of the *ton*," Philip said.

"No, but think of your wife's reputation, cousin. After that scene—"

"I believe I can protect her, cousin," Philip said, an edge to his voice.

"Of course you can. I simply feared that since it's been so long since you've been in company you may have forgotten how to go on."

"Ah, but I'm no fool. Sarah? Is aught wrong?"

"Hm? No." Sarah had been shifting from foot to foot, uneasily listening to the exchange between the two men. Their friendship seemed to have deteriorated since the Pembrokes' arrival in London. "But I think I'd like to sit for a while."

Richard took her free arm. "There must be a chair somewhere for you, cousin. Let me escort you."

"Thank you, Richard, but—"

"It would be my pleasure. You must be upset after what

happened. If you do not object, cousin?"

"Object? Why should I object?"

Sarah looked up at him. "Philip—"

"Go ahead." He released her arm, smiling a bit. "Daresay I'm rather dull company, after your court. Besides," he added, over her protest, "I'd like to talk to Edward Gregory. So if you'll excuse me, Sarah, Richard." Bowing, he turned and left.

"There he goes, leaving you for someone else again," Richard commented, and Sarah rounded on him.

"I won't have you calling him down! Particularly since you arranged this."

Richard had the grace to look sheepish as he took her arm and began leading her across the room. "My apologies, Sarah. But he does seem to leave you alone a lot."

"You yourself pointed out that it's unfashionable for us to be together so much."

"Yes, but—"

"Philip does not have a mistress."

"Did I say he did?"

They had reached a window embrasure where, to Sarah's relief, a gilt and white side chair stood empty. She sank gracefully onto it, opening her fan with a snap and plying it vigorously. "You certainly implied it."

"No, no, cousin, that's all in the past. At least I believe it is." Sarah looked up swiftly at that. "But I must talk to you."

"About what?"

"I've heard from the woman."

"Who is she?"

"That is of no moment." His voice lowered. "The trouble is, she does indeed have proof."

Sarah's hands went cold inside her gloves. "What kind of proof?"

"Letters Philip wrote to her."

"Philip wouldn't be so stupid!"

"A man in love, Sarah."

The words stabbed her to her heart though she didn't show it. "We must get them back."

"I agree. She's willing to part with them. For a fee."

"How much?"

"Five thousand pounds."

Her breath drew in sharply. Good heavens. A fortune, but worth it, for Philip's safety. "I can raise it."

"You can?"

"Yes. I've a substantial portion of my own, you see."

"That vastly relieves my mind, cousin."

"Does it?" Sarah's tone was ironic. "I'll be glad to have this whole business done with."

"I'm sure you will. If you give me the money, I'll deal with the woman."

"No," she said, in so stern a voice that Richard looked startled. "I'll deal with her myself."

"Sarah, you don't understand people like this."

"You forget, my father was in trade. I watched him do business often. No. I will deal with the woman, and she will get nothing."

"Sarah, think of the damage that could be done."

"Where does she live?"

Richard looked at her and then shook his head. "Very well. We'll go together. But I think this is a mistake."

Sarah rose. "If it is, it's mine, not yours."

"Is there a problem?" Philip asked, close at Sarah's elbow, and she turned quickly.

"Oh, no, none at all," she said brightly, and Philip's eyes went to Richard.

"If you must know, cousin, we were discussing the Ramsays. Distasteful people, of course, but they could damage Sarah's reputation," he said.

"Oh, nonsense! Everyone knows I was a governess, and no one seems to mind."

"That is because you are beautiful." His look was admiring, causing Philip to take her arm.

" 'Tis late. Shall we go?"

Sarah glanced up at him. Something in his face told her it would be foolhardy to refuse. "I'm ready," she agreed.

"Then let us make our farewells to our hosts. Richard."

"Cousin." Richard bowed his head in acknowledgment and watched them walk away through the crowd. A job well done. After tonight, the seeds of dissension he had been careful to sow between them would begin to grow. Each suspected the other, that much was obvious. Matters were at last beginning to work out for him. He very much wanted to be the marquess.

It hadn't bothered him at first that it was only because of an accident of birth that his father hadn't had the title. He had even genuinely liked Philip as they grew up together. After all, Philip, as the second son, wouldn't inherit. It wasn't until Philip's brother had died, followed soon after by his father, that the idea had come to Richard. Wouldn't it be providential if something were to happen to Philip, too? An accident, of course, and if he helped providence along, likely no one would know. It was chancy, risky, but he'd always been something of a gambler, which was one reason he was having trouble with debts just now. He thought he ran a good chance of success. So long as Sarah didn't conceive an heir. If she did, he'd have to think of something else. He'd come too far to stop now. Someday very soon, Richard gloated, *he* would be the Marquess of Pembroke.

"What were you and Richard talking about?"

"Hmm?" In the gloom, Sarah looked across the carriage toward her husband. There was a constraint between them that hadn't been there earlier, and it wasn't just because of what she had learned this evening, heavy though it lay on her mind. Whatever was the matter with Philip? "Ah, well," she said. "If you must know, we were discussing the rumors."

"The rumors," Philip said sharply. "What rumors?"

"Richard fears the rumors about you are starting up again." That was, at least, mostly true, and it gave conviction to her voice.

"I see. And that was all?"

"Yes."

"I can tell when you're lying, Sarah."

"I'm not lying!" she protested. "Oh, Philip, don't you see? I don't want you hurt."

Philip peered at her through the darkness. Her face was illuminated occasionally by the harsh glow of a passing gas street lamp. He held out his arms. "Come here."

Sarah hesitated for just a moment and then went to him. How good it felt to be held by him like this, how solid, how real. Someone she could lean on after the years of having to depend on herself. Someone she badly needed to protect. "Philip," she murmured, reaching up and feathering kisses on his neck, his jaw, his ear. Philip reacted quickly, tightening his hold on her, bending her backward and bringing his mouth down on hers in a hard, urgent kiss. Her fingers twined in his hair, roved over his shoulders; his found their way past her black velvet evening cloak and the braided neckline of her gown. Sarah gasped with the sensations only he could evoke within her and clutched him tighter about the neck. He was innocent. He had to be. How could such a man have plotted the death of his wife, let alone such a heinous one?

"Sarah." Philip bent his head, and she cradled it against her bosom. "I can't take you here in a carriage like a—"

"Hush. We're nearly home."

"Thank God." He kissed her swollen lips once more and then straightened, adjusting her cloak about her and smoothing down her hair. "What would I do without you?"

"You're not going to lose me."

They were the very models of rectitude as they walked into their house, though Sarah's cheeks were flushed and Philip's eye glittered. But in their bedroom, they fell on each other, heedless of all else. He was losing her, he thought, kissing the slender column of her throat. Just as he had lost Anne, so might he lose Sarah.

She might lose him, Sarah thought, giving herself up to his wild kisses and caresses, and she couldn't bear it. The golden gown fell unheeded to the floor to be followed by petticoat, chemise, a man's shirt. Sarah clung desperately to her husband as he bore her backwards onto their bed, kissing her, his hands searching out all the secret places that made her moan with delight. *I love you,* she thought at the moment of their joining. If she could not say the words aloud, at least she could think them. *I love you.*

"I love you," she murmured into his shoulder sometime later, and Philip stiffened.

"Sarah?" he whispered. Her only answer was a soft sigh. His wife had fallen asleep after that amazing announcement, and Philip was at a loss as to how to react. Her words seemed to reverberate in the darkness in his own head. She loved him. Good God.

Philip lay very still, no longer the least bit sleepy. What in God's name did he do now?

A note came from Richard the following morning telling Sarah the details of their meeting with Philip's former mistress. Very carefully she folded it into precise creases, noting absently that Richard's handwriting was similar to Philip's, though more legible. She was to go into the City, of all places, and meet him at a tavern there. They would then go to the woman and receive, in exchange for a purseful of money, the letters that incriminated Philip in a terrible crime. Once hers, they would be burned, and so no longer present a threat. And then she and Philip could go on as before. She hoped.

"What is that?" Philip asked, walking into the morning room, and Sarah hastily shoved the note into a pocket.

"Nothing. A note from Madame Celeste. I've some gowns that need to be fitted."

"I see." Philip nodded and turned away. After last night, after what she planned to do for him, his coldness was more than she could bear.

"Philip," she called, and he turned. Standing erect in the doorway, he looked forbidding, mysterious, but she had learned long ago to see past that facade. "What are your plans for the day?"

"I expect I'll visit the soldiers in hospital."

"You never have told me about that."

"Would you be interested?"

"Of course I would be! Philip, what's wrong?"

"Nothing."

"You're as bad a liar as I am! Is it the rumors?"

Philip stared at her for a long moment. "No, madam, it is not."

"Then, what? After last night—"

Last night, and the words she had said to him, the words that had sent his usually orderly mind into utter chaos. The words he could not bear to hear were they false. The words he could not bring himself to say, not yet. "We are married," he said crisply.

"Is that all it meant to you? Oh, Philip."

"When I see you with other men, yes. You have turned into a most fashionable wife, Sarah."

"I—!" She stared at him. "I'm not the one with women flocking about me, talking about how mysterious I am and how they would like to know the real man!"

"You and your court," he flung out. "Damn all of them, sniffing around your skirts, all of them healthy and whole . . ."

"Oh, Philip, surely you don't think your eye makes a difference?"

"Ahem." Cooper stood in the doorway, his face impassive but his eyes avid. "The barouche is ready, sir."

"Thank you, I'll walk," Philip snapped, and turned on his heel.

"Philip," Sarah called, and then fell back against her chair, her hand pressed against her stomach.

"My lady? Are you well?" Cooper asked.

"Yes." Sarah looked up. "Cooper."

"Yes, my lady?"

"Tell the coachman to wait for me. I'll take the barouche."

Cooper bowed. "Very good, my lady."

Sarah rose, clinging briefly to the back of the chair against another spell of nausea and dizziness. In a moment her vision cleared, and she straightened. She was all right now, if a bit weak, and her zona, the long band of cloth she used to support her breasts even under her flimsiest gown, felt binding and tight today. She had planned to hire a hackney to take her to her assignation, but, considering how she was feeling, she would rather ride in comfort in the barouche. What in the world had gotten into Philip now, when she needed him most?

Well. She was not going to sit about like some milk and water miss bewailing the situation. Pulling on her gloves, she sailed out through the door, her head held high. She had a mission of the highest importance to accomplish and, when she had, Philip would be safe.

Sarah paid little attention to the passing scenery, concentrating instead on the meeting to come. She was familiar with the City, the area of London where the business of England was carried out. A strange place for such a meeting. Strange, but appropriate, for what was this but a business transaction? Of course she hadn't five thousand pounds with her; she wasn't that foolish. She had seen her father transact business enough to know that people often were satisfied with less than they asked. One thing she was determined of, though: when she left the meeting, she would have those letters in her possession.

The carriage turned a corner, swaying, and started slowly downhill. Suddenly, it lurched, sending Sarah jouncing against the wall. "Goodness!" she exclaimed, hearing the coachman yell, and fell helplessly against the opposite wall as the barouche lurched again, picking up speed. She grabbed at the strap to pull herself up, in time to see the coachman tumble by her window. She went cold. Something was wrong. Holding onto the strap, she leaned out the window and gasped at what she saw. The team of horses was gone. Somehow the traces that linked it to the carriage had let go, on a sharply sloping street. "Oh, dear God!" she exclaimed, as the barouche rolled on, rocking back and forth as it gained speed. She was alone and helpless in a runaway carriage.

Fear paralyzed her for a moment. Dear God, what was

she to do? Ahead, down the bottom of the hill, was a busy intersection. If the carriage plunged into that, she would be killed for certain. There was only one other alternative.

Grabbing the strap, she pulled herself to her feet, bracing herself against the rocking of the runaway carriage. The door opened outward with some difficulty, and there, for a moment, she paused. Then, taking a deep breath, she did the only thing she could do. She jumped out, and the pavement rushed up to meet her.

Chapter Sixteen

Philip strode angrily along South Audley Street, the fierceness of his expression combining with the eye patch to scare many a passerby. He never had been one to hold onto a grudge, but this situation was different. Sarah was the best thing that had ever happened to him, and she was drifting away. God help him, he didn't want to lose her, but he wasn't certain how to hold onto her.

So lost was he in his thoughts that he was nearly upon a party of fashionably dressed people descending the stairs of a house in Grosvenor Square before he was aware of them. Only the chatter of voices made him swerve in time to avoid a collision with the first person in the group, a tall young man just setting his curly brimmed beaver hat onto dark blond hair. Philip looked up, about to murmur an apology. The words died as he met the cold, hostile eyes of his former brother-in-law, Charles Grantham.

One of the ladies gasped; the other began to chatter but then stopped. Time seemed to stretch out as the two men stared at each other, the first time they had come face-to-face in many a long year. The silence grew, lengthened, as well as the tension until Philip reached up to tip his hat. Anne was gone. The past was past, as Sarah had helped him to see. It was time to go on with his life.

He extended his hand, and without a word, Grantham turned sharply away, gesturing toward a carriage which stood nearby. The remaining members of the party looked at Philip quickly, surreptitiously, as they scurried inside: Elizabeth,

Grantham's wife; a man he recognized vaguely as a Grantham relation; a woman he had once flirted with. Friends, all of them, or they had been. The taste of anger grew more bitter as he watched the carriage drive away, his hands clenched. It wasn't the first time he'd been given the cut direct, but that made it no easier. Not at all.

The carriage had driven away with only its dust left behind before Philip moved. That part of his life was over though he had never really forgotten it. It hurt to be cut by old friends and acquaintances, to know that the rumors still likely circulated about him. But, he reminded himself again as he walked on, all that was past. He had a new life now with new friends, and it was all due to Sarah. What would he do if he lost her?

By the time he reached London Hospital, his anger had cooled. In its place was a new determination. Things had changed. He had changed. No longer did he need to stay hidden away; because of his wife, he had found the strength and courage to go on with his life. Life had been simpler, and infinitely duller, before Sarah's arrival.

His nose wrinkled involuntarily as he stepped into the hospital and the familiar odors of blood, suffering, and, inevitably, death, reached out to meet him. Lord, he hated this place, and yet coming here had become almost a compulsion. A charity hospital, this was where those soldiers came who could not afford better care; those who could received nursing at home as he had after the retreat from Corunna. Men Philip had known in the army, men he had fought with, were here recuperating from wounds or, in too many cases, simply dying. And there, but for the grace of God, went him. Had he not come home on leave when he had, he would not have lost his eye. He might, however, have received a worse injury in battle, losing an arm or a leg, or even, God forbid, his life. He had spent three years feeling sorry for himself because of his disfigurement. Now, seeing it in comparison with more serious injuries, he felt merely ashamed. He had been very lucky.

Philip stopped by the bed of Lt. Peter Taylor, who had once served under him when he had commanded his own regiment. Lieutenant Taylor was one of the lucky ones; he was expected to live, if hospital conditions didn't kill him. Because of the high tax on glass, many of the windows had been bricked over. There was thus little air or light, something Philip found essential. Nor was there any standard of cleanliness. Dirty straw littered the floors, and the sheets were obviously changed rarely. The nursing was rough and ready, provided by low, slatternly women who were frequently drunk and who often abused their charges. The surgeons were little better. That anyone survived his stay in this hell hole was a miracle.

It was that which kept him coming back, his fascination and horror at the conditions. For those men he knew, and some he didn't, he had been able to make things better, paying for clean bedding and decent food, the least they deserved. It was not, however, enough. Until every man here enjoyed the same conditions, Philip would not rest. He could no longer do much on an individual basis. Reform was needed at the administrative level. The army was being remarkably uncooperative with him in trying to better conditions, but that only made him more stubborn. Gone were the days of idly tinkering in his workroom, passing time. Philip had a new purpose in life.

"My lord," a voice said as Philip came out from a ward into the corridor and he looked up to see Geordie bearing down on him. "Thought I'd find ye here."

"Is aught amiss, Geordie?" Philip said, tucking his stick under his arm.

"Aye, you might say so. Lady Pembroke's been in an accident."

Philip went very still and then strode down the corridor. "Is she hurt?"

"Aye, sir, but I don't know how bad. The doctor was with her when I left to find you."

"Damn." Philip marched on so fast that Geordie had to run to keep up with him, in spite of his longer legs. "What happened?"

"Something with the carriage sir. The traces let go or something and—"

"The carriage was a runaway?"

"Aye, sir."

"Good God."

"John Coachman's hurt, but I'd say he and the mistress are lucky to be alive." Geordie paused. "The barouche is a wreck, sir."

Philip pulled on his gloves as they stepped outside. "Hire a hackney," he commanded, sounding much more the man he had been before his accident, though he didn't realize it, and stood tapping his walking stick impatiently while he waited. Sarah, hurt. Good God. What would he do without her?

"You're remarkably lucky, young lady," the doctor commented, closing his bag. "Only a few bruises and that ankle. Mind you stay off it, now."

"Yes, doctor," Sarah said meekly. Her left ankle, sprained and swollen, was propped up on a pillow. She *had* been lucky. Someone must have been watching out for her.

"Remarkably stupid thing to do, jumping from a moving carriage in your condition."

Sarah's hand went reassuringly to her stomach. "It was either that or let myself be killed." She shuddered at the memory of the noise when the Pembroke barouche had crashed into the busy intersection, colliding with a large dray and several other carriages. It was nothing more than splinters now. "Doctor, you won't tell my husband?"

The old man looked up at her over his pince-nez. "And why won't I? He has a right to know."

"No, I mean about the baby. You see, I haven't had a chance to tell him yet, and he'll only worry."

"Hmph. Well, daresay you know him better than I do. But, young lady, you'd best tell him soon."

"Yes, doctor," Sarah murmured, lying back in bed and feeling thoroughly chastised as she watched him go. Now how, she wondered, was she going to explain this to Philip?

At that moment he came in, and though to anyone else he might have looked his usual impassive self, Sarah read his true feelings in his eye. "You're all right. Thank God," he said, bending to kiss her hand.

"Yes, I was lucky." She smoothed his hair. "How is John Coachman?"

Philip grimaced as he straightened. "Not good. He took a bad knock on the head, and his arm's broken."

"Oh, poor man!"

"Sarah, have you any idea what happened? John Coachman's in no condition to tell me."

"No, none. I felt a jolt, and I saw him fall, and that was when I realized the carriage was a runaway. So I jumped."

Philip's eye closed briefly. "Thank God you weren't hurt worse."

"Yes. But, Philip, how could it have happened?"

"I've no idea, but I intend to find out." His thumb stroked over her hand. "Sarah, what were you doing there?"

"Shopping," she said brightly.

"In the City?"

"Yes, well, I'd heard of a draper's where one can get the most fabulous fabrics at such bargains, and since we're thinking of redecorating Havenwood . . ."

"I see. Well." He pressed his lips against her hand and rose. "I should let you rest."

"Yes, I am rather tired. Philip," she called as he reached the door, and he turned. "Are you angry about something?"

"What would I have to be angry about, my dear?" he said, and went out, closing the door behind him.

She had lied again. Shopping, indeed! What did she take him for? Why had she been where she was, and why had she lied about it? Philip had the sickening feeling he knew. She was seeing someone else.

"My lord?" Geordie said, as Philip descended to the front hall.

"Yes, Geordie?"

"Come to the stables, sir. Somethin' I want to show ye."

"Oh?" Philip walked with him. "What is it, Geordie?"

"Rather have ye see it yeself, sir."

In the stables, a team of sweating, stomping horses stood, still in harness. Behind them trailed the reins and the traces that attached the team to the coach. "Found them over by St. Paul's," Geordie said. "Lucky they weren't stolen."

"Any idea how the traces came loose?"

"Look for yeself, sir."

Philip carefully edged around the nervous team and picked up one of the leather thongs. He ran his finger over the ends and froze. "It's been cut."

"Aye, sir, but not all the way through. Just so it would let go."

Philip rounded on the groom. "Wilkins, how could you allow the harness to go out in such condition?"

"It weren't me, sir," Wilkins protested. "That tack was in perfect shape when I harnessed the team."

"Well, something happened to it. Good God." He stared at the leather, clearly cut on one side, frayed on the other. "Who would want to hurt Sarah?"

"Not the mistress, sir," Geordie said, his voice unusually serious. "Ye were the one planning to use the barouche today."

"Good God. Are you saying this was meant for me?"

"Aye, sir." Geordie paused a moment to let that sink in. "Sir, I think it's time you faced facts. What happened at Thornhill and then the highwaymen's attack—"

"And the water near the printing press."

"Aye. Sir, looks to me like someone is trying to kill ye."

"Richard." Sarah, her face creased in concern, held out her hand as he crossed the sitting room to her. "Oh, I'm so glad you've come."

"I came as soon as I heard, but Philip wouldn't let me see you. Are you all right?" Richard asked, pulling a chair near and keeping her hand in his.

"Yes, I was lucky. I hurt my ankle, though, which is why you find me reclining on a chaise. Not, I assure you, my usual style."

"My brave Sarah." Richard brought her hand to his lips, and she looked at his head in surprise. "Does nothing ever overset you?"

"Very little. I fear I'm sadly lacking in sensibility."

"Sarah, Sarah." He shook his head, smiling, while Sarah wondered how she could free her hand from his grip. "How did it happen? Had your coachman been drinking?"

"John Coachman? Heavens, no, he's a devout Methodist! Somehow the team broke away, and when I realized the barouche was a runaway, I jumped."

A look of horror crossed Richard's face. "But I thought —"

"What?" Sarah asked, when he didn't go on.

"Nothing. What a terrible thing. Do you have any idea how it happened?"

"No, none. But, Richard." Her voice lowered as she glanced towards her dressing room where her maid was at work. "We missed the meeting."

"I know. When I realized you weren't coming I went to meet with her myself, but she was gone."

"Oh, no. Then she still has them. Oh, Richard, I fear she'll think I'm trying to cheat her and publish the letters abroad."

"Have no fear, Sarah." He patted her hand. "I've reached her since and told her what occurred to you."

"Oh, thank heavens!"

"But you're right, she is getting impatient. She wants her money soon."

She closed her eyes briefly. "What am I to do?"

"Entrust me with this, Sarah. You know I'd do anything for you."

"No. Oh, I realize how good you are to me, Richard, but I can't let you do this. It's something I must do myself."

"Sarah . . ."

"You won't change my mind on this."

Richard sat back, and Sarah quickly pulled her hand free. "Then at least let me come with you. Sarah, you've no idea what this woman's like. I could protect you from harm."

"You think she'd try to hurt me in some way?"

Richard shrugged. "Sarah, one never knows what a jealous woman will do."

"Jealous! Why should she be jealous if the affair is over?" Richard didn't answer. "Richard? It is over, isn't it?"

"Of course it is," he said, a little too hastily. "Don't bother yourself about it."

Sarah straightened. "Tell me the truth, Richard. I'm no green girl who will go all missish on you! Is my husband still seeing . . . that woman?"

Richard hesitated and then nodded. "I'm sorry, Sarah."

Sarah sat as if turned to stone, staring ahead, her hands still on her lap. Philip had another. Philip, who had told her she was beautiful, who made her feel beautiful. Lies, all lies, like that first betrayal, so many years ago, when she had learned that her betrothed wanted her for her money only. Far worse, though. Funny, then, that she didn't feel anything, only this curious emptiness and a sense that her world had just shattered into pieces. And funny that she, who never wept, was crying, great gulping sobs that she noted in a detached way were not the least ladylike and which came from deep within her.

"Oh, Sarah," Richard said, and put his arms around her.

The delicate glass beakers on Philip's worktable trembled melodically as Geordie stomped across the room. "Damn it, man, are ye going to sit there and do nothing?" he demanded.

Philip held a beaker up, checking the measure of its contents. "I am doing something, Geordie."

"Aye. Playing with foolish contraptions while someone is trying to kill ye."

"Geordie. Sit down." There was a note of command in Philip's voice, and Geordie sat across from him, looking discontented. "I understand your need for action, my friend. But, tell me, what can we do?"

"Find out who it is, sir."

"How?" Philip set down the beaker and carefully added a few drops from a vial into it. "Sarah hasn't complained, but I know her ankle is paining her. This should help."

"Sir—"

"I'm thinking about it, Geordie."

"Aye, and while ye're thinkin', this whole house might go up in flames!"

Philip looked up sharply at that, but his voice when he spoke was mild. "I don't think so. I intend to be very careful. I'm no fool, Geordie."

"No, sir."

He set down the glass rod he had been using to stir the mixture, his face grim. "Whoever it is has hurt Sarah. Do you think I'll take a chance of that happening again?"

"So ye'll just sit there and take it."

"Oh, no. Any word yet on the man in the stables?"

"No, sir. All we know is someone was in looking for work, and he likely did the damage."

"And it's probably all we'll ever know. I doubt it's one of the staff, Geordie," he went on, rising and crossing the room. "It's happened too many places—here, Havenwood, Thornhill—and staff is different at all those places. No, it has to be someone I know." From a shelf he took a small glass bottle; from a drawer, a cork. He set both down and stood there, bracing his hands on the table. "Damn it, Geordie who hates me that much?"

"Might not be a matter of hate, sir. Might be you have something that someone wants."

"Ha." Philip paced the room and turned abruptly. "What do I have that people envy, Geordie? This?" he said, pointing savagely to his eye patch.

"No, sir. Your title."

"Good God." Philip dropped onto his chair. "I never thought of that."

Geordie shook his head. That was the kind of man the master was, less concerned with things that others thought important. "Someone else has."

"Who?"

"Who is your heir, sir?"

"Richard?" Philip drew back in horror. "No, I'll not believe it of him. He and I are friends."

Geordie shrugged. "Believe it or not, sir. Who'd have reason?"

"Someone I harmed, perhaps. Grantham, maybe. I saw him today. Damn it, it can't be Richard."

"Who have ye harmed, sir, besides yeself?"

"Grantham thinks I killed his sister."

"Aye, and d'ye really think he'd wait three years for revenge?"

"I don't know. Damn." Philip paced across the room again, his hands shoved into his coat pockets. Not Richard, one of the few who had stood by him after Anne's death. To Philip that friendship meant much, almost like a comradeship forged in war, outweighing all other concerns of fortune and title. But then, Richard had never been in a position where friendship had been so important. More disturbingly, he seemed to pay much too

209

much attention to Sarah.

A desolate sense of betrayal swept over him. First Anne, with her still-unknown lover, and now Richard. He would believe there was something wrong with him to inspire such disloyalty, were there not others like his sister and Geordie. And Sarah. Thank God for Sarah, even if he suspected that she, too, was keeping something from him. If something happened to him, what would become of her?

"Very well, Geordie." He turned, and though his hands were still in his pockets, his shoulders were squared, giving him a new look of purpose. "There's some action we can take."

"Aye, sir, that's more like the major I used to know!" Geordie got to his feet. "What are ye thinkin', sir?"

"I'm thinkin', Geordie, that I'm tired of standing still and being a target. I think—yes, I think what we'll do is set a trap. And we'll catch whoever's doing this."

Sometime later Philip ran down the stairs, his heart lighter than it had been for days. Geordie had protested at first at the plan Philip had proposed, but in the end he had agreed. They had started, now. They were committed, and he felt surprisingly lighthearted. No more would he chafe at the inactivity of waiting for his enemy to make the move. He would seize the initiative and draw his enemy out of hiding.

He was actually smiling as he descended the last staircase and walked purposefully along the hall to his wife's sitting room. The prospect of doing battle again thrilled him in a way he had forgotten. For too long he had been a victim of life, and he now resented the walls he had put around himself. They had shut out the world, true, but they had also kept him prisoner. It was time to break free and make a new life with Sarah. The thought filled him with elation and a hope he hadn't felt in much too long.

He was, therefore, not at all prepared to enter Sarah's sitting room and see her in Richard's arms.

Chapter Seventeen

In a flash, Philip saw it all. Richard *and* Sarah. Of course. Though Sarah herself had been the victim of several of the incidents, that could have been intended to lull him into a false sense of security. Who would benefit most from his death? His wife, would be left a wealthy widow, no longer chained to a man who was scarred. And Richard, his heir, who had always shown Sarah a great deal of attention. Of course.

Though Philip had made no sound, Richard looked up. His eyes held an odd look, almost of triumph, but it disappeared so quickly Philip wanted to believe he had imagined it. "Philip," Richard said, not moving. "I was just comforting Sarah."

"So I see," Philip said dryly.

"Philip?" Sarah pulled away from Richard's arm, digging in her pocket for her handkerchief. "Oh, dear, I must look a sight. My nose always gets so red when I cry."

In spite of himself, Philip felt a smile threatening, and it made his tone gentler than he had intended. "What is amiss?"

Richard at last released Sarah and rose. "She is disturbed about the accident, cousin. I happened to be here and . . ." He shrugged.

"I see. Thank you, Richard. I'll carry on from here."

"Of course, cousin. By the bye." Richard paused in the doorway. "The cigar lighter you made for me isn't working. Shall I bring it by?"

"Yes, yes." Philip waved his hand in dismissal, and at last Richard left. "Sarah?"

Sarah blew her nose vigorously, and again Philip almost smiled. "Yes?"

"What is wrong?"

"It is as Richard told you." Sarah wadded the handkerchief into a ball, shoving it back into her pocket and not looking at him. "I was distressed about the accident."

"You can trust me, you know," he said, his voice tender. "Come, Sarah. What is wrong?"

"Nothing."

"Really. So you turn to him for comfort, rather than me."

Sarah looked up in surprise at the odd note in his voice. *Do you really care?* "He was here."

"Ah. And I wasn't, is that what you're saying?"

"No!" But it was true, nonetheless. *Did* he have a mistress? Part of her ached to ask him though she dreaded the answer. Of course he would deny it. Such a lie would hurt, but if he admitted it, the pain would be unbearable. "I'm not certain why it happened now, but I think a lady might be allowed her distress at such a thing."

"Oh, quite."

"Philip." She twisted on the chaise to look at him, though his back was to her. "What is wrong?"

"Where were you going the day of the accident?"

"I told you. Shopping."

"Ah, I see. Shopping."

"Philip—"

"Are you in love with Richard?"

"What!"

He turned, his face grim. "You heard me."

"Yes, but I can't believe you'd even think such a thing!" Sarah's cheeks were flushed, and her eyes met his squarely. "What a horrid thing to say!"

"Is it?"

"You know it is."

"Then why were you in his arms?"

"Instead of yours? You tell me, Philip. You're the one who's been avoiding me lately."

"I'm not going to let you go, Sarah. You're my wife."

"You're—" She stared at him. "You pigheaded, aggravating, infuriating man! Why don't you go play in your workroom?"

Oddly enough, that made Philip smile. "I think I will." To Sarah's astonishment, he had the gall to bend and kiss her on the cheek. "Until you calm down."

"Ooh!" The pillow she tossed after him missed him by several feet and landed in the hallway where she couldn't retrieve it. Damned arrogant, irritating man! And yet . . . Her temper cooled as quickly as it had flared. Good heavens, was he jealous? He had certainly sounded it, and that only confirmed her instincts. Philip, though he might not seem to, cared about her. Perhaps not as much as she did for him, but he would, she vowed. Someday, he would.

Philip grinned as he took the stairs two at a time to his workroom. She didn't love Richard! Sarah had told the truth about that. That only, though, he thought, stopping at the landing and frowning. There was something she was holding back from him. He didn't want to believe it of her, but she could very well be in league with Richard.

As soon as he had the thought, he dismissed it. Sarah would make an unlikely conspirator; she was too forthright, too honest. He'd as soon think such a thing of her as he once would have of Anne. And that brought back painful memories. He had been betrayed once before; he could be betrayed again, even by Sarah. But he wasn't going to allow it this time. If she thought he would let her go to another man, she would soon learn differently. He would not let her go. Sarah was his.

"How good it feels to be out and about again!" Sarah said, as she and Philip entered the grand ballroom at Montagu House. Autumn was rapidly passing and with it, the Little Season. Soon people would be returning to their country estates to celebrate Christmas. The ball held by Lord and Lady Montagu was, traditionally, one of the last and most glittering affairs, made more festive this year by the news of Napoleon's rout at Leipzig. The long war at last looked to be coming to an end.

For her return to public life, Sarah had chosen one of her favorite and more daring gowns. Of celestial blue watered silk, its bodice was almost scandalously brief, the blond lace at the neckline only drawing attention to her charms, rather than covering them. The silk itself had a tendency to cling as it flowed over her curves, falling nearly to the floor where the hem was trimmed with several flounces of the same blond lace and where white satin slippers with silver rosettes peeked out. She was wearing the Pembroke sapphires at her ears and, unusually, in her hair as well, having chosen to fasten the necklace to her coronet of braids, a most unique headdress. As she and Philip stepped into the ballroom, her hand, gloved in white kid, resting on his arm, she knew all eyes were turned toward her. A heady feeling, indeed, for the woman who just a few months ago had been plain Miss Chadwick. She only wished Philip would look at her in the same way.

The orchestra struck up a cotillion, and he turned to her as they joined a set. He looked so handsome, her heart ached with it. For the first time, she had convinced him to wear other then black, and he was almost as dazzling as she in a coat of dark blue superfine and white satin breeches. "You look magnificent," she blurted out.

Philip's smile was cool. "Thank you, my dear. Are you certain the dancing won't be too much for you?"

"I'm certain." No answering compliment, she noted, and at home his praise of her appearance had been almost perfunctory. It didn't matter that others were looking at her admiringly. It was Philip's approval she craved, Philip's love she needed, and which she was beginning to fear she would never get.

On the surface, things were well between them. Her reason for being in Richard's arms and Philip's subsequent outrageous accusation had never been discussed again. During the week in which her ankle healed, he had paid her more attention, spending time in her sitting room and telling her of his latest projects or reading to her. Yet Sarah couldn't help feeling that, in some essential sense, he'd gone away from her. His confidences were shallow, his expression guarded. As if, she thought, he didn't quite trust her. Occasionally, however, she would see another look in his eye, a possessive, smoldering look that brought back memories of nights past and conjured up dreams of the future, making her feel warm all over. Only these looks, few though they were, kept her going. Her determination that she would win him back from his mistress grew.

Thus she had chosen her ensemble tonight with care, and he seemed not even to notice! Most lowering and quite annoying. Though she had enjoyed being in London, she was glad they would soon be going home. There was her child to think of, but even more importantly, there was Philip. Havenwood was where it had all begun for them. There they would have a chance to start over again, away from other people. Away from his mistress.

The cotillion over, Philip smiled and raised her hand to his lips. Within a moment, one of her gallants came to claim her for the next dance, and she hardly saw Philip for the remainder of the evening. Time passed in a swirl of silken gowns, the glitter of jewels, the sparkling light from the chandeliers. It should have been an equally sparkling evening but for once Sarah was not enjoying herself. Everything had seemed to be wrong since she and Philip had come to London, and she longed for the day when they would return home, away from society and the frenzied socializing. There, perhaps, they could recapture the closeness they had lost.

"You look tired," Richard commented as he came to claim her for his dance.

"How ungallant of you, sir," she said, forcing a smile. The truth was, she *was* tired. Always in stout health, she had felt little different in spite of her condition, but now a wave of sleepiness overtook her, making her suddenly profoundly aware of the life she carried. With matters as they had been between her and Philip, she had delayed giving him her news, but now she wondered if she had made a mistake.

Richard led her from the floor. "I'm only concerned for you, cousin. Would you care for some refreshment?"

"Yes, something to drink would be welcome," she admitted. "Lemonade, please."

Richard gave her a quizzical look, but nevertheless plunged into the crowd and soon returned with champagne for himself and the requested lemonade for her. In the meantime, Sarah perched on a chair of gilt and blue velvet, fanning herself vigorously. She drank nearly half the glass before looking up at him to see him regarding her somberly.

A sense of foreboding made her set her glass down. "You've heard from her," she said flatly.

Richard quickly scanned the room, but apart from a glance or two, few paid pay them any notice. "I fear so," he said.

Sarah stared ahead. "If Philip is still seeing her, why doesn't she make her demands to him?"

"I don't know, Sarah. Unless she is hoping to bring him around for something more."

"I won't give him up!"

"Easy, Sarah," Richard involuntarily took a step back from the sudden blaze in her eyes. "Do you wish this to be public property?"

"No. No, of course not." She sighed and looked down, fiddling with the buttons of her gloves. "What does she want?"

"The same as before. We are lucky she hasn't raised her demands." He paused. "I'll meet with her if you like."

An unaccustomed lassitude settled over Sarah. To have this dealt with, and by someone else, was tempting, indeed. But she was made of sterner stuff than that. "No, Richard. I'll go with you."

Richard stared at her for a moment. "You are a stubborn wench, Sarah." He sighed. "Oh, very well. I'll set up another meeting. Will that satisfy you?"

"No." She drained the last of the lemonade and rose. "But it has to be done," she said, and walked away.

Her husband had a mistress. The mistress held proof that he was a murderer. Yet the only thing Sarah wanted at that moment was to be at his side, to feel his arms slip around her, and to lean against his compact, solid frame. Her world was falling apart, but the only thing she knew she could depend on was him. And he needed her. In the past he had had to rescue her many times. It was now her turn to come to his defense.

Philip was talking with Sir Edward Gregory, but he stopped when Sarah slipped her hand through his arm. "You look tired."

"For heaven's sake, is that all you men can say?" she exclaimed, and Sir Edward, glancing at the two of them, hastily made his departure. "First Richard, and now you."

"Ah, yes. I saw you talking with Richard." His gaze was watchful. "You and he appeared deep in discussion."

"Oh, he was being disagreeable."

Philip searched her face. "Sarah," he said, his voice gentle. "What is wrong?"

"Nothing." She looked down at her hands, than back at him. "Take me home, Philip," she said, her gaze intent, pleading, urgent. "Take me to bed."

Philip glanced quickly around to make certain she had not been overheard, but something kindled in his eye. "A most unusual request, madam."

Sarah clutched at his arm. "Philip, please!" She could think of no other way to hold him, to keep him from that woman, or to shield him from the menace that threatened him. She was fighting for their marriage; she was fighting for her life.

"Of course I will, little one." His voice was unexpectedly gentle as he reached up and quickly, lightly, touched her cheek. "Come, let's get your wrap and summon the carriage, and we'll go."

"Thank you." She leaned on his arm as they made their farewells, pushing their way through the throng to the door and at last taking their leave.

In the carriage Philip put his arm his wife's shoulders and drew her to him. He wasn't surprised when, a few moments later, she fell asleep, her breath soft and even. She hadn't looked well lately, apart from the effects of the accident. There were circles under her eyes, and her usual energy was missing. Something was troubling her. He knew, though, that she didn't love Richard, and at the moment, that was all that mattered. No matter what Richard might be planning.

Sarah stirred in his arms, murmuring something, and he was caught unaware by the flash of tenderness he felt. Sarah. How had he ever lived without her? She had come into his life and shown him how barren it was and then had taken his hand and led him away to a life filled with richness and light. The thought of losing her was so intolerable that he tightened his hold on her,

217

and she murmured again. Sarah was his. He wasn't going to let her go.

When the carriage stopped in front of the house, he stepped out carefully, his sleeping wife in his arms. Cooper looked surprised when he opened the door, but said nothing more than a circumspect "Good evening." Philip nodded and continued up the stairs, Sarah nestled close to him, a soft warm weight he would gladly bear forever. It was only as he laid her down on their bed that she stirred.

"Philip?" she murmured, drawing a hand across her eyes.

"Shh." Philip untied her cloak and carefully pulled it away. "Go back to sleep."

"Where," she yawned, "are we?"

"Home, dear girl. Go back to sleep now."

He bent his head to kiss her forehead and found himself trapped by her arms around his neck. As he tried to pull back, he met her eyes, sleepy but smoldering and very much aware. The invitation in them was too much to resist. He gathered her close to him, and at last their lips met and mingled.

Much later he lay staring into the darkness, exhausted by lovemaking that had been tempestuous and passionate and yet somehow desperate, too. Or had he only imagined that part of it because of all his worries? Someone wanted him dead. Soon, he would know who that someone was, and he would be free to pursue his life with Sarah. And never, ever, would he let himself think that she might be in league with his enemy.

"What are your plans for the day?" Philip asked over breakfast several mornings later, laying down his copy of the London *Times*.

Sarah looked at him over the rim of her teacup. She knew the shadows under her eyes were deeper this morning and that she looked pale. She felt pale. Philip hadn't deemed to notice, but if this morning nausea went on much longer, he would. Then she would have no excuse not to tell him about the baby. She wasn't certain why she was holding back now, except for what still lay ahead of her. Once that had been accomplished, she and Philip could go on with their lives.

"I'm promised to your sister," she said, setting down her cup and crumbling the piece of dry toast which was all she could manage to choke down. "We're going shopping."

"Shopping? Haven't you enough clothes?"

Sarah smiled. "Not to get through the winter. Unless you wish me to pull out my governess's clothes."

"Spare me."

"As I recall, there is one particularly revolting dress in gray merino—"

"Very well. Go shopping and spend all my money."

"Quite ugly, but serviceable and warm." Her smile was bright. "Wouldn't you like to see me in gray again?"

"God forbid. Buy yourself whatever you want. I'd thought to ask you to come with me this afternoon."

"Oh." Sarah's brow furrowed and then cleared. "Oh! You're going to the observatory at Greenwich. I'd love to, Philip, but I didn't realize when I made plans with Rebecca—"

"It doesn't matter." Philip folded his napkin. "The conservatory would probably bore you silly."

"Philip!" She stared at him, unaccountably hurt. "You know me better than that."

Philip, in the act of rising, paused. "Of course I do. I know about your curiosity. My apologies, Sarah."

She nodded, crumbling her toast still further. "Was Anne bored?" she asked, not looking at him.

"Unfortunately, yes."

She raised her eyes to him. "I'm not Anne, Philip."

"I know that." He bent and kissed her on the cheek. "Enjoy your shopping."

"I will." She leaned against his hand for a moment, and then he was gone. She was not Anne, nor could she ever be, no matter how stylishly she dressed or did her hair. That kind of beauty was beyond her. She'd thought she had something else, though, something that made up for the lack. Was it her fault Philip was unaware of it, or was he simply blind? Perhaps it was just as well if he were. She had lied to him again, and he seemed unaware of it.

219

Much later, long after Philip had left for Greenwich, a nondescript carriage pulled up in front of the Pembroke house. Richard stepped out into the November gloom and helped Sarah, very quiet, inside. Still silent, they drove off, each looking out opposite windows. At length, Sarah could stand the silence no longer. Her nerves were stretched to their limit. "What is her name?" she asked abruptly.

Richard glanced over at her. "I think it's best if you don't know that, Sarah."

"I am not a child! If this woman is my husband's—if he prefers her to me, I need to know all I can about her."

"It's hard to fight these things, Sarah."

"I intend to try."

Richard looked at her. "My cousin is a fool."

"He is not! He's—" She stopped, unable to defend even Philip for this. Pain welled up in her, unexpectedly sharp. "He treats me well," she said dully.

"Poor Sarah. By the bye, where is he today?"

Sarah shrugged, unwilling to discuss Philip further. "Out someplace."

"I remember. Greenwich, isn't it? Well, at least he won't be with her today, though I wonder about the other times he's left you alone."

"Oh, leave it, Richard!" Her arms across her chest, she stared out the window. Not for the first time, she wondered about Richard's concern in this. It was useless to ask questions; Richard would tell her nothing. Well, she was no fool. She would size the woman up herself and learn just what it was that made her so attractive to Philip.

The carriage stopped in a section of London Sarah didn't know, of crooked streets and buildings so tottering they looked about to fall down. A strong smell of fish and other, less wholesome, aromas, came to her from the nearby Thames, making her wrinkle her nose in distaste. "Not the best neighborhood, my dear," Richard said, taking her elbow as he escorted her into the tavern, half-timbered with grimy, flaking plaster. "Less chance you'll be recognized. You did wear a veil, did you not? After all, we don't want a scandal from this."

"Yes." Sarah reached up and pulled a gauzy veil over her face from the brim of her bonnet. Before, she'd thought the precaution ridiculous, but now, seeing the lowness of the place into which they were going, she was glad of it. It was old, this tavern, its rafters and beams black with soot from long dead fires, and the uneven board floor was strewn with straw that hadn't been changed in many a day. Long trestle tables with benches filled the low-ceilinged room, and again an odor reached her, so pungent it made her stomach roil: a combination of beer, age, and unwashed bodies. Even at this time of day most of the tables were taken by coarse-looking, ill-kempt men who glanced their way with dead, incurious eyes. Sarah shivered a bit and drew closer to Richard. She would be glad when this business was done.

At a smaller table near the back of the tavern, a woman sat alone. Like Sarah she, too, was covered, though her veiling was heavier and reached past her shoulders. Sarah's curiosity stirred in spite of herself as she slid onto the bench facing her. *This* was what Philip preferred to her?

"You made it. 'Bout time," the woman said, her voice harsh and coarse. In the dim light Sarah could make out very little about her adversary, except that she was overly plump and that her gown of scarlet silk was neither very new, nor very clean. And she wasn't young. Her hands, in darned black net mitts, were broad and work-hardened. Old hands. "You bring the ready?"

"Patience," Richard said smoothly. "You have something we want first."

"Not till I sees what you got to give me."

"Here." Sarah held up a leather pouch, and a greedy hand grabbed out for it. "No. The letters first."

The hand she held out, the tone of her voice, her bearing were those of the governess she had once been. The woman across from her might never have had the benefit of an education, but she recognized the tone of authority when she heard it. Slowly she reached into her reticule and brought out a packet of letters, tossing them onto the table.

Philip's handwriting. That was all Sarah could think of as she looked at the direction scrawled across the top letter: spiky, nearly illegible, and all too distinctive. "So it's true," she murmured, hardly noticing as the leather pouch was snatched from her hand. For a moment she closed her eyes, trying to hold back the horror of it. It was true. Philip had a mistress, and to her he had confided his crime.

The woman was pawing through the pouch, gloating at the bank notes rolled up inside. "Nice doing business with yer. Now you'll 'scuse me—"

"Wait." Sarah held up a hand, and the woman paused in the act of rising. "There are some questions I would ask you."

"I didn't bargain for this, me lord," she muttered, but she sat down again.

"Nevertheless, there are some things I wish to learn."

"Sarah, that's his handwriting," Richard said in a low voice. "Let's not have any trouble."

"How long have you known my husband?" Sarah asked.

"Oh, donkey's ages. Seems his wife couldn't please him. Oh, but I ferget. Yer his wife, ain't yer?"

"Why you? What in the world does he see in you?"

"I knows things, don't I?" she leered. "Else why would he come back to me? And why would he write to me?" She reached across the table and tapped the letters, which Sarah quickly withdrew. "See? 'Mrs. Flo Lambert,' it says."

" 'Lambeth,' " Sarah corrected, and her head jerked up. "It says 'Lambeth'!"

"Ought to know my own name, oughtn't I?"

"You can't read." Sarah stared at her and then turned to Richard. "Richard, she can't read! This is a hoax."

"It's Philip's writing—"

"Yer calling me a liar?" This time the woman did rise. "Well, we'll just see, won't we? Nice meetin' yer. Tell yer foine husband hello for me." And with a laugh and a cloud of stale perfume, she was gone through the smoke and the dust of the tavern.

"Sarah." Richard clamped his hand on her arm, preventing her from rising. "It's no good."

"Richard, this is a hoax."

"Come, let's get out of here and discuss this outside."

"But she's getting away—"

222

"And we'd best let her go. We've no friends here."

Sarah looked up and saw that the other occupants of the tavern were staring at them, some looking belligerent, some merely curious. Common sense won out over her anger. Without a word, she let Richard escort her back to the carriage.

"A hoax, Richard!" she exclaimed, pushing back her veil and glaring at him as they drove away. "Five thousand pounds, and these might not even be authentic!"

"Let me see them, Sarah." Richard held out his hands for the letters and flipped through them. "It does look like Philip's handwriting."

"I know," she said, in a muffled tone. "Richard, how could he prefer her?"

"I've always said he's a fool — ah!"

"What?"

Richard refolded the letter he had been reading and placed it back in the envelope. "He admits it, Sarah. He's regretful, but he admits it. It doesn't matter how that woman got these. He admits killing Anne."

Sarah had gone white. "No."

"For God's sake, Sarah, open your eyes! Here is the proof. You're married to a murderer."

"No!" she cried again, but the letters, hastily shoved back into her reticule, seemed heavy, weighty, irrefutable proof of the one thing she did not wish to believe. "No."

"Sarah, I'm sorry."

"Oh, God, Richard." She put her hands to her face. "How can face him?"

Richard's face was sober. "You may be in danger."

Sarah's hands slowly dropped. "Philip wouldn't hurt me."

"No one would have thought he'd hurt Anne either."

"No, I won't believe it!"

"Sarah, the man's dangerous. He always has been. The scar only made it worse."

"But what can I do?"

"Come with me," he urged. "I'm leaving Town tomorrow and 'll gladly take you wherever you wish."

"No, I couldn't."

223

"Sarah, I love you."

The right words, the wrong man. Sarah stared at him for a moment and then sank her face into her hands again. "Richard, I can't handle anymore of this."

"I'm sorry, sweetheart. I wouldn't add to your burden. But I do love you. I have from the beginning, and I want to be there for you."

"Oh, God. I don't know what to do."

"Leave him, Sarah. Leave him before it's too late."

"No." She straightened as the carriage drew up before the Pembroke house. "I can't. At least, not yet."

"Sarah—"

"Richard, I appreciate all you've done for me. Truly I do." She laid her hand on his. "But I need time to think. There are reasons."

Richard scanned her face, and then shrugged. "So be it. But if you need me, Sarah, I'll be there for you."

"Thank you," she said, and went into the house, her heart heavy. In the past, Philip had rescued her many times, but who would save her from this?

In her sitting room, Sarah asked that the fire be built up and then dismissed both her maid and the footman. Slowly, methodically, she read each letter and then tore it into tiny shreds, the sounds, sights, and smells of this afternoon's excursion whirling in a kaleidoscope of images. Two stood out: Philip's guilt, written in his distinctive penmanship; and his mistress. How could he prefer that woman to her? Worse than all else, though, were her own feelings. He was a murderer and an adulterer, and she loved him still.

Scooping the fragments of the letters into her hands, she crossed to the fire and dropped them in, watching as the paper caught and burned. The evidence of Philip's crime, such as it was, had been destroyed. Now no one would ever know of it except her. The knowledge was bitter. For the sake of her child she would make peace with it, but she wouldn't trust Philip again. No. She would never trust him again.

Chapter Eighteen

Philip swung off his horse, handing the reins to Wilkins. A few moments later Ned, the undergroom whom he had taken into his confidence, rode in behind him. "Anyone?" Philip asked.

"No, my lord, not a one," Ned said, dismounting.

"I saw nothing either." He frowned. It had seemed the perfect plan, too. "Never mind. We'll just have to try again another time."

"Yes, my lord." Ned glanced after Philip as he left the stables. "Though why the man wants to get himself killed, I don't know," he muttered, and then recalled himself to the task of unsaddling his mount.

Philip entered the house by the side door, still frowning. Damn. There was nothing wrong with his plan. Announce to those whom he suspected — Richard, and, reluctantly, Sarah — that he was going alone to Greenwich on horseback rather than by the river on a dark November day and plan for what might happen. There were certainly enough long, lonely stretches of road where an ambush against a lone rider might be mounted, and Philip had been on his guard. His pistols had been at hand, primed and ready to fire at the first hint of danger, and he had had Ned, following closely behind, to make the fight more even. Thus, the trap had been set. The bait, however, had not been taken. Philip had made it to Greenwich and back without mishap, and he was rather sorry for it. He would relish a good fight just now.

Geordie was in the workroom when Philip came in, his face serious. "Thank God ye got back safe," he said, as Philip sat across from him. "Any trouble?"

"None, damn it." Philip drummed his fingers on the table. "We'll have to come up with something else, I think."

"Say what you like, sir, I'm glad nothing happened."

"Damn it, Geordie, I have to do something to bring him out."

"You could talk to the mistress."

Philip's head came up sharply. "What do you mean?"

"I mean that she went out with Mr. Thornton this afternoon."

So that was why the trap hadn't worked. Richard had been busy elsewhere. "I see."

"No, sir, ye don't. He took her to some low tavern down by the river, and they stayed there awhile."

"So?"

"Are ye blind, man?" Geordie slammed his hand down on the table. "I don't like it anymore than ye, but they're in it together, I'd wager on that!"

Philip rose abruptly and went to the window. "What did they do in the tavern?" he asked, his voice reasonably normal.

"I don't know, sir. I didn't want to be recognized, so I didn't go in."

"You did right." Philip turned. "I'll deal with this, Geordie."

"Aye. Can't believe it of the mistress, but—"

"Sarah's not in it," Philip said sharply. "Just continue to watch my cousin."

"Aye, sir," Geordie said, and watched as Philip stalked from the room. He'd got Lord Pembroke safe through the war, and all that had happened since. He'd get him through this.

Philip's face was impassive as he walked down the stairs. So Sarah had been with Richard when she had told him something else entirely. Damn it, she was lying to him, and he was tired of it! He'd been careful with her, hoping she would confide in him of her own will, but apparently she would not. The time for such gentleness had passed. If he were to survive, he would have to find out what her involvement was. He wasn't

226

certain, though, that their marriage would survive.

"Sarah," he said at the door of her sitting room, and she looked up from the fireplace where she stood. Her face was so filled with misery that some of his angry determination faded. "What are you doing?"

Sarah stirred the fire with a poker. "Burning some old letters."

"Oh." He leaned against the doorjamb. "How was your shopping?"

"Shopping? Oh. Fine. Philip?"

"Yes?"

"Do you think I'm pretty?"

An odd question at such a time. "You'll do."

"I'll do! Am I attractive?"

"What, has your court deserted you?"

Sarah set the poker down with a clang. "Oh, never mind. You don't understand," she said, and turned away toward the bedroom door.

"Sarah," he protested, but she was gone, the door closing behind her with sharp finality. Damn, now what was that all about? He could go after her, demand to know what she had been doing with Richard and at last learn the truth, but he'd lost all desire to do so. She wouldn't tell him, that much was obvious. He'd lost her, just as he'd lost everything else he'd ever valued. But damned if Richard would have her, he thought, heading with purpose down the stairs. He'd die before he let that happen.

Richard knocked again, impatiently, on the rickety door of the tenement, with the gold knob of his walking stick. This time the door opened, and the woman he and Sarah had met at the tavern stood there without her veil, giving him a gap-toothed grin. "Couldn't wait, could yer, love," she said, closing the door behind him. "Knew yer'd be here soon."

Richard glanced around the shabby, messy room, none of his distaste showing on his face. A narrow bed stood in one corner, its covers pulled back, its sheets wrinkled; it obviously had not been made up for days. Various articles of clothing were tossed about on the other bits of furniture: a chemise, a petticoat, a gown in a particularly revolting shade of green. If Sarah were to see this room, she would entertain serious doubts about her husband's infidelity, but Richard thought he had chosen well. Flo had played the part assigned her with, if not style, at least a kind of cunning greediness that rang all too true. And she had a certain kind of attractiveness, enough he suspected, to make someone already uncertain about her looks even less secure. Like Sarah.

"Expect yer wants yer share," she said cheerfully behind him, and he turned.

"Where is it?"

Flo looked down at her ample cleavage. "Now, where do yer think, love? Oh, no," she protested, laughing, as he took a step toward her. "I don't give it away for nothin'."

Richard held out his hand. "The money, Flo."

"Yer a hard one, yer are. Never could figure out what yer wanted. But five thousand pounds, that's a lot of the ready."

"One thousand for you." Richard opened the leather pouch she handed him and peeled off several bank notes. And four thousand for him. "Of course you'll forget all about me."

"Yes, love. This'll set me up nice." She turned away, tucking the bank notes back into her bosom. "Did I do all right, love?"

"You did fine, love," Richard said, and brought the knob of his walking stick down hard upon her head. The woman crumpled to the floor and lay there, very still. "But you forgot your name was Lambeth, not Lambert." His face twisted with distaste as he reached for the money she had just hidden, feeling her chest rise and fall and then wiping his fingers on his handkerchief. So he hadn't killed her. A pity, that, but he'd been here long enough and couldn't stay, even to tidy up this one loose end. Not that she was likely to come after him; he'd been careful to conceal his identity. Nor could he see any reason why she should have the money, even if he had promised it to her for her part in the charade. What would a whore do with a thousand pounds, after all?

Back in the hackney, Richard settled against the squabs, a small smile of satisfaction playing about his lips. A good day's work. Sarah was convinced now that her husband was both a murderer and a philanderer. It didn't matter that neither were true, that Richard had written the incriminating letters himself, carefully imitating his cousin's handwriting, or that Flo had only played the part of Philip's mistress. Sarah believed both were true, and that was all that mattered. It was certain to lead to an estrangement. Little chance now that Philip would have an heir. Richard's position was secure.

Resting his hands on the knob of his walking stick, he thought back over all he had done and all he had yet to do, looking for flaws. Philip had played into his hands, of course, going off on his own pursuits and neglecting his wife. Ah, the temptation to go after him today on his solitary jaunt to Greenwich. If his own plans hadn't been in train, he might have done so. Thank God Philip was so stupid. The man never had known how to handle women. And Sarah. For all her common sense, she had been ridiculously easy to dupe. Of course he'd seen that right away when he'd first met her; she'd been gauche, naive, plain. Ripe for the picking and susceptible to Richard's lies. He had little doubt that she would come to him tomorrow, asking for the help he had offered.

Richard smiled. All was going well. He was five thousand pounds to the richer and more awaited him: the marquessate, which would have been his had his father been born first; Thornhill; even Havenwood, which he intended to pull down as soon as possible. And it would all come to him tomorrow. He'd waited long enough.

They would be leaving London soon. Philip had a bit more business to transact, both with his publisher and the soldier's hospital he was talking about founding, and then they would be free. The Little Season was over, and people were already returning to their country homes for Christmas. Once Sarah had looked forward to their own departure. Now she was no longer so certain.

Sitting at her dressing table the morning after the world as she had known it had ended, Sarah leaned forward and tried to pinch some color into her cheeks. Nausea, or perhaps unhappiness, had left her unnaturally pale. What would happen next, she didn't even want to think.

"Be still, my lady," Millie said behind her, tugging at the laces of the pink sprigged muslin morning gown Sarah had chosen. "This gown's getting snug. If you'd only stand so I could do this right . . ."

"If I stand I'm likely to faint, and I'm not as poor-spirited as that," Sarah said tartly. "It's a good thing, after all, that we're returning to the country."

Millie sent her a look of womanly sympathy but held her tongue. Thank heavens, Sarah thought. She was in no mood for Millie's prattle this morning, well-meant though it was. Likely it was common knowledge throughout the house, the estrangement between Philip and her. Probably everybody knew that she and her husband had not shared a bed last night for the first time since coming to London.

Sarah raised her face and looked at herself, pale, gaunt, hollow-eyed. Not the most attractive of sights for a man to face across the breakfast table. For the sake of her child, however, and even for her own happiness, she would have to make the effort. She loved him, damn it! she thought, pounding her fist on the dressing table and causing Millie to look at her in surprise. Nothing was going to change that. But she wasn't going to sit by and let him go to his mistress. Nor would she let the memory of Anne come between them. For she had accomplished something Anne hadn't. She would give Philip an heir. It was high time, she decided, getting shakily to her feet, that she told him that.

Philip barely glanced up from reading the *Times* as she entered the breakfast parlor. "What is the news?" she asked, as she sat.

"More news about Leipzig. Bonaparte looks finished at last," he said, not looking at her.

"But that's wonderful! The war might end soon."

He turned a page, rattling it ostentatiously. "Yes, and we'll have to deal with floods of wounded and unemployed soldiers."

"Your scheme to found a hospital for them should help.

What more have you done on it?"

Philip glanced at her over the top of the paper and then went back to his reading. "As if you care."

"Philip! That's unfair. You know that what concerns you concerns me."

"Really?" Philip folded the paper and laid it down. "Where were you yesterday?"

Sarah looked up from her tea, her eyes wary. "I told you. Shopping."

"Oh, yes. Shopping. With nothing to show for it."

"Madame Celeste is making up some new gowns for me."

"You're a very bad liar, Sarah."

"Philip!"

"If you wish to be convincing, you should look directly at a person, not away. And don't blush. It's a dead giveaway."

"All right. Where do you go when you tell me you're going to your publisher's or to the hospital?"

"What?"

"You heard me. What is it you're really doing?"

Philip let out a mirthless bark of laughter. "My God. Are you accusing me?"

"Yes." Sarah stared at him. The time for lies was past. If they were to have any chance for a future, they needed to tell the truth. "You tell me where you go and whom you see, and I'll tell you."

"I already know."

"What?"

"Who you're seeing. Richard."

"Richard!" Sarah exclaimed, but the memory of Richard's declaration of love made her face color. "Of all the ridiculous things—"

"I can't say I blame you. He's a handsome devil. And what woman in her right mind would want me, with this?" He pointed savagely to his eye patch.

"Philip—"

"Oh, stop lying Sarah. I've had enough of it to last me a lifetime."

"All right!" Sarah threw her napkin onto the table. "I'll tell

231

you where I was yesterday, then. I was with Richard. There. Does that satisfy you?"

Philip rose abruptly, his chair scraping back. "I don't know what I did to deserve this. First Anne finding another, and now you."

"It's not like that!"

"No?" Philip turned from the doorway. "How is it then?"

"Ahem. Excuse me," a voice said behind Philip, and he turned to see Cooper. "Mr. Thornton has called."

"Is he here for me or for Lady Pembroke, Cooper?"

"Why, for you, sir." Cooper's eyes flicked avidly towards Sarah. "At least, I believe so. He's in your workroom."

"I see." Without a word, he turned and walked out, leaving Sarah staring at the breakfast she hadn't really wanted, feeling sick and hollow. So. The truth, or at least part of it, was out, and it had only made things worse. She didn't want to learn he had a mistress! She didn't want it confirmed. She wanted to go back to the early days of their marriage, after the Harvest Home, when the future had stretched before them and it seemed Philip might actually care for her. Now that would never be, and how she would deal with that, she didn't know. Strange, she hadn't known that a broken heart was so physical a pain.

Like a sleepwalker, she rose from the table and drifted toward her sitting room. She couldn't take anymore of this, the tension, the heartache. There was only one thing left for her to do. She would leave as Richard had suggested. This afternoon when he left for the country, she would go with him.

The look of grim determination on Philip's face as he strode into his workroom wasn't lost on Richard as he rose from his stooping position near the window. The flimsy muslin curtains trembled a bit and then were still. "Just picking up a scrap of paper," he said cheerfully, picking up a piece of metal from Philip's worktable and tossing it up in the air. "Good morning, cousin. I thought to bring the cigar lighter with me but I forgot."

"If that's how you treat it, it's no wonder it doesn't work."

Philip perched on a stool at his worktable, his attention seemingly focused on something there. His rage toward Richard was so overwhelming that he feared if he so much as looked at him, he would explode. Damn the man! Was it fair that he should have everything, health and the easy charm that had always escaped Philip, even before he had been scarred, and Sarah as well? He wasn't giving up this time. Not without a fight.

Richard pulled up a stool across from him. "I treasure anything you give me, cousin," he said, and Philip's eye came up, unexpectedly cold and hard.

"Sarah is mine."

"Is she? You might want to ask her about that." His voice was mocking. "You've made a mess of things again, old boy."

"Oh, no. Everything was fine until you came along."

"And if you'd been husband enough, she wouldn't have had to turn to another, would she? Like Anne."

Philip rose, his face white and pinched with anger. "Get out. Get out, and by God, if you ever come near my wife again, I'll—"

"Kill me? Like you did Anne?"

"Damn you, you know I didn't!"

"Couldn't stomach it when you learned she'd found another, could you?" Richard taunted. "But why fire, cousin? Surely strangling would have been more civilized?"

"Is tampering with my carriage civilized?"

Richard went very still. "Well, well. Are you accusing me of something?"

"I know damn well what you've been up to. I tell you, it won't work. You may still be my heir, but in name only. I'm disinheriting you, Richard. You'll get my title, but nothing else. Not one penny, do you hear? You and Sarah can starve together."

Richard's face had gone dark with rage. "I should be the marquess! If my father had been born first, but damn! An accident of birth, a mere five minutes difference, and you—you!—get all this."

"So." Philip's voice was calm. "So. Now we come to it.

233

You've never been my friend. It's my position you've always wanted."

"Of course." Richard rose, pulling on his gloves of pearl gray kid, perfectly coordinating with his darker gray morning coat. "That, and everything else."

"You won't get it." Philip faced him across the room. "Not my position, not my money, and not Sarah."

"We'll just see about that, won't we?" Richard said, and slipped from the room.

Philip stared after him, his hands bunching into fists. "Oh, will we?" he murmured. It was clear to him now that they were locked in a struggle to the death. Why hadn't he seen it before, the animosity, the jealousy? All this time he'd believed his cousin to be his one true friend while Richard was likely the one responsible for the "accidents" which had befallen him in the past. And a varied lot they'd been, a highwaymen's attack, near electrocution, a runaway carriage, perhaps even fire—

He sat down abruptly at that. Could it be? Was Richard responsible for the fire which had taken Anne's life? Good God, why? But, no, that had been an accident, a candle igniting the bed curtains. Or so he'd always believed. To think otherwise meant that Anne had, indeed, been murdered, though by accident. The fire had been meant for him. That meant that Sarah should be safe. Shouldn't she?

That got him to his feet. Running down the stairs, he burst into his wife's sitting room, stopping short at the sight of several trunks standing open on the floor. Both Sarah, her face pale, her eyes red-rimmed, and her maid looked up, startled by his precipitative entrance. "Philip?" Sarah said.

"You will excuse us," Philip said to Millie, who bobbed a hasty curtsy and made an even hastier retreat at the cold, cutting command.

"Philip—"

"Be quiet." Hands in pocket, he meandered into the room. "Where are you going?"

Sarah turned away, placing a neatly folded stack of chemises into a trunk. "Back to Havenwood."

"Ah. Not going off with Richard, then?"

234

Sarah looked up sharply. "As it happens, yes. He's going to bring me there."

With several quick strides, he was across the room, grasping her arms. "Do you think me a complete fool?" he grated. "I know what's between you."

"You're hurting me!" she cried, but the pressure on her arms didn't let up.

"You're running away with him. Admit it, damn it."

"You *are* a fool, Philip. When I think of what I've done for you . . ."

"What have you done? Made a cuckold of me again. A wonderful gift, Sarah!"

"No! I've saved you from being branded a murderer."

Philip's hands dropped to his sides. "I beg your pardon?"

"You killed Anne. But don't worry," she said, her voice bitter. "I've destroyed the evidence. Now no one else will know."

"You think me a murderer?"

Sarah stepped away, folding a petticoat and not looking at him. "I know you are."

"My good God." He sank into a chair, staring sightlessly before him. "Of all people, you're the last I'd expect that from, Sarah."

"Why not? I'm cuckolding you, aren't I?"

He looked up. "Are you?"

"What do you think?"

"I don't know what to think anymore." He rose, his face strangely defenseless, his hand outstretched. "Sarah. The truth. For once, tell me the truth."

"Oh, Philip." The pain that had lodged near Sarah's heart eased. There was still a chance. If they could clear matters up between them, perhaps she wouldn't have to leave. "I'm with child."

He stiffened. "Whose child?" he demanded, and her hand shot out and caught him across the cheek.

Chapter Nineteen

Philip barely flinched, but stayed as he was, glaring at Sarah. "You idiot," she said bitterly. "I can't take anymore of this. I'm going back to Havenwood. When you're seeing things more clearly—"

"When *I* see more clearly?"

"Oh, get out." She turned away, her hand folded protectively across her stomach. "We've nothing more to say to each other."

"No, we've said it all, haven't we?" He stared at her, the knowledge of her betrayal a bitter taste in his mouth. "But I never thought you'd betray me, Sarah."

Sarah paused in the act of folding a petticoat and then went on with her task. "Someday you'll see."

"If you think to foist this child on me as my heir—"

"I don't want to talk to you anymore, Philip. Please go away."

"And let you go with Richard?" The thought chilled him. The child might very well be his. If so, she could be in danger. "Does he know?"

"About the child? No. And he's not going to. I'm not eloping with him."

"Ha." He could see it all now, what Richard had wanted from the beginning, Sarah and the estate. Look at all the efforts Richard had made to separate them, from courting Sarah to planting seeds of suspicion in Philip's mind. Richard had succeeded quite well in estranging husband from wife, so well that Sarah had taken him as her lover.

Sarah dropped the petticoat in a heap in the trunk. "Oh, believe what you want!" she snapped, her temper finally getting the best of her. "I'm tired of this, Philip. I can't take anymore, living with your suspicions and knowing that you —"

"Murdered my first wife? Then go, Sarah." He turned on his heel and strode to the door. "Go to your lover. But, by God, don't expect to come crawling back to me when he deserts you!"

"He's not my lover!" Sarah cried, but he was gone, slamming the door behind him. "Oh, damn you, Philip." Her knees suddenly too weak to support herself, she sank to the floor amid a froth of cotton lawn and lace, her face in her hands. Damn him for his suspicions, for his having a mistress; damn him for making her love him.

Wiping her eyes with the back of her hand, she lifted her head and looked around the room. She would survive. She'd gone through hard times before and survived them; she would survive this. But it would never again be the same, she thought, getting somewhat unsteadily to her feet. The joy that she'd known was gone, and there was no getting it back.

She was gone. From his workroom Philip watched as Sarah climbed into the carriage and was driven away. Strange that it didn't hurt. He'd felt worse when she'd left Havenwood that first time, but then, he hadn't had this numbness wrapped around him then, like cotton wool, protecting him. Then he had begun to see a glimmer of hope for the future. Now he knew there was no chance for him ever again. What was wrong with him that he was fated to love women who didn't love him in return?

The carriage turned a corner and was gone. Head down, Philip walked over to a stool and sat, toying with a fragment of metal. He loved Sarah. For the first time he admitted it, though he'd known for a very long time what he felt. Now, when it was too late, when she had found another, he could put words to his feelings. If only he had said them earlier, if only he had told her. . . . But he had told Anne, and she had found another, just as Sarah had.

Bewildered, he put his head in his hands. He'd not have

thought it of Sarah; she seemed so straightforward, so honest. But find another she had, a person who had somehow managed to convince her of his guilt in Anne's death. And she had thought she was protecting him! The irony was so bitter, he almost laughed. Well, why shouldn't he? It was a joke on him, wasn't it? No wonder there was moisture on his cheeks. Tears of laughter, of course. What else could they be?

Philip rose, angrily rubbing at his cheeks. To hell with her; to hell with all women! He was a man, and he needed nobody. He was better off without her, concentrating instead on his various projects. They were what had gotten him through before, and they would get him through again. It would seem strange at first, not to have anyone to share them with, but he would soon grow used to that again. He was alone as he had always been, as he was meant to be. Sarah had made her choice, and it wasn't him.

No, damn it! He jumped to his feet, disgusted by his self-pity. He wasn't going to sit idly by and let his wife go, not when she carried his child. For he was certain that it was his child, not Richard's, and that fact put her in danger. He couldn't let Richard win, not this time. Sarah was his, though he wondered if she would ever forgive him for the things he had said to her. This time, he was going to fight.

"Sarah!" Richard stopped in surprise at the door to the drawing room of his lodgings. "You *are* here. When my butler told me, I didn't believe him."

Sarah, sitting on the sofa, her hands folded in her lap, and appearing somehow very small, looked up. "I had no choice. Richard, please, will you help me?"

"Of course I will, dearling." He was by her side in an instant, taking her hand in his and patting it. "You know I'd do anything for you."

Sarah squirmed. "Richard, this is not an elopement."

"I know that, dearling, but in time — ah, well, we needn't talk about that just yet. I'm glad you're here. How can I assist you?"

"Take me to Havenwood."

"Havenwood!" Richard pulled back, though he didn't release her hand. "Good God, Sarah, of all places!"

"Where else am I to go?"

"There are plenty of places. I have friends who would be happy to take you in."

"No." Sarah shook her head vigorously. "I want to go home. I want to go to Havenwood."

"Think, Sarah. He'll come after you there."

"I haven't left him, Richard. At least, not permanently."

"Yet."

"Ever. But I had to get away. Matters have gotten so bad. It's not good for the child."

"The child?" Richard said sharply.

"What? Oh, of course, you didn't know. I'm carrying Philip's child."

Abruptly Richard released her hand, pulling back even farther. "Good God, Sarah, this is a nightmare! A murderer's child—"

"Don't you ever say that!" Sarah's voice was low and fierce, and her eyes flashed with fire. "My child is innocent, and I'll not have you, or anyone else, say differently."

"Of course not, of course not." Richard patted her hand again; this time, she pulled away. "Well. I must say this is a facer."

Sarah looked up. "Why?"

"Because—never mind. Very well. I'll take you to Havenwood. But you must promise me something, dearling." He caught her chin in his hand, though she stiffened. "While you're there, you must give serious thought to leaving him." Sarah didn't answer, but only returned his gaze. "You are stubborn. Very well, I won't ask you to make such a promise. Yet." He rose. "I'll see to the rest of my packing, and then we'll leave. Strange, isn't it?"

"What?"

"How a man like Philip, so intelligent and concerned for others, could so completely neglect his wife. Ah, well, his loss." He flashed her a gleaming smile. "I'll be with you in a few moments. In the meantime, Fawcett will bring you tea."

"Thank you."

Richard bowed and then strode into his room to finish packing. He had won! After all his scheming and planning, he had won. He was rather surprised that Philip hadn't put up more of a fight, but then, the man had always been a weakling. He must be suffering now, Richard thought, with a mixture of anticipation and satisfaction, but he'd be out of his pain soon. And Richard would be the marquess.

Except, damn it, except for Sarah's child. That was a facer indeed. In spite of all he'd done, she might very well be carrying Philip's heir. That would be cosmic justice, wouldn't it? He would have to bide his time still further; perhaps he could get himself appointed the child's guardian. And then, who knew what might happen? Nothing was going to stand between him and his goal.

In the drawing room, Sarah leaned back against the sofa, stripping off her gloves, suddenly weary, and yet seeing things with an odd clarity. This room, for example. Small, shabby and old-fashioned for a leader of the *ton,* and she could swear she'd smelled liquor on the butler's breath. There were lamps everywhere, most of them lighted, odd for this time of day; and several instantaneous light boxes, glass bottles coated on the inside with sulfur that, when struck, produced a flame.

Hypnotically, she stared at one of the lamps. Soon she would be on her way, away from everything. The day had been a fire storm of emotion, and ahead she faced a long journey. For a moment her courage flagged, but then she raised her chin. She was a Chadwick, after all, and Chadwicks did not give into fear or weakness. Even when they wanted to.

Strange, though, wasn't it, she thought, stirring sugar in to a cup of tea she didn't want, that Philip was as he was. Since she'd known him, she'd seen him do nothing but good: the devices that made Havenwood run smoothly, the improvements in farming, the primers for the village children, primers that now would be used all over England.

A tear escaped down her cheek. It was not like her to give into mawkish sentiment, but lately the oddest things set her to crying. Those primers. They were so typical of Philip, of the

240

genuine concern he had for others. Look at what he'd done for her. When she had needed a home, he had taken her in. He'd done more than just that, though. Knowing she'd never had a London season, he'd set out to give her one, though he could easily have transacted his business from Havenwood. He had not complained once about the money she had spent on clothing, and he had always called her beautiful. More importantly, he had made her feel beautiful, cherished, desired. No one else had ever been able to do that. Why, oh why, she wailed inwardly, wiping away more tears, did he have to be a murderer, too?

Wait. It was wrong. *This* was wrong, her being here. Philip was no murderer, not a man such as he, with so much love to give — yes, she knew he loved her. He'd never told her, but he had shown her instead in a thousand different ways. No, a man such as he could never, ever have done the things he stood accused of. As for his mistress — for heaven's sake, she had been stupid about that one! Philip surely had better taste than to choose so low a person as his companion. How the woman had got the letters no longer mattered. Their authenticity no longer mattered. What did was that she loved her husband, and when he needed her most, she was leaving.

What are you doing? She'd never run away from anything in her life. Whether Philip was innocent or not, she loved him. She had to go back. If she didn't, she would be forever haunted by the look of complete and utter misery that had so briefly appeared in Philip's eye when she had gone. He needed her. Her place was beside him.

The teacup rattled as she hastily set it on its saucer and rose, drawing her cloak about her. No time to leave a note for Richard to thank him for his misguided help; she would simply have to tell his butler and trust him to pass her message along. She was going home. It might be the wrong thing, but, oh, it felt so right!

Richard's butler protested when she asked him to find her a hackney, saying that Mr. Thornton wished her to wait. Sarah, however, was adamant. She knew finally what she wanted. "I'm going back to my husband," she said, sailing past him and out the door. "There, that should give you something to gossip about!"

"Yes, my lady. I mean, no, my lady!" the butler stammered, frowning after her and then reaching inside his coat for his flask. Flighty little thing. Ask him, Mr. Thornton was better off without her. Not quite the master's type, either, though she was right. This would make for interesting gossip with the other servants.

"Fawcett." Richard's voice from the drawing room was sharp. "Where is Lady Pembroke?"

"Gone, sir, these past five minutes."

"Gone? Where? Tell me, damn you, or —"

"Sir!" Fawcett backed up a few steps, startled by the sudden murderous rage that swept over Richard's face. "I tried to stop her, but I couldn't. Perhaps you could still catch her," he added.

"Where did she go?"

"I'm not sure, sir. She said something about going back to her husband."

Richard's breath drew in sharply. "My good God," he said and ran out.

"Philip!" Sarah called as she ran up the stairs to the attic, and he paused in the act of pulling on his coat. Good God, now what? He sat down again to await events. But, so help him, if Sarah tried to leave again, he would do anything he had to, to stop her.

"Philip?" She burst through the doorway. "I'm back."

Philip gave her a cool, measuring look. "What, did your lover decide he didn't want you?"

"No, silly, and he's not my lover." She put her arms around his neck and kissed his cheek, though he was stiff and unresponsive. "What are you drawing?"

Philip looked down at the sketch on the table without seeing it. "A design for a balloon."

"To the moon?"

"Yes."

"Oh, Philip." She kissed him again. "There'd be problems

here, too."

Philip pointed his pen at her, conceding the point, as she went to perch on the stool opposite him. "True, but no people."

"You won't make it big enough for two? Excuse me, three."

"For you and Richard? Damned if I will."

"Why, Philip. I do believe you're angry. I don't think I've ever heard you swear before."

"Sarah . . ."

"Philip—oh, heavens, I don't know how to say this!" Sarah flung her hands in the air, frustrated. "And you've no intention of helping me, do you?"

Philip's gaze continued cool. "With what?"

"With apologizing. With working out our problems and going on with our marriage."

"I'm not the one who walked out."

"But you told me to go, Philip." Sarah's lips compressed for just a moment. "And that hurt, knowing you don't want me."

"Don't want you!" Philip slammed the pen down. "My God, Sarah! I'm not the one with a lover!"

"No, just a mistress."

"I beg your pardon?"

"You don't have to deny it. I've met her, you see."

"No, I don't see." His brow wrinkled with a frown. "Sarah, who told you I had a mistress?"

"Richard."

"Richard. Ah, now I see."

"What?"

"Is he your lover?"

"I told you, no! And since you say you can tell when I lie, you must know I'm telling the truth. There's been no one but you. Ever." She looked directly at him. "I don't want anyone but you."

"That bastard," he said softly. "Look what he's done to us. But there is something between the two of you, Sarah."

Sarah fiddled with the strings of her reticule. "Well, yes. But I did it for you, Philip, I swear."

"So you said before. I think you'd best tell me just what it was you did for me, Sarah."

There was no disobeying that steely tone of voice. She took a deep breath. "I burned the letters."

"What letters?"

"The ones you wrote to your mistress, admitting you killed Anne."

"Holy God!"

"But I don't believe them, Philip. I don't care what you wrote. I don't believe it. I know you couldn't do something like that. And, even if you did," she shrugged helplessly, "it doesn't matter to me."

The look he gave her was searching. "You'd stay with me even if you thought me a murderer?"

"Yes. But I will not countenance your having a mistress, Philip!"

Unforgivably, he laughed, and then sobered. "Sarah." He reached across the table, grasping her hand. "These letters. Tell me about them. Where did you get them?"

"Richard heard from your mistress," she began, and went on to tell him the entire story. When she was done, she sat back, feeling curiously light. He would likely be angry with her, and she couldn't blame him. Still, she was glad it was out. Now they could find a way to deal with their problems.

"Interesting." Philip rose. She watched, puzzled, as he crossed to the bookshelves, pulled out a book, and withdrew from it a sheet of paper, which he handed to her. "Is this what the handwriting looked like?"

"Yes. No!" She studied the letter, for such it was, more carefully. "This is very close, but it's not quite like your handwriting."

"Look at the signature."

Sarah turned the letter over and gasped, her gaze meeting his. "Richard? But why—"

"Would he do such a thing? Sarah, the letters were a hoax, just as you thought."

"Then you didn't kill Anne."

"I didn't kill Anne."

"I knew it!" She jumped up from her stool and hugged him exuberantly. This time, he returned the embrace. "Oh, I knew

244

t. And you don't have a mistress either."

Philip's lips twitched. "Not Flo Lambert or Lambeth, certainly. Credit me with better taste than that."

"Philip . . ."

"There's no one but you, Sarah." He pulled back, studying her face. "There never has been."

"There had better not be, or I'll—"

"What?"

"I don't know, but something pretty terrible, I think."

"Sarah." He was suddenly serious again. "Do you . . . that s, I mean—oh, drat—"

"I love you, Philip," she said simply, framing his face in her aands. "I love you!"

The look that came over his face was sunshine. With a laugh of pure joy, he picked her up and whirled her, shrieking with surprise, around the room. "She loves me! Did you hear that, everyone? Sarah loves me!"

"Put me down!" Sarah laughed. "Oh, Philip!"

"My God." He set her back on her feet as quickly as he'd lifted her. "I'd forgotten. The baby. Are you—?"

"I'm fine." She smiled up at him, reaching up to smooth the lines of worry from his forehead. "Really. Feel." And she took his hand, guiding it to her still-flat stomach.

A look of wonder crossed Philip's face. "My Sarah. No one's ver given me anything so precious. But."

"But?"

"Did you come back to me just because of the baby?"

She could get angry with that, Sarah supposed. For an intelgent man, he could behave remarkably stupidly! Again, hough, she remembered the misery on his face when she'd eft. "No. I had a choice, and I chose you. It's been you all long. And, by the way," she smiled at him, "when someone ays 'I love you,' it's customary to say it back."

Philip's arm settled about her waist. "I was coming to that," e said, when the door burst open.

"Sarah!" Richard stood there, his hair disordered, his reathing rough. "Thank God, I made it in time."

Philip moved swiftly, stepping forward and thrusting Sarah

behind him. "What do you want?"

"You've got to get out of here. Before God, I never meant any harm to come to you, Sarah."

"Never?" Philip walked forward, his hands bunched into fists. "What do you call telling her I was a murderer, you bastard?" And without warning, his fist shot out, catching Richard squarely on the jaw.

Richard rocked back with the force of the blow, his arm raised. "I don't want to fight you, Philip, but you have got to get Sarah out of here."

"Why?" Philip was circling his opponent, looking for another opening. "So you can try to take her away from me again? Not this time."

Richard danced away. "Listen to me. You're in danger—"

Philip's left fist shot out, and Richard dodged it just in time. "No, you're the one in danger, my friend. My good friend. My cousin. Always standing by me while trying to kill me."

"No!" Sarah gasped. She had taken refuge on the other side of the table, uncertain whether to call for help or not. Richard looked strange, mad, and in such an unpredictable state, who knew what he might do? If something happened to Philip when they had finally found each other, she didn't know what she'd do.

"We both know I'd make a better marquess than you." Richard, too, was circling, his fists raised. "Very well, cousin, if you want a fight."

Philip jabbed with his left again, this time connecting with Richard's cheek. "I do."

"Fine. Let's go outside."

"Right here suits me fine."

"Damn you! Why do you always have to be so dense?" Richard exclaimed, and launched himself at him. Sarah shrieked as the two men engaged, fists flailing. Richard clearly had the advantage; he was larger than Philip, and he lived a more athletic life. Philip, however, looked as she had never seen him, his eyes burning, his lips pulled back, scaring her almost as much as Richard had.

"You tried to kill me," he growled.

"You have everything I ever wanted. The title," Richard gasped, as another blow landed squarely in his midsection. Bent double, he lunged forward, using his head almost as a battering ram and pushing Philip back into the table. "The property, everything, and it should have been mine."

"I don't—give a damn." Philip's breath was coming in gasps now, and Sarah, pressed against the wall and watching in horror, her hands to her mouth, wished he would save his breath. Somehow the accusations were more vicious than the physical fighting.

"You've always had everything," Richard panted. He had Philip pinned against the table, and the two men struggled against each other. "A beautiful wife—"

"And you would have hurt her, damn you!" Philip roared, and with a mighty effort, threw Richard off him. Off balance, Richard stumbled back, falling against the wall and into the draperies. For a moment nothing happened, and then there was an odd sound, a whoosh. Suddenly the draperies were a wall of flame.

Chapter Twenty

"Good God! Sarah, get out!" Philip shouted. It was his worst nightmare come true, fire, in his house again.

Richard was screaming, a horrible, high-pitched sound. "We've got to get him out of there!" Sarah cried.

Philip had picked up a carpet and was beating at the flames. "Get out before the whole place goes up."

"I'll get help." She covered her mouth with her hand and ran out of the room, coughing and choking. Someone rushed by her as she reached the top of the stairs, and then someone else, and she fell back against the wall, eyes streaming from the smoke. Philip. Oh, God, Philip. If anything happened to him, what would she do?

The terror, the heat, the smoke were too much. A wave of dizziness and nausea swept over her, and she sank to the floor.

A long time later, an eternity later, she felt arms lifting her, holding her. She moved convulsively. "Philip!" she cried, as the memory of how she had last seen him, silhouetted in flames, came to her.

"Hush, darling. I'm here." The beloved voice came from somewhere near her ear, and she relaxed, leaning her head against Philip's shoulder as he carried her down the stairs.

"Silly thing for me to do, to faint," she muttered, and in spite of the grimness of the situation, Philip's lips twitched as he laid her down on the bed. "Philip! Don't leave me!"

"I'm not." He came back across the room with a damp cloth, wiping her face. The cloth came away grimy and stained, but the coolness revived Sarah. For the first time she noticed that, underneath its coat of smoke, Philip's face was pale and strained. "Philip. You're all right?"

Philip coughed. "Got some smoke in my lungs," he explained, "but yes, I'm all right. If Geordie hadn't got there—"

"That was Geordie who ran by me?"

"Geordie and Cooper, of all people. When Geordie realized what happened, he got water." He shook his head. "I owe that man my life. Again."

"Philip." Sarah laid her hand on his arm. "Richard?"

He shook his head. "He's gone, Sarah."

"Oh." In spite of what had just happened, in spite of all that Richard had tried to do, tears came to Sarah's eyes, making her turn her head away. "But, why—"

"Would he want to kill me? Jealousy. I never realized how jealous of me he was. If his father had been born first, he'd have had the title, not me."

"Yes, but . . ."

"And he would have had Anne. Or so he thought."

Sarah stared at him. "Philip, you're not saying—"

"Richard was Anne's lover. He confessed it before he died." He closed his eye. "The fire was meant for me, not her. And today . . ."

"You're not saying he started the fire!"

Philip nodded. "Yes. And the one that killed Anne, too."

"No!"

"I fear so. This time, he'd set up the cigar lighter I made him—ironic, isn't it?—to start a fire when he thought I'd be in the room. When he fell against it, he set it off."

"Oh, my God." Sarah closed her eyes, sickened by the horror of it. "But if he knew about the danger, why did he come?"

Philip's smile was crooked. "Because he didn't want you to be hurt. I think he cared more about you than even he realized. He said," he played with her fingers, "he told me to take care of you."

Tears flooded Sarah's eyes again. "Oh, Philip."

"God, Sarah!" Philip suddenly swooped down and caught her in his arms, holding her close. "I love you so much, and when I saw you lying there, I thought I'd lost you, too."

Sarah clung to his neck. "Say that again."

"I couldn't bear losing you—"

"No. What you said before." She smiled up at his bewildered face. "The word that begins with *L*."

Philip grinned, and suddenly, none of it mattered, the horror of the last hour, the grime that still covered his face. "What, love?"

"Philip—"

"I love you, sweet Sarah," he said, and kissed her, hard. Sarah responded eagerly, her mouth opening under his. It was a kiss of love, of passion, a kiss that celebrated being alive.

"But I must look a sight," she fussed when he released her at last. "All smoky and dirty."

He laughed, the low, sensuous chuckle that she'd only heard during their most intimate moments. Then, as now, it sent a shiver down her spine. "My sweet Sarah, don't you know how beautiful you are? Inside, where it really counts?"

Her breath caught. "Am I?"

"You are."

Her eyes were wide and wondering as her fingertips reached up to brush his forehead, his cheek, and, finally, the eye patch. "Like you."

"Sarah." He caught her up in his arms again, kissing her tenderly, passionately, binding them together for all time. The terror, the misery of the last weeks receded as he held her close to him. How lucky she was. She could have gone with Richard, making the worst mistake of her life. Instead, here she was, safe and secure and cherished for what she was—herself. All that had gone before, his first wife, her own checkered past didn't matter. All that counted was now.

"My heavens," she said, when she could speak again. "This is so much better than being a governess ever was."

And Philip laughed.

Epilogue

"Well, what do you think, my lord?" Sarah said sleepily.

Philip brushed hair still damp with sweat back from his wife's forehead. "I think he looks like a little monkey."

Sarah pulled back, her nose wrinkling, and regarded her son, not quite an hour old, nestling in her arms. "He does, doesn't he? But a beautiful little monkey."

"Oh, quite." Philip's finger found a tiny, flailing fist, which held onto him with quite amazing strength. "And you're beautiful."

"Oh, nonsense." Sarah yawned. "I must look a sight."

Philip smiled, his gaze filled with love. She did look tired, but there was a radiance about her that made it unimportant. "You gave me quite a scare, you know."

"It wasn't so bad. He was worth it." Sarah cuddled the baby. "What shall we call him?"

"Hmm. We can't go about calling him 'Monkey,' can we."

"Heavens, no! And if we shortened it to 'Monk,' people would surely misunderstand."

Philip grinned. "True. We'll name him after my father. Augustus Edward."

"How perfectly revolting! I'll not have a child of mine called 'Gus'!"

"Then you suggest something."

"Benjamin, for my father. And Philip."

"Lord Benjamin Philip Thornton, Earl of Thornton."

Philip considered it. "Rather a lot for a little monkey, but I like it."

"Then Benjamin Philip it is." Sarah and the baby yawned together. "A good choice."

"Quite." And as her husband's arms came around her, cherishing both her and their son, Sarah knew she had made the best choice of all. She had chosen love.

Author's Note

As an author of historical novels, I strive to make my use of historical details as accurate as possible. However, as a fiction writer, I also take some liberties. Therefore, I would like to acknowledge that the following inventions and innovations were actually produced by Thomas Jefferson: the dumb waiter; the leather swivel armchair with removable desk; the clock that tells the day as well as the time; the compass on the ceiling. The stained-glass dome, cigar lighter, and electrically operated printing press Philip came up with on his own. I had no more idea than Sarah what that thumping noise was as she crept down the corridor in Chapter Two until she reached Philip's workroom!

I'd love to hear from my readers, and I'll gladly answer all letters. Please write to me care of Zebra Books, 475 Park Avenue South, New York, NY 10016.

ZEBRA'S HOLIDAY REGENCY ROMANCES CAPTURE THE MAGIC OF EVERY SEASON

THE VALENTINE'S DAY BALL (3280, $3.95)
by Donna Bell

Tradition held that at the age of eighteen, all the Heartland ladies met the man they would marry at the Valentine's Day Ball. When she was that age, the crucial ball had been canceled when Miss Jane Lindsey's mother had died. Now Jane was on the shelf at twenty-four. Still, she was happy in her life and accepted the fact that romance had passed her by. So she was annoyed with herself when the scandalous—and dangerously handsome—Lord Devlin put a schoolgirl blush into her cheeks and made her believe that perhaps romance may *indeed* be a part of her life . . .

AN EASTER BOUQUET (3330, $3.95)
by Therese Alderton

It was a preposterous and scandalous wager: In return for a prime piece of horse-flesh, the decadent Lord Vyse would pose as a virtuous Rector in a country village. His cohorts insisted he wouldn't last a week, yet he was actually looking forward to a quiet Easter in the country.

Miss Lily Sterling was puzzled by the new rector; he had a reluctance to discuss his past and looked at her the way no Rector should *ever* look at a female of his flock. She was determined to unmask this handsome "clergyman", and she would set herself up as his bait!

A CHRISTMAS AFFAIR (3244, $3.95)
by Joan Overfield

Justin Stockman thought he was doing the Laurence family a favor by marrying the docile sister and helping the family reverse their financial straits. The first thing he would do after the marriage was to marry off his independent and infuriating sister-in-law Amanda.

Amanda was intent on setting the arrogant Justin straight on a few matters, and the cozy holiday backdrop—from the intimate dinner to the spectacular Frost Fair—would be the perfect opportunities to let him know what life would be like with her as a sister-in-law. She would give a Merry Christmas indeed!

A CHRISTMAS HOLIDAY (3245, $3.95)

A charming collection of Christmas short stories by Zebra's best Regency Romance writers. *The Holly Brooch, The Christmas Bride, The Glastonbury Thorn, The Yule Log, A Mistletoe Christmas,* and *Sheer Sorcery* will give you the warmth of the Holiday Season all year long.

Available wherever paperbacks are sold, or order direct from the Publisher. Send cover price plus 50¢ per copy for mailing and handling to Zebra Books, Dept. 3702, 475 Park Avenue South, New York, N.Y. 10016. Residents of New York and Tennessee must include sales tax. DO NOT SEND CASH. For a free Zebra Pinnacle catalog please write to the above address.